P9-CJK-267

I, Rhoda Manning, Go Hunting With My Daddy

Also by Ellen Gilchrist

ELLEN GILCHRIST

I, Rhoda Manning, Go Hunting With My Daddy

& Other Stories

Little, Brown and Company

BOSTON   NEW YORK   LONDON

Library of Congress Cataloging-in-Publication Data

Gilchrist, Ellen.
    I, Rhoda Manning, go hunting with my daddy, and other stories /
by Ellen Gilchrist. — 1st ed.
        p.   cm.
    ISBN 0-316-17358-4
        1. Southern States — Social life and customs — Fiction.
    2. Manning, Rhoda Katherine (Fictitious character) — Fiction.
    I. Title.

PS3557.I34258 I15 2002
813'.54 — dc21   2001037678

10 9 8 7 6 5 4 3 2 1

Book Design by Robert G. Lowe

Q-FF

Printed in the United States of America

For Abigail

Seymour once said all we do our whole lives is go from one little piece of holy ground to the next. Is he never wrong?

— J. D. Salinger

Contents

Author's Note

In the aftermath of the terrible events of September 11, 2001, in New York City, Washington, D.C., and Somerset County, Pennsylvania, I would like to note that the story "Götterdämmerung, In Which Nora Jane and Freddy Harwood Confront Evil in a World They Never Made" was written in the fall of the year 2000. I am not prescient. I do, however, have a habit of imagining disasters. In these daydreams, I am able to manipulate events to assure that innocent people are not harmed, that bad guys are punished, and happy endings are achieved.

I wish evil did not happen in the world. I wish the world could be populated by people like Nora Jane and Freddy Harwood, fortunate, caring men and women, watched over by a writer who would never let them come to harm.

Ellen Gilchrist

October 1, 2001

Fayetteville, Arkansas

I, Rhoda Manning,
Go Hunting
With My Daddy

I, Rhoda Manning,
Go Hunting
with My Daddy

IN NINETEEN FORTY we were living in Mound City,
Illinois, because my daddy was building levees on the
Mississippi River. He was chief engineer for the Louisville
District of the Corps of Engineers and he loved piling dirt
higher and higher and laying revetments and having big yellow
tractors and tractor drivers at his command. On Sundays he
would take my brother and me out to look at the tractors
and let us sit on them and touch the wheels and gear shifts
and marvel at the huge tracks they left in the red dirt. It was
different from the black mud of the Mississippi Delta where
we were from. It was dense red clay, stained with iron, and it
made a perfect medium to pile up and pack down, as the
Mound Builders had proved a thousand years before. Several
times Daddy had taken us to see Indian mounds and let us

climb on them and pretend we were Indians and think about what it must have been like to live on dirt mounds when the water rose and covered the land.

The water wasn't going to rise anymore in southern Illinois if my daddy could help it. He got up at dawn every day and worked until dark and expected the same from his men. It was men against the Mississippi River, a good fight and an unending one. When my daddy was in college he had worked summers at a levee camp in the Delta. This was before they had tractors and had to pile up dirt with mule teams. When the depression ended and the government sent tractors to the river it made my father a happy man, and the years we spent in Mound City were exciting years because he was an exciting man. I thought he was the strongest man in the world and I wanted him to like me as much as he liked my brother, Dudley, but that was a doomed desire because Dudley was a boy and he did what Daddy told him to do. I was incapable of doing what I was told to do no matter how much I wanted someone to like me and think I was nice. Alas, sixty years haven't changed that much, as my failed marriages attest.

Another wonderful thing about my daddy was that he thought up everything to do. He thought up trading some old bicycles for quarter horses and teaching us to ride. He thought up getting roller skates. He brought some men one day and built me a swing so high I could swing to the skies. No matter how high I swung I could never fall because the poles were sunk in four feet of concrete and I got to watch the men dig the holes with post-hole diggers and pour the concrete in and then I got to watch it dry and write my initials on the top.

When winter came to southern Illinois he thought up going ice-skating although none of us had ever lived where water froze or seen it done until we got the skates and cleared a pond and started trying.

Daddy and Dudley usually let me in on anything they thought up to do but they had never taken me hunting and I was mad about that. I was mad about several things the year I was five. I was mad because I could never win at poker and I was mad because they didn't take me camping in the woods and I was really mad because I never got to shoot the guns or go hunting.

If I was mad about something I never stopped thinking about it and telling my mother it wasn't fair. My mother didn't like to live the fast hot life my father lived. She was from the Delta and liked to dress up and have servants and practice French and go to the Episcopal church. She didn't like to go outside and get her shoes dirty and have any bug bites on her. She was teaching me to make doll clothes and read books and say my catechism and cook and write letters to our relatives and have a dollhouse on the back porch and make doll furniture out of cardboard boxes. She couldn't understand why I wanted to go hunting but she felt sorry for me for being left out and she told them so.

"She can't even shoot," Dudley said.

"We'll have to show her how," Daddy said. "Come on, Son. Bring the BB gun and let's go out back and find a bale of hay." He could not resist showing someone how to do something they didn't know how to do and it never occurred to him that we were too young to learn anything. He thought we were perfect, to tell the truth, despite my being "hardheaded" and "a tough nut to crack."

It was Sunday afternoon and they put on my boots and we all went out to the pasture and Dudley pushed a bale of hay into place and pinned an oilcloth target to it.

"This is a gun," my daddy began. "Come here, Sister. Pay attention to me."

"I'm paying it."

"This gun is loaded. Every gun in our house is always loaded. That way there are no mistakes. Any gun is assumed to be a loaded gun, in this house and anyplace you go. Understand?"

"Yes, sir."

"This is the barrel. The bullet comes down this and is directed at the target. This is the stock or handle that you hold it with. This is the trigger. You pull this to fire the bullet through the barrel and at your target. In here is the explosive device that hits the bullet and starts it on its way."

"Am I going to shoot it now?"

"No, you are going to listen to me if you are capable of listening. When Dudley was your age he could hit a bull's-eye with the four-ten. But you have to start with the BB gun, which is different from the gun I just showed you because it has a magazine." He put down the four-ten and took the BB gun and explained all the parts of that.

"Let me try it," I said.

"Not yet. Take these now and tell me everything I just told you about how they work."

★   ★   ★

It was half an hour later before I was finally standing in front of the target and was shooting into the bale of hay. I did so well with the BB gun they decided to let me shoot the over and under, but only three times because it spooked the horses.

"Okay," Daddy said, when we were back at the house and sitting at the kitchen table eating scrambled eggs and cinnamon toast for supper. "Next Saturday you can go with us. If you don't bother your mother all week and do everything she tells you to do without arguing. Ariane, it's going to be up to you. On Friday night if she's been good we'll get her ready. We're going bird hunting over on Mr. McGehee's property. We can take her there. If she's been good all week."

"I'm good," I said. "I'm a lot better than Dudley is."

"That's another thing," my daddy said. "You're always saying bad things about other people. I don't know where you get the idea that you're better than other people. No one wants to be around someone who's always throwing off on their brother and their little friends."

"Carleen Dee is not my friend. You just bring her over here because her daddy works for you. She's dumb and she smells funny."

"There she goes," Dudley said. "She can't stop it. I don't think she ought to get to go. She's already being bad."

"You stay out of this, Son. Your mother and I will settle this."

All week long I was so good you wouldn't believe it. I was five and a half years old and I could think and plan as well as I could when I was thirty. Better, because I didn't have to waste time wondering if what I was doing was a good idea. If there was something I wanted, I was after it until it was mine. So on Saturday morning they got me up before dawn and dressed me in jodhpurs and two sweaters and my boots and put me in the truck between them and took me hunting.

We drove out of town with the sun just beginning to light up the sky to the east. It was November and the leaves were gone from the trees and you could see the lay of the land and the way the fields stretched out to the woods and the river. You need to imagine that part of the country in nineteen forty. How narrow and crooked the roads were and paved with asphalt. We were the only vehicle on the road, and our headlights cut through the fog in the low places and lit up the picked fields and the farmhouses near the road.

We drove along with the windows rolled up because there was no heater in the truck, but after a while we had to roll them down because the windows were fogging up.

Behind the seat was a shoe box containing our lunch. Meatloaf sandwiches with mayonnaise, carrot sticks that had been soaking all night in salt water, apples, and homemade oatmeal cookies for dessert. I had helped make the lunch the night before and I was thinking about it as we rode. I wasn't thinking much about hunting. I figured we would go out and kill something and bring it back and then eat the lunch. Still, you could never tell with my daddy. We might be stopping off at an apple orchard or to buy some goat milk. Going off with him in the truck was always full of surprises.

★ ★ ★

Daddy started talking about hunting and he kept checking to see if I was listening. "Listen to this, Sweet Sister," he would say. "I'm not going to tell you twice."

Then he talked about how to keep the gun broke over your arm at all times if you were walking and then he got off on people he knew about who had been killed by going hunting wrong and then he was talking about hunting dogs my granddaddy had raised in Alabama and how one time he had to borrow a car and leave college and drive all the way to Courtland, Alabama, to get one of my granddaddy's dogs and take it back to Auburn so some men could use it to teach other dogs to hunt.

Then he got off on snakes and watching out for them in the woods and then he said, Goddammit, we should have some dogs but he hated to have them around because he had to take care of them all the time when he was little and haul them around the whole South the whole time he was in college.

"When are we going to eat lunch?" I asked. "I'm getting hungry."

"Don't start complaining, Shorty," my brother said. "I said you'd just complain the whole time."

"We'll eat lunch at lunchtime," Daddy answered. "You just had breakfast. You couldn't be hungry again."

"She throws up when you feed her in the car," Dudley put in. "Remember last summer when she threw up on the way to the Delta?"

"Well, we're almost there," Daddy said. "Right up there where that gate is. Mr. McGehee said there are quail by the dozens. He's coming out later with his pointers and let us see him work them. His son's driving a tractor for me now. He owns eighty acres and he's keeping this all for hunting."

We stopped the truck by a wide sloping place on the shoulder of the road and got out and took the guns down from the gun rack and Daddy checked them. A four-ten for Dudley, a shotgun for Daddy, and the BB gun for me. They showed me how to remove the magazine containing the BBs and put it in my game bag and sling the bag on my shoulder over my sweaters.

"I have to take off one of these sweaters," I said. "I'm burning up." So Dudley took off my game bag and then one of my sweaters and put the sweater in the truck and came back and got the bag situated so I could grab the magazine and load it in the gun if I needed to. "Be sure and screw it in tight," he said. "But don't do it until we tell you to. Just carry the gun with the barrel pointing at the ground. Pretend like it's broke over your arm to practice for later but don't point it at your feet. Sometimes people shoot their feet if they aren't careful."

When we were suited up and equipped, we walked down to the gate and Daddy opened the lock with a combination and we went through and closed the gate behind us and locked it and started walking out across a field toward a stand of oak and maple trees. Other trees were along the fencerow to our left, completely barren, not a leaf left on a tree. Beyond the field the early morning sky was gray with soft white clouds and a full moon in the east turning palest silver. "Those clouds are over the river," Daddy was telling Dudley. "Take out your compass and get a bearing. You must always know where you started and where the sun is and the way to the river. Then you can't get lost, but don't take bearings by the moon unless you have to." He turned to me. "If you get lost, Sister, stay where you are and wait for us to find you. When children get lost it's always because they didn't stay put and wait to be found."

"I know it," I said. "Sit down and make a mark on a tree and don't panic. You'll come and find me."

"That's it." Daddy and Dudley walked ahead of me. Daddy had started in telling Dudley how God made the world for men to live in and enjoy and all about what a great job God did putting animals around for us to hunt and dirt to build levees and all the blessings of our lives. I had heard that enough so I dropped behind to think my own thoughts. They were about thirty feet ahead of me, talking about how beautiful quail were and how the mother quail would sacrifice her life to save her babies, when I saw a crow on the high branches of an old tree beside the fence. It was just sitting there, waiting for somebody to shoot it, and I reached in my bag and got the magazine and fitted it into the gun and screwed it in and pumped the gun and raised it and shot.

Dudley hit the dirt and Daddy turned and put his arms up in the air and started yelling. "Drop the gun, Sister," he was yelling. "Drop the gun. Don't shoot. Please don't shoot."

The crow had flown away. I didn't know if I had hit him or not and my daddy was running across the field yelling at me. "I shot a bird," I told him. "But it got away."

"Oh, no, Sister," he was saying. "You can't shoot until we tell you to. You can't shoot when someone's in front of you. That's how people get killed, Sweet Sister. Give the BB gun to me."

I handed it over. Hunting was turning out to be a lot like a lot of other things they thought up to do. A lot of work for nothing, like catching grounders or throwing footballs. It was cold in the field and the stubble was sticking my legs and I was hungry.

"I wish we could eat that lunch," I was saying. "I think it's time to eat the lunch."

Dudley had gotten up from the ground and was coming toward me. "You're crazy, Rhoda," he was saying. "You can't shoot a bird when it's sitting on a tree. It isn't sportsmanlike. You have to wait until it's on the wing."

"Well, I don't see why," I answered. "It was just sitting there. You said we were hunting birds." He screwed his mouth into a line and kept from saying anything. He looked so grown-up, standing there with his shell cartridge around his coat and his four-ten rifle he got for his ninth birthday and his short haircut and his privileged position as the oldest male heir, not to mention being named for my father and my grandfather and my great-grandfather who had been the governor of Mississippi during the Civil War. I was proud of him, to tell the truth, and glad I didn't shoot him by mistake.

"Let's mosey back to the truck and see if Mr. McGehee is here yet," my daddy said. "If he brings his grandchildren maybe there'll be somebody for Rhoda to play with."

We started back across the field in the direction of the truck. There were some sparrows picking at stalks in the field but that's about all the wildlife we saw.

When we got to the gate Mr. McGehee was just pulling up with two of his grandchildren but they were big boys Dudley's age so Daddy let me stay in the truck and take a nap. An old black man who worked for the McGehees had come along to oversee the hunting dogs and he said he'd stay and watch me because his rheumatism was bothering him and he didn't want to be out in the cold. He climbed in the front of the McGehees' truck and I climbed in the front of ours.

The rest of them marched off to the fields. Daddy and Mr. McGehee and Dudley and the two McGehee boys and two thin brown-and-white dogs running in front of them and smelling for quail. I didn't care if they left me. I'd had plenty of hunting for one day. As soon as they were out of sight I got a meatloaf sandwich out of the shoe box and took off the waxed paper and sat behind the steering wheel eating it. I was a pretty strong little girl. I was sure of that. I did everything there was to do. I rollerskated and ice-skated and rode a bicycle and rode a quarter horse with a western saddle and wrote letters to my grandmother in Mississippi who liked me as much as she liked Dudley and sent me lamb cakes on my birthdays.

I fell asleep with my sandwich half eaten across my chest and slept until the sun was shining in the windshield of the truck. When I woke up I started thinking up a letter to write to my grandmother telling her everything that had been going on. This is the letter I wrote.

Dear Dan Dan, I went hunting and shot a crow but it flew away. I don't know if I wounded it or not. When I come down there this summer we can go in Aunt Roberta's closet and get out her Effanbee doll and I will play with it. I miss you. Your loving granddaughter and namesake. Rhoda Katherine Manning.

P.S. It's getting cold here and we are waiting for snow so we can have some winter sports.

About the time I finished thinking up my letter I started wanting to go to the bathroom and of course there are no bathrooms where you go hunting so I got out of the truck and walked over behind a tree and looked around to make sure there wasn't any poison ivy or any ants nearby. Then I took off my second sweater and pulled down my pants and peed on the ground. It was very pleasant to watch the pee make a little river running down the tree roots and running off to make tributaries. Dudley and I knew all about river systems and tributaries. We had a map of the Mississippi River system on our bedroom wall that was made by the National Geographic Society. Only people who worked for the Corps of Engineers ever got to have one that fine or understand how rivers are upon the earth.

A couple of ants showed up on the banks of my river so I hurried to pull up my pants and button them and shook out my sweater before I put it back on. Then I got some dirt clods to throw on the ants. I was just finishing off the second one when I heard the hunters' voices in the distance. I walked back over to the fence to watch them coming in.

"What did y'all shoot?" I called out.

"Three quail," Dudley calls back. "Three big ones."

The McGehees got their lunch out of their truck and we got ours and we made a table on the back of our truck and everyone shared their food. I sat up on the truck bed on a tire and finished off my sandwich and told Mr. McGehee all about what I had been doing.

"These are fine children, Dudley," he said to my daddy. "No wonder you're proud of them."

"She's a rough cob but she's learning how to ride this year real good. She'll ride any horse you show her."

He reached up in the truck and patted me on the head. It was as close as he came to showing affection and I was basking in it. "She almost shot us right before you showed up. We let her get behind us with the BB gun and she put in the magazine and shot at a crow on a tree." Mr. McGehee and Daddy started laughing. The more they laughed the harder they laughed.

"It wasn't funny," Dudley said. "It wasn't funny at all."

"Calvin almost shot me once when he was six or seven," Mr. McGehee said. "He didn't know it was loaded."

"You got to keep them loaded," Daddy said. He stood back and put his hands in his back pockets and started in. "I keep every gun in the house loaded and they have signs on them that say, Loaded Gun. That way no one makes any mistakes about them."

"Who shot the quail?" I ask.

"Calvin shot one and Mr. McGehee shot the other two," Dudley answered. "I got a shot but I missed."

"We want you all to take the birds home," Mr. McGehee said. "Go on. We get plenty of them. You think your wife knows how to clean them?"

"We got a woman who can do it." About that time the old man in the McGehees' truck woke up and got out of the cab and came over and talked to us and ate some of the lunch plus the cornbread he had with him. It was pleasant sitting on the bed of the truck with the low clouds covering half the sky and the sweet smell of the land and river all around us. Daddy and Mr. McGehee talked about President Franklin Delano Roosevelt and what a good job he was doing in Washington and how many tractors he had sent to the levee jobs and then they talked about President Theodore Roosevelt and his Rough Riders and Mr. McGehee told Daddy about some cutting horses he could buy and not to get me a pony because ponies are too mean but just to keep me on a quarter horse until I got finished learning. Then Daddy told him all about his grandmother who rode to hounds sidesaddle and then they said some things about women and then Mr. McGehee said they had to be getting on and he hoped we enjoyed the quail.

We waited until the McGehees got in their truck and started it up and then we got into ours and started home. Daddy put me in the middle with my legs stretched out beside his long one and the cold, hard feel of his vest beside my face. Everything about my daddy was hard and strong, and his voice was as strong and beautiful as a river. When he started talking anyone would listen because no matter what he was saying somewhere in his voice was laughing, somehow he was always bringing it down to earth, making sense of it, telling you where you were. A long time later, when I knew he wasn't always going to be alive, I saved some tapes from my telephone answering machine so I would have the sound of his voice forever. It's been a long time since he died but I have never looked for the tapes. I don't need them. The sound of his voice is part of my mind forever. Just because he isn't here to say it doesn't mean it's gone.

We rode along home in the truck with the November sun

getting lower in the sky and Dudley napping with his head propped on the window and after a while Daddy started in telling me about the land around us and how the middle part of the United States where we were living was called the stable interior craton and that it was the hard, strong part of the United States and all the other parts of our country depended on it for food and for good people who worked hard and took care of their families, plus we had the river which could take us all the way to New Orleans and out to sea or up to Minnesota where strong people from Germany and Norway and Sweden lived in the snow and went ice-skating every afternoon when they got through work and school. "I went up there once when I was playing ball," he told me. "But it was summer and I only got to see the places where they do it, because the ice was mostly melted. They make some cheeses up there that will melt in your mouth, Sweet Sister."

That's about all that happened on our hunting trip except we drove on home and showed Momma the quail and then we sat out on the back porch in the cold and cleaned them and tried to pick all the buckshot out of them and Momma cooked them and we had them for supper with some grits and biscuits and a nice new pot of butter our neighbor had brought over for a present. Then they bathed us and washed our hair and dried it and put on our flannel pajamas Momma had made us on the sewing machine and put us in our beds and turned off the lights and made us go to sleep. I never did like to sleep back then. There was so much going on I didn't want to miss it for a minute.

POSTSCRIPT

I wouldn't want to miss this opportunity to tell you what it's like to go hunting with a man who would kill or die for you. A strong man that other men seek out and love. It's a gift for a girl to have that kind of father and it's also a curse. It's a gift because you have a safe and fortunate childhood and can grow up strong and unafraid. It's a curse because you cannot reproduce it in the adult world. No man can be that wonderful ever again because only a child's mind can really comprehend wonder.

My daddy's dead now, buried in the ground in Rankin County, Mississippi, and I never even go and visit his grave. He wanted people to come visit his grave and expected that they would so I guess I'm still not doing what he told me to do. But I am mourning him.

The other day I found a letter he wrote me. It was in answer to my asking him to write down things about all the rivers he had known. He sent me back a list of the rivers and their characteristics and where they rose and where they ended. Then the letter said:

Now if we could only get you to stop thinking you know everything about the world and its background and history. It would do you good to listen just a little bit to someone who does definitely know and then pick up any additional knowledge you think good for you. You need to learn more about the major things of life. You seem real interested sometimes in the little things I know about, like rivers, but please be interested in a few of the big things I now know or at least listen when I try to tell you things that will be invaluable in the long run for you and your loved ones.

Then he got off on talking about why eating too much meat is bad for your health and where to order macrobiotic food and why the Department of Education is the worst thing that ever happened to the United States.

Entropy

MY NAME IS RHODA MANNING and sometimes I think too much.

It is the hot heart of summer in these soft old mountains where I spend my time now that I am old and gray. In the early mornings there is an hour of coolness and I go out that time of day and walk for miles up and down the steep hills. Crows call out and are chased by redbirds. I saw a rabbit chasing a crow the other day. The crow would hop toward the rabbit's nest, then the rabbit would chase it away. Nature is red in tooth and claw and we are part of nature. Hard to believe that in the easy life of the United States in the year two thousand.

Of course, battles still rage in our hearts. I watched a television show about recalcitrant teenagers being dragged off to boot camp as their parents watched from the stage. It threw my mind back to nineteen seventy-four and the day I let the men take my sons away. They were smoking marijuana and the men thought they could make them quit. I don't regret letting them be taken away. If I had it to do over I would chain them in the basement and make them live on bread and water. If I had it to do over I would be ten times as mean as I was then. Still, I can't forget the day they left.

It does no good to think about the past. I did the best I could given the information that was available to me at the time. Still, I think about it and it spoils the day. It even spoils the first fine hour of morning with its golden light and quiet hills. Young people are wild and crazy. That's the plain truth of that. Here in this land of plenty we have lost the means to calm them down. If we ever had the means. Perhaps all we ever had was fear. When there was less prosperity you could make them afraid they would be starving and homeless.

One of my sons is practically homeless now. The one called Jimmy in this story. He works for several months, then he travels around the world spending the money, then he comes home and goes to work again and makes more money, then goes back to France or Alaska or Africa. He's on the Internet so at least I can find him now. Before that I had to wait for postcards. He doesn't smoke marijuana anymore. Now all he does is drink. He is my sweetest, kindest, funniest child. I'm sick of his drinking and he's sick of me talking about it. We have an impasse. He does what he wants to do and I tell him not to do it. Nothing has changed between me and Jimmy. He is thirty-nine now. It's the same thing that was going on when he ran away and I let my father take him to Wyoming.

I spend a lot of time thinking about what I should have done rather than let the men take my sons away. I should have quit drinking myself. That's for sure. Then I should have hired a guard and handcuffed them and taken them to AA meetings. My father thought he knew what to do. He thought he could take them to Wyoming and let them ski and ride horses and go hunting and they would come to their senses and stop wanting to get high. It never occurred to my father that there was something he couldn't do if he set his mind to it. But there are things it takes a whole culture to achieve, and the culture was against us in nineteen seventy-four. I guess it's against those poor parents I saw on television. They were on a stage and right below them the sergeants walked in and grabbed their kids and started yelling at them. Even when the sergeants were right up in their faces screaming, the teenagers looked like they didn't give a damn. Those were the exact looks Malcolm and Jimmy were giving me the year they ran away to Mardi Gras and then got dragged off to be straightened out.

We were living in New Orleans. We had moved there when I married a wealthy lawyer to get my children away from my father. He had had a heart attack the year before and I guess he was starting to go crazy. He subscribed to all sorts of right-wing journals and believed the world was coming to an end sometime soon. The End Time, he called it. It scared me when he talked that way and I made up my mind to marry the richest person I could find and get my children away from him. I had divorced their father so I could go home and live with my parents and send my children to good private schools. I had no sooner gotten home than my father went crazy and helped start a right-wing Christian school near our home. He was sending my brilliant children to this school and I was powerless to stop him so I married a wealthy man and took them to New Orleans. I was uninformed, half educated, and half crazy myself from the fourteen schools and colleges he had sent me to while he moved our family around the South making money. Also, I drank too much. What did I think was going to happen to children with no father and a mother who had never grown up? Why was I surprised by anything that happened when I got them to New Orleans?

I had married a darling man who wanted to love them and be their father. I had moved them into a beautiful house in a nice neighborhood. I had enrolled them in the best schools in New Orleans and worked hard to make friends with the parents of their new friends.

So they started smoking marijuana and then they ran away to Mardi Gras. It was the year all the hippies in North America came to New Orleans for Mardi Gras. They were camped out two blocks from our house, in Audubon Park, and first Malcolm and then Jimmy went to the park and did not come home. We searched for them for nine days. My aunts came into town from Metairie and drove around in their Lincoln Continentals searching for them. My cousins searched for them. My husband's law firm went out en masse to search for them.

We begged the police to search for them but the police

thought it was a joke when we asked them to find two teenage boys in blue jeans. They had thousands of teenage boys on the loose that week. All they were doing was trying to keep order.

Finally, on Mardi Gras day, my father flew in from Mississippi, rented a car, and in two hours had them in his power. No one has ever found out how he did it.

Then my brothers took them to my mother's apartment on Henry Clay Avenue and held them down and cut their hair. Then their father came from North Carolina and took the oldest one to live with him and my father took the second oldest one to his ranch in Wyoming. That was that. My beautiful sons were gone. I had created a beautiful life for them and they had run away to smoke dope with the gypsies.

It was a block from my mother's apartment to our house on Story Street. My youngest son and my husband and I walked back to our house. As soon as we got to the bottom of Mother's stairs, I started crying. My husband, Eric, was crying too. Only Teddy wasn't crying. Now he would have the house to himself. Now Malcolm and Jimmy wouldn't hit him and tease him and drive him crazy.

Nineteen seventy-four. The kids were on a tear and the grown people were helpless in their ignorance and fear. There were no drug treatment programs, no Tough Love groups, no place to send hair samples to prove they were smoking dope. No one knew what to do. The worst thing you could say to anyone at a cocktail party was, "How are your kids?" It was an epidemic. No family was immune.

So I walked along the sidewalk crying bitter tears. I felt like someone had died. Remorse fell like rain from heaven. The golden rain trees were putting out their leaves. The crepe myrtle trees were sending flowers from bare stalks, but my fruit was wasted and lost and gone.

Except for precious, scrawny Teddy. He had gone home and let the sheepdogs out and they ran along beside us. Two Old English sheepdogs with their wonderful faces and half-blind eyes. Great sheepdogs are as smart as dolphins. They know what you are feeling.

It was the day after Mardi Gras when the men drove off with my sons and the trees were festooned with beads and here and there along the street were scraps of confetti and crepe paper and abandoned doubloons.

"It won't be forever," Eric said. "As soon as we get them straightened out we'll bring them back."

"It is forever," I cried. "They're gone. They're really gone."

"Jimmy's hair was on Grandmother's rug," Teddy said. "I had to get out the vacuum so Sally could clean it up."

We came to our house and walked up the stairs and went into the kitchen and got out food and began to make sandwiches for lunch. I don't think I'd eaten anything in days, but since I was always on a diet I probably thought of that as a lucky thing.

Eric went into the bedroom and turned on the television to watch a ball game. Teddy went downstairs to play in Malcolm's room. I went out to the garage and looked at Malcolm and Jimmy's bicycles. We had packed so hurriedly for them we had forgotten to send half the things they owned. All their baseball equipment and skis and everything they treasured was still in our house.

What would I do with the rest of my life? I went upstairs and went into my workroom and wrote two or three poems. Then I found a diet pill and took that and in a few minutes I started feeling better, lots better. I didn't have many diet pills. They were very hard to get. I had to beg and beg to get our friends who were physicians to give me a few.

After the diet pill kicked in I called my best friend and told her I'd taken it. "Come over and I'll give you one," I said. "Then we can go run in the park."

"How many do you have?" she asked.

"I thought I had ten but there are only five. I think Jimmy stole them right before he ran away. Anyway, I have five left and I'll give you one."

"Sure," she said. "If Mother will take care of my kids." My best friend was a beautiful, tall society woman. My husband, Eric, adored her. We both loved to have her at our house.

I went into the bedroom and got up on the bed with him and tried to cheer him up. He was still in a sad mood because he never took any diet pills so if he felt bad he just had to ride it out. "Janet's coming over," I told him. "We'll cook dinner and watch *The White Monkey* on PBS. We did what we had to do, Eric. There was nothing else to do."

"I still don't know how your father found them," he answered. "Do you think he bribed someone?"

"No one knows how he does anything. He did find them, that's the thing. He found them in the park."

"Where we had looked for them a thousand times. Maybe they came back there."

"He found them both. And they weren't together."

"We had to get them out of here. There won't be any dope in Wyoming or in North Carolina. It's in New Orleans because New Orleans is a port."

I gave him a hug and a kiss, then I got up from the bed. I was feeling much better now. I was from a rich and powerful family and we could solve our problems. If our children went crazy we just took them somewhere and got them well. My father had been a famous baseball player. He could do anything, even find lost teenagers on Mardi Gras day. Any animosity I held toward him for his methods was dissolved in my relief that he had found the boys.

"Don't leave," my husband said. "Stay here with me."

"I want to get out some wine. Janet loves that Piesporter your uncle sent us. She adores that wine."

Teddy had come upstairs with some of Malcolm and Jimmy's phonograph records and was listening to them on the stereo in the den. He was listening to a recording by James Booker, the famous heroin addict who was called the Piano Prince of New Orleans. Teddy looked so cute, standing in front of my stereo listening to music and shuffling his feet. I wanted to give him a big hug and a kiss but he didn't like to be interrupted when he had started something so I left him alone.

Then I went down to the basement to find some wine for dinner. White wine on top of Dexedrine is a wonderful way to get rid of the blues.

★   ★   ★

Now it is twenty-six years later and it is Jimmy's birthday and I don't know where he is. I called my ninety-year-old mother and we talked about the day that he was born. I was living in a small apartment in Atlanta, Georgia, and my husband was at Georgia Tech. Malcolm was ten months old and Jimmy was not supposed to be born for another month but at ten in the morning I went to the doctor for a checkup and he said the baby was on its way. Since I had to have a cesarean section, we had to hurry. I went back to my apartment and called my husband's fraternity house and told them to find him. Then I called my mother-in-law to come take care of Malcolm when the maid left. Then I packed a suitcase and took a taxi to the hospital. I was excited. The excitement was so intense it kept me from being afraid. I was twenty years old, in luxuriant health, and I was on my way to have a baby and save myself the last boring month of a pregnancy.

There were no seat belts in the nineteen fifties. I leaned up into the front seat of the cab and told the cab driver what we were doing. There was no reason for him to drive at breakneck speed across Atlanta but he did it anyway. When we got to the hospital I paid him and he wished me luck.

Then I went inside and they began to prep me for surgery. I refused to let anyone else shave my pubic hair, so they let me do it myself. Then I was trundled into the operating room and given a shot that made me believe I was God.

I watched with great interest as they gave me a spinal block and as they cut me open and pulled my baby from my womb. A long, thin baby boy with dark red hair, abundant hair, a laughing happy person I would always love. Maybe he got addicted in the womb to that great shot they gave me before he came. Maybe he has been trying ever since to find that shot, that exultation and nirvana.

"Where is he now, for whom I carry in my heart this love, this praise?"

This all has much to do with that television program on which desperate parents watched as their children were dragged off to boot camp. Maybe the children secretly want to go somewhere where they will be yelled at and forced to mind, forced to protect themselves from the traps and pitfalls of the modern world. Maybe Malcolm called my father and told him to come get him. After twenty-six years of mindfucking over this story I finally decided that's the only way it could have happened. I will never know. My father's dead and Malcolm isn't telling. He adored my father and looked up to him. He keeps their secrets. Their secrets are about high testosterone and not letting women run their lives. Their secrets are about living on the edge of being civilized, a precarious edge that keeps them free. They will never be ashamed of the violence and madness and freedom in their hearts. Watch nature videos. See who rules a group of chimpanzees and why. Then decide if you want your president to keep it zipped.

I don't know. The main thing is I quit drinking and taking diet pills. Diet pills ruined a lot of lives in the fifties and sixties and seventies. And alcohol is the most dangerous drug in our culture. I was to blame for my children's madness as my parents were to blame for mine. Maybe. Either we are all to blame or we are all blameless and just doing the best we can in a situation where we are all doomed to die. Two things I know for sure. Alcohol is to blame and so is lack of information. Not being able to see clearly what is going on. Being caught up in the thing we wish to examine.

"There was more dope in Wyoming than there was in New Orleans," Jimmy tells me now. "All you did was throw me in the briar patch."

Two months after the men took Malcolm and Jimmy away, my father had both of them with him. As soon as he got to North Carolina with his father Malcolm started plotting to leave. He tried several strategies. Then he took his father's shotgun and went out into a pasture and shot a neighbor's cow. His father called my father and my father said, "Send him to me. I've about got Jimmy straightened out. I can take one more."

My father was beating Jimmy to make him mind. The rest of the time Jimmy was smoking dope with a Navajo Indian he met at school. The Navajo had bales of marijuana and his parents let him smoke it.

When Malcolm got there my father tried beating them both but they were stronger than he was by then and besides they could make him laugh and besides now it was a game and Malcolm and Jimmy together were two against one. Now my father found out what Eric and I knew, what it was like to be double-teamed in a game where the young are the only ones who understand the rules.

Not that they needed it with the Navajo meeting them every day at school, but just to keep his hand in Malcolm started growing marijuana under lights in an abandoned trailer beside the barn. It was two feet high before my father found it. My older brother was there when he found it. He says my father sat on a chair and cried like a child.

When they weren't fighting with my father, Malcolm and Jimmy were hunting antelope and deer or going down rivers in canoes or skiing. My father let them have Wednesdays off from school to ski when they pretended to be minding him.

A couple of months after Malcolm got there he called me and told me he was unhappy. I got on the next plane and flew to Wyoming and brought him home. I tried to bring Jimmy too but he wouldn't leave. Too much was going on for him to leave. My father's nephew was on his way to spend the summer. My brothers were flying in to go hunting. The ranch had become the favorite hangout for all the high-testosterone males in the family. They were flocking out there carrying hunting rifles.

This is all true. This really happened. Why do I think this is funny? Why in the name of God after all these years have I decided this is funny?

Because everyone lived through it. Because no one died or was maimed or had their lives ruined. Malcolm is a grown man with wonderful children and his addictions tamed. Jimmy loves his life and wouldn't change it. He has traveled around the whole world and had adventures most men would die to have.

★   ★   ★

I am going to be wiser than my father was. I am going to learn to watch life without caring. This is what happens. This is how it ends, only it never ends because by some divine miraculous luck we are all still breathing.

A Christmas
in Wyoming

BIG DUDLEY WOKE UP on December 17 and put on his long johns under his ski pants and pulled on his cowboy boots and went out to the garage to make an inventory. All fall he'd been buying skis and ski clothes at yard sales. Half of the garage was taken up with the Jeep station wagon he had bought for getting to the ski resort and the other half was taken up with ski paraphernalia, including three pairs of short, beginner skis. He had learned to ski on short skis the year before and had decided it was the only way to learn. He was up to six-foot-long skis now and that was as far as he was going. He was seventy years old. He couldn't afford to start breaking bones at this stage in the game.

He turned on the light in the garage and took a yellow legal pad down from the wall and started writing names on small pieces of paper and sticking them with Scotch tape to various pairs of boots. *Teddy,* the notes said, *Dudley Three, Malcolm, Jimmy, Juliet, Ann Marie, Rhoda.* He stopped and put the pad away and opened a box of long underwear he had ordered from a catalog. It contained nine pair of long underwear in three sizes, enough for everyone. He didn't need any for his sons, they already knew how to ski and had bought expensive clothes at ski resorts.

He wasn't starting his grandchildren at expensive ski resorts. He was starting them right here on Casper Mountain, a local resort run by local people. In the early fall he had flown his daughter and her youngest son out to visit and they had walked all over the mountain to see the lay of the land and the moguls the local kids built to wait for winter. The manager of the slopes had even allowed them to ride on the lift and the T-bar so they could get a feel for that.

When he had finished sorting out the long underwear and arranging it on a shelf with the sizes marked by taped notes he turned off the garage light and went back up to the kitchen and started making breakfast. It was barely beginning to be light outside and the piled snow in the backyard was smooth and white and stretched out half an acre downhill to the neighboring yard. It would make a good practice run when they got here.

Big Dudley was a happy man as he put water in a skillet for poached eggs and put on the oatmeal in a double boiler and started the coffee and got out a tray for toasted bread. He had escaped the South and all its troubles and he was going to save his children too. As God is my witness I'll get them out here with some white people, he swore to himself. If I can live long enough I can do it.

His wife came into the kitchen wearing a long pink silk dressing gown and the expression she had been wearing for six months. "It's freezing in here, Dudley," she said. "I'm going to turn up the heat."

"If you'd put on some clothes you wouldn't be cold," he answered. "Where are those long underwear I bought you?"

"I am not wearing long cotton underwear as long as I live," she answered. "If you want an old, fat country woman go and get one. I'm doing the best I can with all of this, Dudley, but you ask too much."

"Come and eat some breakfast. I'm going out and look over the mountain later. Come on, get dressed and go with me. We'll have lunch up there in their little restaurant. And wear those boots I ordered you."

"I'll try. My God, I'm doing everything I can."

In New Orleans, Louisiana, his daughter, Rhoda, was in her bedroom packing. She put all the ski clothes she had bought into the suitcase and then she added some dress-up clothes for Christmas Day and then she decided to go back to Gentry and buy the ski jacket she had decided against because it cost too much. We're rich, she decided. I can have what I need.

Her youngest son, Teddy, came and stood in the door to her bedroom and watched her packing. He had already finished packing his suitcase and had put it in the front hall. She had taken him to Gentry with her and he had new ski clothes also.

"We have to have those boots that clip onto the skis," he said. "Trip Healy said the way the skis stay on is they clip on the boots."

"Granddaddy has some," she answered. "He said he has everything we need. Why don't you go and wake your brothers?"

"They'll get mad if I wake them up. I don't want to do it."

"Okay. Never mind. I'll do it in a minute. Come here and let me see what you're wearing. Okay, that looks nice. You look very nice, Teddy. Come here and give me a kiss." She stood waiting and he came to her and let her hug him *for a second*. His thin, strong body never stopped moving. He could barely hold still long enough to be hugged. He was a funny, intense little boy with a cowlick of bright red hair. Spare, her father called him. The extra blessing.

Her two oldest sons were downstairs sleeping. They had gotten stoned the night before in preparation for going to visit their grandfather, whom they loved and feared in equal measures and against whom they would measure themselves as long as they lived. "You can't put anything past him," they told their friends. "He can read your mind." They and their mother had lived with him on a country place in Mississippi for four years before their mother married their stepfather and moved them to New Orleans. He had taught them to ride horses and shoot guns and drive farm equipment and play baseball. When their mother took them to New Orleans he was so brokenhearted he had gone to Wyoming to live. He had managed to keep the older boy, Malcolm, with him for five months after she married, but in the end he even had to relinquish him.

Now they were going out to spend three weeks with him in Wyoming learning how to ski, but Rhoda's two oldest sons knew better than to think that was all there was to it. They knew what he really wanted was to get them away from her and keep them. When Rhoda divorced their father, their grandfather had told him he would never have to pay child support or alimony if he would let him adopt them and make them his heirs and their father was so young and broke and confused he had agreed to that. So not only were they the old man's grandsons, they were his adopted children. If their mother died in any of her escapades, he was their legal guardian.

Malcolm and Jimmy knew this and they knew something else. Messing with the old man was not like messing with any of the other grown people they knew. He could not be fooled and he could not be manipulated and if they made him mad he would hit them.

So they were glad they were going to Wyoming to learn to ski but they were wary. "We better get stoned," Malcolm had said the night before. "We'll never be able to do it when we get out there."

"We might be able to," Jimmy said. "If we could find some pot and take it with us."

"There might be some out there. George said everyone was stoned when they went to Vail last year. He said his ski instructor was stoned every day but he wouldn't give them any. If we had enough money we might get some."

"We can get all the money we want from Eric. Just tell him you want to buy something."

"I don't want anything from Eric. I'm not taking money from him."

"Well, I'll take it from him. I like him. He's nice to us. I don't know why you want to be so mean to him."

As soon as their mother and stepfather Eric were asleep they had gone out in the backyard and smoked a joint by Teddy's turtle pond. It was a perfect night in New Orleans, cold and clear, you could even see some stars between the liveoak trees and rooftops. After they got high they went back inside and went to sleep in their clothes listening to Little Feat. Life was good in New Orleans even if they did miss their grandfather's farm and their horses and the easy White Citizens' Council School he had supported so they could go there. They didn't miss him bossing them around and hitting them. But they missed him. There was something about him that was more fun than being in New Orleans. They would be much older before they understood what it had been. They would be burying him before they knew what they had lost.

"I'll get dressed," Big Dudley's wife was saying. She had finished her breakfast and was drinking the last of her coffee. She looked up at her husband, who was sitting across from her pretending to be patient. He was her husband and she had followed him out here to Wyoming, his last wild goose chase, and she didn't know what to do now but live each day as well as she could and try to trust in God to get her through it. "I'll do the dishes and then I'll get dressed, but don't hurry me. I wanted to go to church this morning."

"Then go to church. Do what you want to, Ariane. It's good to go to church and meet people and start to feel settled."

"I will never feel settled here. This was too much, Dudley. This is more than I can bear." She was going to start crying again.

"Get ready for church and I'll drop you off there and then I'll go on out and come back and get you or I'll go with you. Do you want me to go with you?"

"Yes, I do."

"Then get ready and we'll go. What time does it start?"

"At eleven. You don't have to go. I know you don't like my church. You don't need to go."

"Then I won't go but I'll drive you there and pick you up."

She got up and began to clear the table and put the dishes in the new dishwasher. The new kitchen was very modern, well equipped and easy to use. Ariane hadn't had to do any of her own housework in many years, but doing some of it was better than having the old German woman they had found to work for them there every day. She was a depressing woman with a mole on her face.

"I can't look at that on the weekends," Ariane had said. "I'd rather do dishes than look at that mole."

She tied a long apron over her robe and began to run water in the sink. "I'm going out back and start scoping out a practice run," Dudley said. "Goddamn, it's hot in here. I don't know how you can stand it this hot."

He pulled a long white jacket on over his sweater and fastened two of the front fasteners and stuck his ski cap in his pocket and went out the back door. When he was at the bottom of the back stairs he stopped a moment to take in the beauty of the morning. The air was as clear and clean as mountain air. It had snowed in the night and the cover was perfect and untouched. As far as he could see the snow lay in its perfect state. There was not so much as the track of a bird on the snow near him. Only near the house, on the eaves and windows, a few icicles were forming from the heat within. Except for that, only snow. Dudley walked around to the side door to the garage and went inside and found a pair of ski boots and put them on. Then he put on the five-foot-long skis and took two ski poles and slid out the door and back to the bottom of the stairs. When he was ready he took his hat out of his pocket and put it on. He added a pair of small black goggles. Then he buttoned up the jacket almost to his neck and put on his gloves and began to ski down the hill. From the window Ariane watched him disappear down the yard, bent at the knees, moving at a steady pace, using the poles. "He is absolutely crazy," she said out loud. "He has lost his mind."

The phone was ringing. It was ten o'clock in New Orleans and Rhoda was calling to make sure they knew when to meet the plane.

"Your father's skiing down the backyard," Ariane said. "He can't wait for you all to get here."

"I think I have everything we need but I don't know what to bring to wear. How cold is it?"

"It's freezing. You can't believe how cold it is. Bring all the warm things you have. Bring that white coat and hat I bought you to take to New York. He got a lot of ski coats for the children. I don't know if they'll fit. He has six or seven of them."

"My God. Well, we can't wait to try it. We're all excited. When is Dudley getting there? When is Ingersol coming?"

"Tomorrow sometime. Dudley's bringing Juliet and Ann Marie and Stella and Stella's little girls."

"Don't remind me. Well, I have to go wake up Jimmy and

Malcolm. Teddy's been up since dawn. He's been packed since yesterday morning."

"We can't wait until you get here. I've been so lonesome, Rhoda. I feel so far away."

"Well, don't worry about that. We're coming." She hung up the phone and went up to the front of the house where her husband Eric was sitting at his desk paying bills. "I talked to Mother," she said. "Daddy's out skiing down the backyard. Can you believe it? Well, I can't wait to go. I hope I don't break my leg."

"He's doing what?"

"She said he's skiing down the backyard. I can't believe they're out there. I can't believe he made her move to Wyoming."

"I wish I could move there," Eric said. "Listen, Rhoda, what is this bill from the tennis club? Did you take all these lessons?" He handed it to her and she glanced at it.

"I take two a week. Why, do you want me to stop?"

"No, it's all right. I just want to make sure they're yours. Why don't you pay for them with checks? That way I don't have to worry about the bookkeeping."

"All right. I will." She bent over and kissed him on the cheek and gave him the bill back. "Well, I'm going and wake the boys. The plane leaves at two. We better stop fooling around and get ready."

After they were up and dressed and had eaten breakfast Malcolm, age fourteen, and Jimmy, age thirteen, were downstairs packing suitcases and deciding what to do next. "I'm going over to the park and try to find Rio and get some weed before we leave," Malcolm said. "You finish packing all this stuff for me and I'll do that."

"I'm not packing your stuff."

"Well, if you don't I won't have time to try to find him. Just put in all the stuff on the bed." He picked up a pair of boots and threw them the pile. "Come on, Jimmy, help out."

"Okay. I will. Are you telling them you're going?"

"No, tell them I'll be right back." Then Malcolm was gone, out the back door and over the fence to Webster Street and Hurst and down it and across to Henry Clay and the park. He was walking as fast as he could in the direction of the liveoak tree that was Rio's office. If Rio wasn't there sometimes he left a number you could call, but Malcolm was in luck and Rio was sitting on one of the big roots of the massive tree eating a sandwich and talking to a lanky girl with a British accent who had showed up about a month before and was living somewhere on Magazine Street in a van with some other kids.

"What you need?" Rio asked.

"Something to smoke. What you got?"

"I got a baggie for twenty dollars or two for thirty-five. How much you got?"

"I got seventeen dollars. Can I get two for that?"

"Since it's you. Since it's you." Rio opened his vest and took out two small bags of grass and put them in a paper sack and handed them over as though it were his children he was surrendering. He was a small black man of uncertain age, maybe nineteen or twenty, certainly no older. "Where's your brother?"

"He's packing our bags. Our mother's taking us to see our

grandfather. He's out west. He says he's going to teach us to snow ski."

"It's snowing out there?"

"That's what they say."

"Ain't that the shits? Ain't that the shits."

Malcolm handed Rio the money. He took the paper bag and put it in his jacket pocket. "I got to get going," he said. "They didn't know I was leaving. You take care of yourself, Rio. Stay out of trouble."

"Bring me some of that snow." Rio started laughing. He was laughing so hard he reached out a hand to the British girl for support. "Bring some home with you."

"I'll be lucky to get home," Malcolm said. "They made me go live with that old man the last time they caught me smoking weed." Rio kept on laughing. He'd smoked some Arkansas Redbud with the British girl about an hour before and it was just now getting ripe in him.

Rhoda was standing on the front steps to the house when Malcolm turned off of Hurst and started down Webster Street. She was wearing a long wool pantsuit and a turtleneck sweater and high-heeled boots. She looked like some kind of model in *Vogue* magazine instead of a mother and she was mad. "Where in the hell have you been?" she said. "Get dressed. We have to leave in fifteen minutes. We've got the car packed and everyone is ready. Please hurry, Malcolm, don't make us miss the plane."

Malcolm bypassed her and went through the gate and the backyard and went in the back door and to his room and transferred the package to the inside pocket of his heavy jacket and changed blue jeans and put on a plaid shirt and took off his tennis shoes and looked for his boots. Then he remembered they were in the suitcase so he put the tennis shoes back on and went upstairs.

"Did you lock the back door?" Eric asked. Eric tried to have as little conversation as possible with Malcolm. He tried to sound kind and friendly.

"Yes. Let's go."

Malcolm walked by Eric and went out the front door to where his mother and his brothers were getting into the station wagon. Eric went down the stairs and locked the back door and then came back up the stairs and down the hall and out the front door and got behind the steering wheel and started driving. "We're off to the ski slopes," he said in a cheerful voice. "Let's get going."

"I don't believe you're wearing those filthy shoes on the plane," Rhoda said, turning around on the seat to face Malcolm. "Where did you go? Why did you leave when we were getting ready?"

"I had to tell someone goodbye. My boots are in my suitcase. I couldn't find anything but these."

"We'll buy him some shoes out there," Eric said. "Come on, everybody, let's just have a good time."

They arrived in Casper, Wyoming, at nine o'clock at night Casper time. Rhoda's brother Dudley had arrived at eight and rented a van and was waiting at the gate for them. With him were two of his daughters from his first marriage, his third wife, and her two little girls. The older daughters were fifteen and fourteen and had been good friends of Rhoda's sons since they were born. They embraced them now and made a foursome to stand against the poor little blond stepchildren. Rhoda tried to make up for their snubs by making a fuss over the little girls. They collected the luggage and got a cart and hauled it all out to the waiting rented van. It was so cold outside the building that Rhoda felt her mouth freeze. "Good, God," she said. "How cold is it?"

"It's five below," Dudley said. "This is just the beginning."

"This is just like Daddy," she chattered. "To bring everyone out to some goddamn place so cold you can't be outside. How will we ski in this?"

"It's in the daytime." Dudley laughed. "Come on, quit worrying. Get in the car. I've got the heater going."

At ten fifteen they pulled up in front of their parents' new home, a three-hundred-thousand-dollar brick house on a large lot with three or four small trees. Covered with snow and with their mother's Christmas tree blazing in the window it looked all right. Maybe it was all right to have their parents move off to the middle of nowhere and trade in a beautiful antebellum house in the country for a brick house in a frozen city called Casper, Wyoming. There was no point in caring. It had been done. It was a done deal.

They pulled into the driveway and all piled out of the van and went trooping into the kitchen. Inside it was better. Their mother's furniture was in the rooms, her paintings and photographs and china and silver candelabra and silver tea set. Photographs of them were on the walls. The rooms had been painted the same soft beige as the house in Mississippi and the same soft expensive carpet and rugs were on the floors. In the bedrooms were the same comfortable cherry beds and dressers, the same lamps and lamp tables. This was now their parents' home. This was where they went now for Christmas.

Rhoda and her youngest son, Teddy, had seen the house when they visited in the summer, but that was before the interior was repainted and the carpets changed. That was before Ariane had made it look like their old home.

"Well, the house looks better," Rhoda said, brushing off her mother's embraces. "Let me see the rest."

Ariane led Rhoda around the house showing her where things were and assigning rooms. There were five guest bedrooms. Rhoda and Eric took one. One was for the boys, one for the girls, and one for Dudley and Stella. That left one for Rhoda's unmarried brother, Ingersol, when he arrived.

Rhoda left her suitcase on the suitcase rack and followed her mother out to the living room. It was as much as possible like the one in Mississippi except that had been a square room with fifty-foot ceilings in a house that had been built in 1830 and this was a rectangular room with twenty-foot ceilings that had been built the year before.

"Is it all right?" Ariane asked.

"It looks just like you." Rhoda took a seat on an old blue velvet loveseat that had been her favorite reading spot when she was a child. "Good old loveseat. Imagine this in Wyoming."

"I don't know if I can make it," Ariane began. "It's so cold I can't go out. I'm afraid to drive in it."

"Well, just do the best you can," Rhoda said, watching her

mother's face begin the shrinking, weakening thing it did when she talked about the lives Dudley made her live. Rhoda had no patience with weakness, no sympathy for it, refused to enter into her mother's helplessness, as if to acknowledge it would make her vulnerable too.

Her father was at the door. "Come on, Sister," he said. "I want to show you the ski things. Come out to the garage."

Rhoda got up, grateful she didn't have to talk to her mother anymore or hear her troubles. She followed her father out to the garage where her brother and his wife and children and her husband and her children were already trying on ski boots. After a long time her mother came out and stood in the door to the kitchen. She was smiling now, at the sight of her two oldest children and her grandsons and her two oldest granddaughters. Malcolm and Juliet were sitting on the running board of the Jeep trying on boots. "I got some weed," Malcolm whispered to her. "But I forgot to get some papers."

"We can use plain cigarettes," she said. "I know how to do it."

"How are those boots fitting?" their grandfather asked. He had spotted them whispering and come over to see what they were up to. "Rough cobs," he was always telling people about his grandchildren. "Especially the oldest ones. They're tough nuts to crack. Well, I'm going to teach them to ski so they'll want to stay out here."

"We're going to start off on short skis first thing in the morning," he was saying to Malcolm and Juliet. "By noon we'll be ready for the mountain. Then we'll practice on the bunny slopes. That's the one with the T-bar. You're going to love this. I've been going out three times a week. They put a picture of me in the paper for being the oldest person to learn to ski since they built the slopes. Did I show it to you?"

"You sent us a copy of it," Malcolm said.

"I haven't seen it, Granddaddy," Juliet said. "I want to see it. Where is it now?" She got up and gave him a kiss and a long sweet hug. She was a startlingly beautiful girl and very, very sweet. Juliet worked on the premise of you catch more flies with honey. No one had ever yelled at her or hit her in her life, not even Big Dudley in his deadliest rage.

Everyone slept well their first night in Casper. One thing about Ariane Manning. She could make people comfortable and she could make them feel at home. Her beds all had fine new mattresses and were made up with the finest linens. There were electric blankets on every bed and comforters and quilts on closet shelves for people who didn't like electric blankets. There were soft down pillows in fine cotton pillow slips. In the room she had made for the girls there were twin beds for her older granddaughters and a bunk bed for the little stepgranddaughters from Texas. They were sweet little girls. By the time they had put on their little gowns and gone to sleep Juliet and Ann Marie had decided to stop being mean to them. They weren't as beautiful or smart as their father's real children. They weren't any threat even if their father did hug them and pretend to like them. No one could like little girls that quiet and plain. Juliet decided to be nice to them first and then Ann Marie decided she would too.

"Malcolm's got some pot," Juliet whispered to Ann Marie,

after they turned off the lights and settled down into their beds. "He brought it from New Orleans."

"He's the worst boy that ever lived," Ann Marie whispered back. "If Granddaddy catches him with that, he'll kill him."

"Well, he's got it. I'm just telling you."

"I'm not doing it. You better not either."

"You never do anything. You're afraid of them."

"Go on to sleep. Let's go to sleep. Grandmother's beds always smell so good. This is just like sleeping on the farm. I'm glad we're here."

"I am except for mother. She's really sad we won't be there for Christmas."

"We can't be everywhere at once. Go on to sleep, Juliet. I'm really tired."

"You want to smoke a little now?" Malcolm was asking Jimmy, in the room where they were sleeping.

"Hell, no. It's too dangerous. They'll smell it. Don't do it now. Save it for tomorrow when we're out in the snow. We don't have enough to smoke it every night."

"Okay. But we'll try to get some more. How much money do you have?"

"I have twenty dollars Eric gave me for the plane. I'll get some more. I'll get some from Granddaddy."

"Don't get it from Granddaddy. Don't do anything to make him think."

"Okay, go to sleep. Go on to sleep."

★   ★   ★

Big Dudley got up before dawn and built a fire in the living room fireplace and went into the kitchen and started getting things ready for breakfast. He made a pot of coffee and laid out pans for biscuits and put the skillets on for eggs and tried to be patient while he waited for people to wake up.

At seven Ariane came in the kitchen and joined him. At seven thirty their youngest son, Ingersol, drove up in the snow-covered driveway and parked his rented Lincoln and came into the house through the garage. He had been in Casper the night before but he had spent the night with a woman he met in a bar the week he was out there helping the old man move into his house. He was in a good mood and looking forward to showing his nieces and nephews how to ski. He had an apartment in Casper he'd rented several months before but he hadn't told his parents about it. He didn't mind having to come out to Wyoming all the time to talk business with his father but he wasn't going to sleep in the house with him and have him at him morning, night, and noon.

"Go wake up your brother and sister," Big Dudley said. "Let's start getting some people up around here."

Ingersol went down the hall and woke his older brother. Then he went to Rhoda's room and knocked on the door. "Who is it?" she called out.

"It's your brother. Get up. The old man wants to get started."

Rhoda opened the door and pulled her brother into the room and hugged him. In the bed Eric sat up and pulled the covers up around his chest. He liked his younger brother-in-law. Everyone liked Ingersol. He was a good man to have around, sweet and smart and funny, elegant, good-looking.

"Hello, brother-in-law," Ingersol said. "What do you think about Wyoming?"

"I haven't seen it yet. Is it always this cold?"

"It's cold all winter. Come on, get up. Momma's got breakfast ready. Dad wants to try the kids out in the backyard before we go to the mountain. Did you see the garage?"

"It's amazing." Eric laughed.

"He's been going to garage sales. He's met everyone in town going around buying that stuff. You can't ski in those old boots. We'll buy you some when we get out to the slopes. Or rent some and buy some next week when we go to Jackson Hole and Targhee. He's taking you to the big resorts next week. Did he tell you that?"

"He never tells anyone what he's going to do." Rhoda was pulling on her new ski pants, totally oblivious to her brother watching her get dressed. He was her baby brother. She had no modesty around him. "He just expects everyone to go along with anything he thinks up."

"Well, pretend to go along with the boots. I'll fix you up with some good ones later."

Ingersol left the room and Rhoda put on her new turtleneck undershirt and her new red, white, and blue ski sweater and looked at herself in the mirror. She looked great in ski clothes. This was going to be a great sport for her.

They were all gathered at the breakfast table by eight. Rhoda's mother had cooked scrambled eggs and biscuits and bacon and sausage. There were three kinds of juices and four kinds of jellies. There was whipped butter. Everyone ate and then Big Dudley sent the children back to their rooms to put long underwear on under their clothes. "What about you, Sister," he said to his daughter. "You're going to get cold out on the slopes. You've got to layer your clothes. You really need some long johns."

"They make you look fat," she said. "I've got a new down jacket. It will keep me warm. The lady in Gentry said it will keep you warm to twenty below."

"So you're going to let some saleslady in New Orleans, Louisiana, tell you how to dress to ski in Wyoming in December? Is that what you're telling me?" He was standing by the door to the garage holding a set of the long underwear he had ordered. He kept on holding it.

"No," Rhoda answered. "I'm going out to that garage and get some of those little skis and take them out in the backyard and start learning how to ski."

"Come on, Sister," her younger brother said. "I'll show you how."

"Wait for me," Eric said. "I'm coming too." Eric took the long underwear from Big Dudley. "I'll put them on," he told his father-in-law. "I'll wear them when we go out to the mountain. Give them here."

"This is the wrong size for you," Big Dudley said. "I'll put your pair on your bed. Go on out with Ingersol. He's a good skier. He'll show you how."

They went to the garage and found boots that almost fit and put them on and picked up the short skis with their old-fashioned fittings and carried it all out to the backyard. Ingersol had left his own boots and skis by the garage door. He brought them around to the backyard and put them on, then he helped Rhoda and Eric and Malcolm and Jimmy and Juliet and Ann Marie put on the things they had found. "First, be very quiet," Ingersol said. "Snow has a sound. Listen to it, get to know it. It's the medium."

"I hear it," Juliet said. "It's beautiful. Like a whisper."

"You three first," Ingersol said, meaning Rhoda and the two girls. "I want you to bend your knees and hold your poles lightly and follow me down. Don't be afraid of the speed. Speed is the control. Come on." He skied lightly down about twenty feet and turned and waited for them. Rhoda came first and almost made it before she fell. The hush was broken. Everyone started laughing and Juliet came next and went almost to the bottom of the hill before she started yelling. "How do you stop?" she yelled. "How do you stop these things?"

By eleven in the morning everyone in the family except Stella's little girls had made it down the hill at least once without falling and had learned to turn and stop and walk sideways up the hill. In the process they had turned the backyard snow into a mess. It was getting dangerous to ski on it because of all the packed places and holes from falls. "Get some dry clothes and let's go up the mountain," Big Dudley said. He had been standing by the back steps watching his sons teach the others how to ski. He was a completely happy man by the time the morning was over. His children were strong and capable and not afraid to try anything. They were fine athletes. Any sport you taught them they could conquer.

Rhoda's boys were even stronger than his own sons had

been. Even little, skinny Teddy, even Rhoda herself, were doing good. Everyone was doing good. He had them there. They were in Wyoming and they were learning how to ski.

They all went into the house and changed into dry socks and gloves and then piled into the Lincoln and the van and the Jeep and started off for Casper Mountain. Even Ariane was in a good mood, wearing her fur coat and hat and sitting beside him in the Jeep acting like she was having a good time. He had the heater on at full blast to keep her warm. If you could keep Ariane in a good mood it was worth burning up while you were driving.

Malcolm and Juliet and Jimmy were in the backseat of the Jeep with Big Dudley and Ariane. Rhoda and Eric were in the Lincoln with Ingersol, and Dudley was bringing up the rear with Stella and the rest of the children. Stella's little girls, Amy and Beth, had some puzzles Dudley had bought them in Las Vegas in the pockets of their coats. They were letting Teddy and Ann Marie play with them. Teddy loved intricate toys and puzzles. He was a lot happier than he had expected to be in Wyoming. He was in the back of a van with two little girls who were letting him play with their toys and the only grown person in charge of him was his uncle Dudley, who was patting his new wife on the leg and talking about elk hunting in Montana. Teddy liked Amy and Beth. They were pretty and they had on little matching pink out-fits and they had ski pins on their jackets from all the places Uncle Dudley had been skiing. It was then that Teddy got the idea to have a collection of such pins for himself. For the rest of the week he would be spending a lot of time in ski shops picking out the pins and getting Eric to buy them for him.

Casper Mountain was packed. It was the first day of vacation and every teenager in town was on the slopes hotdogging and tearing down the black runs and standing in line at the snack bar to get doughnuts and hot chocolate. Malcolm and Jimmy allowed themselves to be kept on the bunny slope until about three in the afternoon, then they took their skis and went off to the lift. "Let them go," Ingersol kept saying. "They're okay. They can't get hurt on five-foot skis. That's how you learn." The only people left on three-foot skis by three in the afternoon were Eric, Stella, and Ann Marie. Rhoda, Teddy, and Juliet were going down the bunny slope on old pairs of five-foot skis. Amy and Beth had quit trying and were on sleds.

Big Dudley made a few runs by himself, then settled down to coach on the bunny slope. At three forty-five he started concentrating on his son-in-law. He loved Eric Pais and was always telling people Eric was "the best Jew he'd ever known, one of the good Republican Jews, not the kind that want to take over the world."

He convinced Eric to change skis with him and they went up the T-bar together, Big Dudley on Eric's three-foot skis and Eric on Big Dudley's six-footers. When they got to the top Big Dudley gave Eric some instruction with the poles, then they started down, Eric first and Big Dudley following. Eric bent his knees, marshaled his will and his pride, and made the run without falling. He had played football and rowed double sculls at

Andover. He was not without athletic skills. He just had not used them in a while.

When Eric came to the end of the run, all the Mannings stopped and applauded. He got back on the T-bar and made the run again. He did fall the second time but not until he reached the bottom. After that he didn't fall again.

That night they had a meeting in the living room after supper. "Everybody's doing real good," Big Dudley said. "So here's the plan. We'll ski Casper Mountain two more days. By then everyone should have been on the big lift and come down the big runs at least once or twice. On Saturday we'll pack up and go to Jackson Hole. It's so beautiful up there you can't imagine. It's the Grand Teton Mountains, the big range. It's God's country, that's for sure. You're all doing good, real good."

They basked in Big Dudley's praise. Rhoda even helped do the dishes and offered to read a bedtime story to Amy and Beth. Ingersol even waited until his parents were in bed before he left and went to his apartment.

On the second day on Casper Mountain, Malcolm and Jimmy found a dealer. They didn't even find him. He found them. They were on a green run and had veered off into a stand of aspen and pine trees to take a break and smoke a joint. Juliet was supposed to be with them but she'd been waylaid at the top by her father and stepmother and had agreed to ski down with them.

Rhoda was skiing with a ski instructor she had hired. Eric and Teddy were going down blue runs with Ingersol. Stella was at the lodge with Ariane and Beth and Amy. Big Dudley was staying at the bottom of the mountain near the bunny slope where he could watch his children coming down the runs.

Malcolm and Jimmy stopped between two pine trees and Malcolm got out the joint he and Juliet had made the night before using the paper from one of Ingersol's cigarettes. It was squashed pretty badly but they'd smoked worse in Audubon Park. Malcolm lit it, took a drag, then passed it to Jimmy. They started laughing before they even got high. They were laughing so hard they could hardly breathe. They kept on laughing and smoking the joint and just standing in the trees watching skiers go by. Some teenagers went by in a group, bent over their poles, trying to beat each other to a chute that led to a black run. A group of blind skiers went by led by a pair of sighted skiers giving voice commands.

"Did you see that?" Jimmy howled. "That's the best. That's the best thing I've ever seen. They're blind. Those guys are blind."

"Let's go," Malcolm said. "Let's follow them." He took one last drag on the joint, passed it to his brother, waited, then took it back, put it out, and stuck the remains in his jacket pocket. As he was doing so a tall boy with long braided hair skied up beside them and stopped.

"You want to buy some weed?" the boy asked. "I've got some."

"What do you have?" Jimmy asked.

"Good stuff. Colombian. You want it? It's twenty dollars."

"I've got twenty dollars," Jimmy said. "Give it here. Let me look at it." They moved further behind the pine trees and the boy took out a small baggie full of raw weed. It was half twigs.

"I don't know," Jimmy said. "This doesn't look like much."

"You want it or not?"

"We want it," Malcolm said. "Give him the money, Jimmy. It's okay."

Jimmy fished around in the interior pockets of his jacket and found the twenty-dollar bill and handed it over. The boy saluted them and skied off down the hill.

"You keep it," Jimmy said. "I don't want the stuff on me. I'm too scared of him. He'll beat the shit out of us if he finds out."

"How can he find out? He doesn't think it's happening. He thinks we quit."

"Maybe we ought to quit." Jimmy looked off into the beautiful skyscapes all around him. In the distance the Laramie Range lay on the horizon, mountains so beautiful you could never imagine them in Louisiana or Mississippi.

"You think that kid was a Shoshoni?" Jimmy asked. "Granddad said they lived out here."

"You're stoned," Malcolm said. "Come on, let's go." He put the baggie in his coat and pulled down his goggles and put on his gloves. "I'm skiing down to where the old man is waiting. Come on. Let's go talk to him while we're stoned. I like to talk to him. He's not going to catch us doing a goddamned thing. He's too busy getting people to ski."

"He's not too busy with anything. He can read our minds. He can, Malcolm. You know he can."

"Not if we don't want him to." Malcolm started down a broad field of snow that led to the area where his grandfather was waiting. When he saw him, he bent lower over his skis and skied as fast as he dared to the bottom of the hill. Jimmy was right behind him.

Big Dudley watched, so happy he thought he might have another heart attack at the sight of his grandsons coming down a mountain in this beautiful, clean country, boys so strong and agile they could learn any sport as fast as you taught it to them, boys so like himself and his brothers that the only thing that made him sad was that Rhoda was too selfish to let him change their names to Manning. Well, it might hurt their father's feelings. He had to be careful about that. Well, to hell with it. He'd just be glad they were here. Now if he could only make them stay.

On Saturday they woke before dawn and ate a hurried breakfast and packed to go to Jackson Hole. They were all caught up in the excitement now. No one had to be dragged out of bed or made to check their equipment. Ingersol had bought better boots for Eric and Malcolm and Jimmy. Rhoda had bought herself a pair of expensive skis and boots and everyone had started to get territorial about hats and gloves and goggles and poles. It was turning into an expedition. It was going good.

An hour out of Jackson Hole they stopped below a small, local resort to look at the mountains. The Wind River Range of the Bighorn Mountains was just coming into view. The small resort was built on one of the first high rises of the range.

They stopped the vehicles by the side of the road and got out to stomp around in the snow and look up at the ski runs, festooned with lifts and skiers in bright red and green and yellow ski outfits. Many of them were wearing blue jeans. It was the style that year to wax blue jeans and prove your toughness by skiing in them.

"Let's go down one of the runs," Jimmy suggested. "Come on, Granddaddy. We're just wasting a whole day riding in the car. Let's go down one."

"What the hell," he said. "Why not?" So they got back into the cars and drove up to the parking lot of the resort. They all got out and started collecting their gear. Everyone was for the idea. Even Ariane seemed to think it was sane.

The name of the resort was the Arapaho. It had been in operation long before the big resorts had been built at Jackson Hole and had the feel of a local place like Casper Mountain. The mountain and the ski slopes came almost down to the highway with a sheer drop from two of the black runs that would challenge the most advanced skier.

Malcolm, Jimmy, Juliet, and Ann Marie collected their skis, took the money their grandfather handed them, and disappeared into the press of holiday skiers. "Do you think they're ready to go off on their own?" Eric asked Big Dudley. "You think they'll be all right?"

"Hell, Son, they've got kids out here five years old skiing by themselves. Who do you think was on the Lewis and Clark expedition? Kids younger than this bunch and not as big."

It took the grown people longer to find their things, disentangle their skis from the tops of vehicles, and get ready to ski. Ingersol and Dudley took Eric and Stella off to ski with them, and Rhoda was left with her parents. Ariane stationed herself in the restaurant so everyone could check in and gather there later. Rhoda and her father took their skis and went off to buy lift tickets and make a run. She felt shy being alone with her father in such a strange situation. She waited while he bought the tickets. Then they went off to the lift and rode up together. He was strangely quiet, not bossing her or lecturing her or trying to talk her into anything. They rode up the lift in the ice-cold air. The sun had moved behind the clouds since they got out of the cars. At one point the lift passed a large thermometer. It said the temperature was five degrees above zero. "Did you see that?" Rhoda asked her father. "It doesn't seem that cold, does it?"

"Just be quiet, Sweet Sister," he answered. "God will speak to you out here if you let him."

At the top of the lift they got off and moved in freshly falling snow to the crest of a run. Big Dudley fished a map of the slopes out of his pocket and studied it and showed her where they were going. "Follow me," he said, "and don't get too close behind. Just take your time and enjoy going down. We're going across a wide moraine and then down a chute. I love the chutes. Just keep your knees bent and don't lose your poles."

"It's snowing," she said.

"That's good," he answered. "It's not much snow. It makes the skiing better. It will stop halfway down. If you get in trouble, bend your knees some more." Then he was gone and Rhoda followed.

The slopes were almost deserted now. He led her down a broad field of snow and around a mogul field and down to an icy curving path that led to the clubhouse. She followed him. It was a thing she would not forget. Many years later, long after he was dead, she would wake one morning and remember following him down that field of snow and know for the first time, really know, not just accept or half believe, that he was gone and would not come again. That it was over, the part where she was a child and he was her father.

Ariane was on the porch of the clubhouse watching for them, and they waved to her as they finished the run. "Let's go down again," Rhoda said. "That was so much fun. We might never come back here as long as we live. Let's go down it one more time." Big Dudley looked at his watch.

"You go on, Sweet Sister. I better go in and take care of your mother. We've got another hour to drive. We better start collecting our gear."

Rhoda rode back up on the lift. This time when she passed the thermometer it said ten below and she laughed out loud. She was in ten-below-zero weather under a dark gray sky skiing down a mountain. It was fabulous. Maybe she would move out here, she decided. Why not? They were rich. They could do anything they wanted to do.

What they couldn't do was find Malcolm and Jimmy. When Rhoda got to the restaurant, Dudley, Ingersol, Stella, and Eric were there and so were Juliet, Ann Marie, Teddy, and Stella's little girls. No one had seen Malcolm or Jimmy for an hour.

"They'll come in," Big Dudley said. "Stop worrying. I'll go out on the porch and look for them. I can always find them. It's getting cold out. They'll be in. If they don't we'll send the ski patrol to find them." He walked out on the wide porch and stood by the railing looking up at the trails that came down from the top. The others bundled up and came out and stood beside him. After a long time Big Dudley pointed to the top of the mountain and there, with a stand of fir trees behind them, were the boys. They were at the top of the most difficult run on the mountain. They waved their poles and started down, Malcolm first and Jimmy behind him.

It was a defining moment. It was the moment when the old man knew his life had been worth living, when Rhoda knew she would never control her sons, when Eric admitted to himself he had bitten off more than he could chew, and when the skiing expedition began to have a life and momentum all its own.

The old man stood almost without breathing and watched his grandsons tearing down the black run, hatless, crazy, as much like him as his own sons because his daughter had married a man as strong as he was, with a dick as big and with the same harddriving intensity that made them hate each other.

He watched his grandsons moving down the mountain and it was all worthwhile. Anything he'd had to do to get them into the world to begin with and anything he had to put up with from Rhoda to keep them was worth it. They were his even if she did insist on calling them by someone else's last name.

When they started off again in the cars, Big Dudley changed who was riding with whom. He took Malcolm and Jimmy in the Jeep station wagon with him and Ariane. He asked Teddy to come too, but Teddy begged off and stayed with Eric and his mother.

As soon as they left the resort and were back on the highway, Big Dudley let the other cars get in front of him. Then he stopped the car and let Malcolm drive. He had taught him to drive tractors and trucks on the farm when he was ten years old. "You got to learn to drive in the snow," he told him now. "You never can tell when I might need you to drive me if I fall asleep. Just keep it at fifty miles an hour and pay attention to what you're doing. Don't put on the brakes. No matter what happens, don't brake with snow falling on the road. Be going slowly enough so you can steer yourself out of trouble. And be ready to gear down if it gets worse."

"Do you think you ought to let him drive in this?" Ariane began.

"Don't start that, Ariane. He knows what to do. He's got to learn to drive in the snow. All the kids around here drive at four-teen. They got a law that fourteen-year-olds can drive to school."

"They get driver's licenses?" Jimmy asked.

"They sure do if they live on a ranch like the one I'm trying to buy right now."

"What ranch?" Ariane asked. "You didn't tell me you were going to buy a ranch."

At Jackson Hole, they moved into two suites of rooms at the old-est resort hotel and spent the first night in the ski boutiques buy-ing things. Rhoda bought a white ski jacket with a fur collar. Teddy bought five ski pins with the names of different resorts on them. He had already bought two at Casper Mountain and one at Arapaho so altogether he had eight now. The front of his little jacket was festooned with pins. Also, he was getting Eric to buy him different kinds of goggles. He had three different sets by the time the trip was over.

Malcolm and Jimmy were buying weed with money they got from their mother and money Juliet and Ann Marie got from their father. Ingersol saw them on the slopes with a sleazy-looking boy and told Big Dudley about it but he didn't want to listen.

"Don't go throwing off on the boys," he said. "They're doing good. You're as bad as Rhoda throwing off on people. I'm watching them. They stopped all that shit."

"Well, I wouldn't trust them," Ingersol said. "It's all over the place, Dad. You better not give them any money."

"They haven't asked for any. Did you see them coming down that black run at Arapaho? I'll never forget it. I could make a pitcher out of Malcolm if Rhoda'd give him to me."

"They're doing all right in New Orleans, Dad. Eric's a good man. He's a good father to them. They're in the best school in town. It's okay."

"Down there with a bunch of niggers and drunks." The old man's eyes were clouding up. "If I could get them out here with some white people, I could get them on the right road. I wish they didn't have to go to school at all. All they're teaching them is a bunch of liberal bullshit and lies. They're in a Jewish school, Ingersol. There's no God anywhere."

"Well, you better keep an eye out for dope. I don't think they quit it, Dad. Nobody quits it unless you lock them up."

"Well, you better worry about your own life, Son. I'll take care of the boys."

But the doubt was cast. That afternoon Big Dudley left the slopes early and went into the room where the boys had put their things and began to search their bags and clothes. He found some matches and a package of wrapping papers and he thought he smelled something funny on one of Malcolm's shirts. He took the package of wrapping papers down to the lobby of the hotel and waited until the boys came back from skiing. They were with Juliet and Ann Marie.

"What is this?" he asked Malcolm when he came in. "What's this for?"

"I don't know," Malcolm said. "Where'd you get it?"

"I found it in your room," he said. "Tell me what it is."

"It's for rolling cigarettes," Malcolm said. "I bought it some-where last winter. I forgot I had it." He stood very still. If the old man hit him, he hit him. That was that. But Big Dudley didn't hit him. He turned to Jimmy.

"Are you boys doing that dope shit you did last year? Tell me the truth, Jimmy."

"No, sir. No, sir, we are not. We went to that thing at the church. You know about that. We put it in the hands of Jesus. We told you all about it. We'd never do that again."

"He wouldn't, Granddaddy." Juliet came between them and touched her grandfather on the arm. "They've been with us all the time. They aren't doing anything. Don't go getting suspi-cious of them. They love you. We all love you. We love being out here getting to ski."

"We were going to go get in the hot tub, Granddaddy," Jimmy added. "Why don't you come with us? It feels so good."

"Go on, then," Big Dudley said. "But don't lie to me, boys. Whatever you do, don't lie to me."

"We aren't, we won't," Jimmy said, but Malcolm just kept looking at him. If he hits me I'll hit him back, he had decided. If he hits me I'll hit him in the face with my fist. He's an old man. He's getting real old and his back's caving in.

Big Dudley looked his oldest grandson in the eye. He sighed. Then he stood there while the four teenagers walked off to the elevator. They're lying, he decided. But not Malcolm. He's so mean he's about to stop bothering to lie.

So I have to have a plan. I'll lie low and find a way to make Rhoda let them stay out here. If I can't have them both, maybe she'll just let me have Malcolm. If I could keep him out here, I could straighten him out.

Big Dudley was getting tired. It was starting to be a long vacation and in the morning they had to get up and drive up the pass to Targhee and spend another night away from home. I'll find a way to talk to Eric, he decided. Eric has good sense. He'll see what I mean.

Big Dudley went up on the elevator and went to his room and told Ariane he was going to order some oatmeal and whole wheat toast and poached eggs from room service and go to bed.

"What's wrong, Dudley?" she asked. "Are you tired of your adventure?"

"I'm not tired of a goddamned thing," he said. "I'm just going to eat some supper and go to bed."

"You weren't serious about looking for a ranch, were you?"

"Don't start on that now, Ariane. Look up that room service number for me, will you? You go on down and eat dinner with the rest of them. I need to get some sleep."

Malcolm, Jimmy, Ann Marie, Juliet, and Teddy were in the huge outdoor hot tub, soaking in the water while a soft snow fell on their faces. In the distance the mountains lay against the sky like a dream or a vision. "We got to be really careful now," Jimmy said. "He knows we're doing it, Malcolm. You know he does. I think Uncle Ingersol told him. When he saw us at that hot chocolate place with that guy. I bet he told him."

"Don't worry about it. I got the grass in those old boots he gave me. He'll never find it. I'll move it if you want me to. We'll get Juliet to keep it. Besides, he can't do anything with Mother here. She won't let him."

They were alone in the hot tub except for one very fat man soaking in the water and drinking Scotch and water.

"Don't talk so loud," Ann Marie put in.

"I won't keep it," Juliet said. "I'll do a lot for you, Malcolm, but I won't do that."

"He's going to find out," Teddy put in. "If he finds out he'll kill you. You better not do it anymore out here. You're going to make everything go bad."

"Shut up, Teddy," Malcolm said and moved toward him to hit him, but Jimmy and Juliet got in the way.

"Don't do anything to him," Jimmy said. "He's being good. He's been skiing real good." He tousled his younger brother's hair.

"Let's smoke some now," Malcolm suggested. "We could go in and do it in the dressing room."

"People smell it," Juliet said. "I wouldn't do that if I was you." But Malcolm was already out of the pool and moving toward the door to the dressing room.

"Are you coming?" he asked Jimmy.

"I don't know."

The fat man pulled himself out of the pool and wrapped a robe around his disgusting fat and waddled off to the dressing room.

"Don't do it when he's in there," Juliet said when he was gone. Malcolm was still by the door. "Please don't now. It's too scary."

Malcolm went in the door and came back in a minute wrapped in a robe. He was carrying a joint and some matches. He sat down on the edge of the pool and lit it and sat smoking it, looking out across the fields of snow to the sun going down behind the Wind River Range of the Teton Mountains. The smell was everywhere. In a while Juliet took a drag from the cigarette, then Jimmy took one, then Ann Marie. "You want some, Teddy?" Jimmy asked. "Go on and try it."

"I have to go in," he said and pulled himself out of the pool and put on his robe and left. "You're going to get yourself killed. He said he'd rather you were dead than a dope addict. He told it to Mother." Malcolm flipped the butt of the joint at him but it missed and landed on the snow. Then he started laughing and his brother and cousins laughed with him. The dying sunlight on the snow was turning red and violet and every brilliant shade of azure and orange and pink and fuchsia and violet and blue. A world full of mountains and sunsets and skies was too beautiful for ordinary human beings. It was a world for Gods and Big Dudley's four oldest grandchildren sat in the hot tub and celebrated like the gods they thought they were.

The trip to Targhee was hurried but uneventful. They had time to ski for several hours in the afternoon and Teddy even managed to get Eric into a ski shop and pick up one last pin. Then they got into the vehicles and started driving home. It was Christmas Eve and it was two hundred and eighty miles back to Casper and the forecast was for snow.

They started off with Dudley and Stella and her little girls and Rhoda and Jimmy in the van. In the Jeep were Big Dudley, Ariane, Malcolm, Juliet, and Ann Marie.

Ingersol and Eric were last in the Lincoln with the trunk and backseat piled high with bags and equipment. They had decided not to put bags on top of the Jeep because of the snow warnings.

They made it to the long pass between Targhee and Jackson Hole just as dark was falling. In the van Dudley was telling hunting stories. Just as they came to the steepest part of the pass he saw an elk on a precipice and rolled down the window to point it out to Jimmy. Then the van began to slide. They watched helplessly as the van began to move down the side of the mountain. No one spoke. The van seemed to fill with light. They were falling off the side of a mountain and they were helpless to stop it. Little Amy held on to Rhoda's arm. Jimmy was transfixed.

Then, miraculously, the van began to slow its fall. It slowed and came to a stop in a bank of snow it had plowed up as it fell. They were twenty feet from the road in the dark in the snow. But they were alive.

Behind them Big Dudley had seen the accident happening and had put on his flasher lights to signal Ingersol and Eric. A third car stopped to help. Someone took off to find a phone to call the highway patrol.

The inhabitants of the van slowly began to speak and then to move. "All move to the left side," Dudley said. "Dad will have seen us. Stay still. We don't know what's under us. Snow is tricky. Don't try to get out. Get on the left side and be as still as you can."

Stella was starting to cry. So was Amy, but Beth seemed to think it was all right.

"What should I do?" Jimmy asked.

"Nothing," Rhoda answered. "Move over this way very slowly. Be quiet. Be still. We'll be okay. Daddy will save us."

"What if he didn't see us go off the road?"

"He saw us. Of course he did."

"Roll down your window a little bit, Shorty," Dudley said to Rhoda. If snow comes in, roll it back up."

"Okay, it's okay. I got it down. Nothing's coming in."

In a few minutes they could hear yelling up above them. It was Ingersol's voice. "Sister, Brother, we're here. We'll get you out. You're okay, you're dug in. You aren't going to fall anymore. I'll be down."

Before the police arrived with ladders and blankets, Ingersol had climbed down the embankment and was beside the car talking to them. The last thing Rhoda remembered was holding Ingersol's hand through the window. Then the highway patrol was there and carrying her up a ladder.

It was nine at night before everyone had been thanked and the van had been pulled back up on the road by the wrecker and tested and declared driveworthy and the family was back in the vehicles and on their way again.

"God saved us again," Big Dudley kept saying. "He's been so

good to us. No one will ever know what he can do. Did you see Ingersol climbing down that fall, Ariane? He's a goddamn man. He's a man."

"We shouldn't have been out here to begin with," she answered. "We shouldn't be driving now. We should stop somewhere and wait until the morning. We won't be home until the middle of the night."

Rhoda was curled up in the back of the van with three blankets on her back and Jimmy beside her. "We almost died," she kept saying. "I'm freezing to death, Dudley. Let's stop somewhere and spend the night. We almost died back there. What are we doing still driving in this van?"

"There's no place to stop, Sister. Just go to sleep. And for God's sake, stop complaining."

They got to the house in Casper at two in the morning on Christmas Day. "Just take in what you need," Big Dudley said. "Get to bed. We can straighten all this out in the morning."

He turned up the setting on the furnace and fell into his own bed. "I don't know what you think you're doing" was the last thing he heard Ariane say. "I can't believe you, Dudley. They were almost killed. What was Dudley doing driving in that snow? He can't even see out of one eye. What are we doing out here? I can't live like this. I'm not strong enough to see my own children die. . . ."

Dudley and Stella were the first ones awake in the house. They sneaked out of bed in their pajamas and went into the living room to put some presents under the tree for Stella's little girls and Dudley's daughters. He had bought emerald earrings for Juliet in Vegas and a gold lamé bracelet for Ann Marie at a shop in Jackson Hole. For Stella he had bought a new diamond ring. He gave it to her underneath the tree and watched her put it on. Dudley's favorite gifts to women were pieces of jewelry. He had outlandish, extravagant taste and later, when he was broke, many of the women still loved him for the moments when they opened the little boxes from Neiman Marcus and the Sands and Tiffany.

By nine o'clock the rest of the household was waking up. Stella was taking a turn cooking breakfast. Rhoda was in her bedroom rolling up her hair on heated rollers. Teddy was out in the front of the house helping his grandfather spread cinders on the front walkway, and Malcolm and Jimmy were in their bedroom rolling a joint. They had bought some more papers from a boy they met on the slopes at Targhee. Jimmy was weeding and processing the pot and Malcolm was standing by holding the paper. When the joint was finished, Malcolm held it up into the air and they inspected it. "When do you want to smoke it?"

"In a little while. Let's go in the bathroom in the front hall. There's a big fan in there. It's better than in here."

"We better wait till we can go outside. There're too many people in here. Uncle Ingersol will know what it is if he smells it. So will Mother."

"No, she won't. I've smoked it right in the next room and she didn't smell it."

"Well, when she was drunk."

"No, just on a regular day."

"I think we ought to go outside."

"It's Christmas, Jimmy. Well, just wait. I'll tell you when. Let's go see what they're doing." Malcolm folded a Kleenex over the joint and put it in his shirt pocket and they went out to eat breakfast and open their presents.

At eleven o'clock Malcolm and Jimmy found Teddy and told him they wanted him to help them with something. They took him to the wide front hall and stationed him by the stairs to watch for grown people. "We're going in this bathroom and smoke a joint," Malcolm told him. "If anyone comes just start yelling like you hurt yourself."

"I don't want to get in this."

"Well, you're in it. Just stay by the stairs and yell if anyone comes. It will just take a few minutes. Now do it."

Malcolm and Jimmy went in the large guest bathroom and closed and locked the door and got out the joint and started smoking it. Teddy stood by the stairs scared to death.

About two minutes went by. Then Big Dudley came into the hall. "Where are your brothers?" he asked Teddy.

"I don't know."

The smell of marijuana burning was everywhere. It was a red flag in the wind, it was as clear as day, it was the end.

"What do you mean, you don't know. You just walked by with them." The old man was very close to him. He took him by the arm and squeezed his arm. "Where are they?"

"They're in there," Teddy said, pointing to the bathroom door, starting to cry. "I didn't have anything to do with it, Granddaddy. I'm not in this." Big Dudley let go his arm and went to the bathroom door and tried to open it. Then he began to beat on it. Teddy ran from the hall and went to find his mother and Eric.

When Rhoda got to the front hall her father was pounding on the door with his fists and screaming. "You goddamn little sons-of-bitches, you better open this door. I'm going to kill you, you little sons-of-bitches." He was screaming and crying and beating on the door. The smell of marijuana was everywhere and his sons tried to hold him back from the door but they couldn't over-power him. Rhoda ran to the door. "Open the door, Jimmy," she said. "What in the hell are you doing in there?"

In the end Dudley and Ingersol managed to drag their father away from the door and Eric and Rhoda talked the boys into opening the door but when they were out in the hall Big Dudley tore loose from his sons and went to them and started hitting them with his fists, screaming and crying and hitting them both as hard as he could hit them.

Then Rhoda dragged her sons away and she was screaming too and Ariane sat on the stairs crying and Stella took her little girls to her room and sat on the bed comforting them.

Rhoda kept on screaming at her father. She screamed at him all the way down the hall as she pulled her sons into a bedroom and locked the door behind them. Then Eric got on the phone and called the airport and made reservations.

By two in the afternoon Rhoda, Eric, Malcolm, Jimmy, and Teddy were in the van and Dudley was driving them to the air-port. Christmas in Wyoming was over. It would never come again.

On the Wind
River in Wyoming

IN NINETEEN SEVENTY-TWO my father couldn't take it anymore. His five oldest grandchildren had gone to the revolution, the party I guess you should call it, the decision by a lot of people in the United States that life was short, government was unreliable, rules were made to be broken, and it was time to start cashing in two thousand years' worth of civilized chips.

My brothers and I had been at the party all along. We fueled our rebellion with alcohol instead of drugs, but aside from that there was nothing the hippies were up to that we hadn't already tried.

With half his progeny at the party my father began to feel maybe it hadn't been worthwhile after all. He was tired of being the only one who could be depended upon. He was sixty-six years old and he had had a heart attack and he wanted to do what he wanted to with the rest of his life. What he wanted was to leave the decadent South behind and go and live where there were cowboys and wide open spaces and people who believed in God.

So he took a diesel Mercedes and parked it at the Denver airport and started flying back and forth from Jackson, Mississippi, and driving around the West looking for a place to live. He was a Caterpillar Tractor dealer and when he was gone the business was run by my older brother, who was a genius, albeit a mixed-blessing one. Between my father and my older brother ran a river of love so deep and troubled and profound that neither of them could understand lesser loyalties. "Dad," my brother called my father. "Son," my father called him.

On the shores of this great love my younger brother and my mother and myself gleaned what love we could. Not that my father didn't love the rest of us. He did and he gave us anything we wanted and had plenty of energy and attention left over for his grandchildren. What we couldn't have was the unquestioning devotion he lavished on Dudley, who was named for him and for his father.

Still, my father was tired of being the main person who stayed sober and worked while the rest of us had a party. He blamed that on the South and planned on shaking its dust from his heels and pushing on to greener pastures. He was sure that once he made the move he'd be able to seduce the rest of us into following him.

It was a pattern that had developed during the years when my father was making his fortune. The pattern was, get everyone settled and comfortable, then talk them into moving to a

place where they would be richer or better off or have more op-
portunities.

My father liked the pattern but my mother was sick of it. She
had redecorated all the houses she could stand to redecorate. She
thought she had earned a rest. She was as sick as Daddy was of
having everyone at the party but she didn't think moving to the
West was going to change it.

My father came home from his third trip to Denver saying he had
found his place, a new world where our family could make a new
beginning and save our children from the madness that was over-
taking Mississippi, drugs and desegregation and sexual license.
So many children to save, I guess he was thinking, but he believed he was up to the task, as soon as he got his ducks in a row
and his strong sons by his side.

He had bought a house in Casper, Wyoming, he told my
mother, and they would live there while he looked for a ranch in
the foothills of the Bighorn Mountains.

"That's it," she answered. "You have gone too far, Dudley.
This time you have gone too far. I am not moving to Wyoming
and that is that."

So she packed her bags and went off with her bridge club to
the Orient. She was gone five weeks. When she returned she re-
lented and began to pack the china and silver and antique furniture and to say goodbye to her friends. She was in the habit of
giving in to him and once again she did it.

On the first of June she watched a yellow van carry her life
off to Wyoming. When it had left the yard she and my father got

into a second diesel Mercedes, and, with my youngest son riding shotgun, drove off to start their new life.

The historic farmhouse she had spent five years restoring was left in the hands of my older brother's best friend and his new wife. The horses were left in the pastures. The business was left to my brothers to run or sell. My father was on his way to live among cowboys and Mormons and antelopes in the great state of Wyoming. His first choice would have been Utah, which was chock full of Mormons, but he settled on Wyoming because of the mountains and because he thought it would be an easier place to talk the rest of us into wanting to live.

His plots were labyrinthine, and yet, they were also simple. They were always just what he said they were except they were so outlandish it always took us a while to believe he meant it when he made his proposals. The master plan was that one by one he would buy each of us a bank or a dry-cleaning establishment or a filling station, whatever was for sale, and one by one we would come and live there and run the businesses and do outdoor sports instead of cocktail parties and Mardi Gras. We would all learn to ski and the men would hunt the Bighorn Mountains and we would have horses and ride on western saddles into the sunlight of a new beginning for our family.

It didn't turn out like he planned. Within a year my mother was living around the corner from me in New Orleans. She had brought all the silver and china and antique furniture back to the decadent South and moved into a duplex apartment on Henry Clay Avenue and was going out to dinner with one of her old boyfriends from Ole Miss.

My father had bought a ranch and was living there with a woman who had been his bookkeeper the year he made his first million dollars. She was, not incidentally, the other grandmother of his first four granddaughters, as her daughter had married my older brother. She and my father had been hot for each other the whole time he was making that million dollars but instead of consummating their love they had bred their oldest children to each other. The marriage didn't last but the girls were nice and my father loved them. Now, with my mother pouting in New Orleans and Valerie's husband dead, Daddy and Valerie were making this stand in the foothills of the Bighorn Mountains. My brothers said it was my father's first experience of oral sex but I think it was about the million dollars. My father was a Scot. He loved money more than he loved anything in the world, except maybe his father and his sons.

He loved *my* sons with the same passion and had been plotting for years to take them away from me. Sometimes I wish he had succeeded. He was a man. His influence on all of us and the genes he gave us may be a mixed blessing but I don't know anyone in my family who wants to give any of it back or change it for any other influence or set of genes. It's a gift that will stand by you when the chips are down or when your back's against the wall or when you need to make a stand. I feel it in me every day, a force I can call on when I need it. He didn't back down and he couldn't be intimidated. We don't all have it to the extent he did but we have it when we need it.

That's the back story of how my youngest son and I ended up on the Wind River in a canoe with no idea where we were going or how long it was going to take to get to wherever it was we were going. We were alone on that river for five hours and fifteen minutes. A twelve-year-old boy and a thirty-eight-year-old woman in a Grumman canoe with three paddles, a loaf of bread, and a bottle of water. It was Daddy's idea of trying to seduce me into moving to Wyoming. He was seducing the men with hunting trips. He had decided to seduce me with canoe adventures.

Well, I did love canoes and so did my youngest son, Teddy. Teddy had won blue ribbons in canoeing every year at Camp Carolina, and he was, in his way, as fierce and tenacious as any man in the family. He was always working at a disadvantage by being the youngest male of his generation in our tribe, but he fought on no matter what they did to him. I think now I should have protected him more but he never acted like someone who needed protecting. He acted like a fierce little redheaded boy who would live up to the Manning code of honor. It was Gaelic or Scots. Loosely translated it said, No one fucks with us with impunity.

From the moment my father thought up making a stand in Wyoming, Teddy was one of the main ones he was trying to seduce. My older sons ended up living there for long periods of time because we were trying to get them to stop smoking marijuana but that was expediency. The boy Daddy most wanted to take away from me was Teddy. "He's little," Daddy would say. "But he will stand. He's tough as a cob."

All the men in our family are small when they are young. They don't get their height until they are fifteen or sixteen and they keep on growing into their twenties. Teddy fit this growth mold perfectly. He had the Scots-English version of our male family body, elegant and powerful and energetic. More important to my father, he had the voice, the tongue, the powerful imagination and quick wit and sense of humor. That wit was my father's saving grace where human relationships were concerned. He was one of the funniest men who ever lived and could sum up a situation or a cultural zeitgeist in phrases that would be repeated by everyone he knew.

When I first began to make my mark as a writer he came to my house and put a story I had published down on the table and said, "Why would anyone want to write a story about a thing like this? This could lead a young person to think it's all right to break the law." It was a story about a young man who robs a bar.

I have not forgotten him saying that and I've decided he was right. Raising the young and keeping them out of trouble is the main thing a culture should be doing. Why would I want to add to the confusion and lawlessness of the world?

He was always turning out to be right, and when we abandoned the clear paths he wanted us to travel we were always sorry.

My daddy loved to talk to Teddy. When he was three years old, Daddy would put him in a car riding shotgun and talk to him about things. He used to take Teddy out to the family graveyard and show him the place where he planned on being buried. There was a huge granite stone he had quarried out of the Kentucky hills. On it were carved the names of his male ancestors going all the way back to Scotland. "After I'm dead I'll still come back and watch over you and make sure you're doing good," he would tell him.

"You won't be able to get out," Teddy would reply. "There'll be little devils down there holding you down."

"I'll get out," Daddy would say. "They can't hold me."

"Yes, they will," Teddy would answer. "You can't get away from them. You'll be old."

"I won't get old," Daddy said. "I'm doing my exercises."

I thought about that when Daddy was dying, when the morphine had him under. It was the first time in his life he had ever been powerless. Eighty-nine years old and he was still fighting every minute until they started the morphine. He had fought his way out of a hospital and fought his way out of the bed and then he fell and took all the skin off his arm so they put him down and gave him morphine. I was there. I should have stopped it. I should have let him get up and die standing on his feet even if he bled to death. I don't know what we thought we were doing. He wouldn't stay at the hospital and he didn't want to be treated and he wouldn't stay in bed and his heart was giving out so we chose not to let him be in pain but I think now we should have let him be in pain or bleeding or anything he wanted instead of lying in a bed on morphine listening to gospel music. He could still squeeze our hands. He could still grip my hand as hard as when he was young. I was terrified he would tell me something I didn't want to hear so I didn't stay in the room very much. When I was there I talked incessantly.

Well, that's how he died and we thought we were doing the best we could but it was ourselves we were serving. I don't want hospice coming to my bedside. They're too much like those little devils Teddy warned us of.

★　　　★　　　★

Daddy timed the move to Wyoming to take place when school was out so he could take Teddy in the car to act as a buffer between him and my mother's rage. He was taking her away from her family and friends and expecting her, at age sixty-five, to homestead to the West and talk to cowboys and chunky women who wore men's coats in the winter. He was expecting this from a woman who had her hair done every Friday and wore heels to garden in. A woman who grew hybrid roses and played bridge at the country club and had been a Chi Omega at Ole Miss. "You don't know where to stop," she was always saying to him. "You always go too far."

So Teddy had been on the initial trip to Wyoming and also on the Christmas trip when Daddy taught twenty people how to ski and also had gone out there once for two weeks alone. He was already an expert on Daddy's Wyoming adventure, so, when Mother moved back to the South, and Daddy bought the ranch and moved Valerie in, Teddy and I flew to Wyoming to visit them. I had not seen my father since the famous skiing trip, and, although I was trying not to think about him at all, I couldn't help being curious about the ranch. "We've got two pretty riding horses," he told me on the phone. "And there's a country club with tennis courts and you've got to see these mountains. They're the prettiest ones in the world."

"I saw them when we went skiing."

"But you haven't seen them when the snow melts. There's a river here you can go down for days. It's the prettiest water you've ever seen. Come on out and visit me, Sister, and bring the little boy with you. I'm lonesome for him."

★   ★   ★

"You want to go out to Wyoming and see Granddaddy's ranch?" I asked Teddy.

"Sure," he said. "When can we go?"

"As soon as school's out," I said. "I'm not going there anymore unless it's warm."

"I want to go," my husband, Eric, said. "I want to see this ranch."

"Can you leave in June?"

"No. If I leave then I can't go diving in July. You two go on and I'll come spend the last weekend. I need to go to Oregon anyway. I'll figure it out so I can come there afterward."

"What will we do with Jimmy and Malcolm?"

"I'll take care of them and your mother will help."

Malcolm and Jimmy and Teddy were my sons from another marriage. Malcolm was sixteen and Jimmy was fifteen. It was the last summer they would go to Camp Carolina but they didn't leave until the middle of June. Still, they had to go and see their father anyway. Plus, Mother was around the corner. Plus, Eric's parents would take care of them. Plus, I had a full-time maid. Plus, they did whatever they wanted no matter who was taking care of them. I suppose I had given up on keeping them from doing anything as long as I didn't know about it and as long as they passed in school. My mind had leaped over the problem of my two oldest sons. It would grab at anything rather than admit they were out of my control.

"They could visit their father while I'm gone," I suggested. "He wants them as soon as they can come."

"We'll figure it out," Eric said. "Go on and see your father. Call my secretary. Tell her to get you some airline tickets."

So, on the third of June, Teddy and I rose before dawn and threw our suitcases in the car and Eric drove us to the airport and put us on a plane to Denver. At Denver we changed planes and flew to Sheridan, Wyoming. Daddy met us at the airport and we got into a Mercedes and started driving south to Buffalo. As soon as we got in the car he started lecturing us about geology and elevations and river basins and mountain ranges and wildlife and the indescribable beauty of the world God had made and given us. "I'm going to send you and the Little Boy down the Wind River," he said. "It's a beautiful canoe ride, past wide pastures lined with willow trees. It's the prettiest river I've ever seen and not a bug on it. You can float for miles without touching a paddle. I took Valerie on it about a month ago. Ask her about it."

"How is Valerie?" I asked. "Does she like it here?"

"She's made some friends and she likes playing tennis at the little country club we joined. She's playing some with one of the bankers' wives."

"Mother's mad at us for coming. She thinks it's disloyal of us to visit you with Valerie here."

"Well, don't say anything against your mother, Sister. I don't want to hear that."

"I wasn't. I was just telling you."

"She said you were out here with your hussy," Teddy put in. "She told me not to come."

"Well, she shouldn't have been saying that to you." Daddy

sighed and rolled down the window. "Keep on the lookout for wildlife, Ted. There are herds of buffalo around here and antelope that look like the lilies of the field. I'd like to take you on a side trip over to the Bradford Brinton home and let you see the Remington paintings but I promised Valerie we'd get back in time for dinner. Everywhere you turn in this state there's something gorgeous to see. This is just a four-lane going to Buffalo but you'll be able to see the mountains in the distance. Just taste this air, Sister. The mean elevation in the state is six thousand, seven hundred feet. This air is as clear as God meant air to be. I hate to think what you're breathing down in that swamp where you live. Goddamn, I wish I could get you out of there before it's too late."

"It's not a swamp," Teddy said. "It's nice in New Orleans, Granddaddy. We got a dog, did we tell you that? A real English sheepdog. Eric got him from Atlanta. He came on a plane."

"And I guess you keep him in the house like you did that last one. Goddamn, that's what kills me about that place. People keeping dogs in houses and white trash and drunks asleep on the streets. I don't know how you can stand to live down there. How are Malcolm and Jimmy doing in school, Sister? Did they pass okay?"

"Just barely. Don't talk about them. I need a vacation from thinking about them. They're supposed to go to camp in two weeks but Jimmy says he isn't going."

"He came home after a week last year," Teddy said. "It wasted all of Eric's money."

"Granddaddy pays for camp," I said. "I don't let Eric pay for things like that."

"Jimmy's going to Georgia to see our father," Teddy added. "He's going to work for him painting Grandmother Alice's house."

"Well, that's good. I'd rather have him working than going to some pantywaist camp in Carolina."

So the trip went on for forty miles, plus stopping every fifteen minutes to look at livestock or wild animals or to examine road cuts for geology lessons or just to stop and walk around and look at the land. It took an hour and a half to go forty miles. Then, finally, we were on the outskirts of Buffalo, Wyoming, then down the main street and out of town again and then we turned onto an asphalt road and went up a hill to a white wooden house with barns and buildings all around it. There were very few trees and no flowers.

Standing in the door of the house was my father's new *wife,* the pudgy, sweet-faced Valerie, mother of my sister-in-law, keeper of my father's books the year he made his first million dollars, and, according to my brothers, his Aphrodite of exotic sex.

She was smiling. She was hoping for the best.

The house was a log cabin painted white with rooms added on either side and chimneys pointing to the sky like horns. The front door was a thick wooden slab surrounded by a small concrete porch with nothing on it but a broken bentwood chair. Above the chair was a small black mailbox. It was stark.

We drove to the side door and walked through mud to a set of concrete block steps leading to a small enclosed porch with thick storm windows, a box for firewood, a freezer, and an extra refrigerator. There were two empty Cutty Sark boxes filled with files, sitting on a kitchen table painted white. On the floor someone had thrown a horse blanket to use to wipe our feet. Beside the door was a device for removing cowboy boots and a hat rack. Valerie had left the front door and come to open the door from the porch to the kitchen. I was going to be nice to her because I was always nice to everyone, even Valerie Kerrigan, who had broken up my parents' marriage and even though I had been dreaming lately of stabbing her in the chest with knives. I had been dreaming it ever since I started packing to go to Wyoming. The dreams didn't seem to need much explanation. Mother had left Wyoming because she didn't want to live on an ugly ranch in the middle of nowhere, and as soon as she left, Daddy went to Memphis and brought Valerie back. He said he had gotten a Mexican divorce and married her but my brothers and I only half-believed it. While I was in Wyoming I met an older couple who said they had been at the wedding ceremony. Also, there was a photograph of Daddy and Valerie together and Valerie was wearing a pretty dress and holding flowers so whatever the truth of the Mexican divorce might be, Valerie thought she was married to him and he wanted us to act like we believed it too.

After all, she was the other grandmother of his four oldest granddaughters. So, either she was married to him or he was pretending she was married to him. A few years later, when it broke up and he went down to New Orleans with his hat in his hand and convinced Mother to forgive him and take him back, they got married again in the Episcopal church, so maybe it was true about the Mexican divorce and the Wyoming marriage. I didn't care one way or the other. I was surprised, actually, that I had dreamed of stabbing Valerie as I felt no real animosity toward her. She was too short and chunky to pose any real threat to my mother, who was tall and very beautiful. Also, she cooked and cleaned up the log house and had agreed to live with Daddy under these primitive conditions. She even went skiing with him and let him take her down rivers in canoes. I admired her for that and didn't blame him for wanting a change from Mother. "My vacation," he would later call it. "Your mother won't let me have a golden anniversary party because of my vacation," he would say. "Your mother's still mad because I took a vacation."

Anyway, we were here and I was going to make the best of it. If my father wanted to live in Wyoming, I would go and see him because I loved him and I sure wasn't quitting being his daughter. He had seen me through three marriages and gotten me an illegal abortion when I needed one and given me anything I asked for since the day I was born. I wasn't giving him up for anything or anyone.

It would be many years later, after twenty-four years of psychotherapy and four years of recovering from the psychotherapy before I realized how much I loved the man. I was him. I was more like him than either of my brothers. If I stopped loving him I would have to stop loving the most powerful parts of myself. He was my daddy. I loved him more than I would ever love another person but I never told him so or did one thing he wanted me to do. If he told me A, I did Z. He knew this, but he couldn't stop telling me A, so I kept on doing Z.

★   ★   ★

He was always offering me treasures and I was always turning them down, although some of the things he offered me were too good to refuse, like learning to roller-skate and ice-skate and ski, or jumping horses over fences or swimming them across ponds or how to survive in the woods or to use a compass. This trip to Wyoming was going to be one of the things I couldn't refuse. I was being shown the most beautiful and unspoiled land in the United States, the Bighorn Mountains before the spoilers found out about them.

Even when I tried to turn down things he offered me he never gave up, he kept on coming. On this trip he kept on talking and showing us antelope and mountains and river basins and road cuts, talking, pointing out, teaching, and, finally, when he'd exhausted everything in the immediate area, he put us in a camper with a canoe tied in the back and took us off to meet the Wind River. This was nineteen seventy-four. No one had messed with this country yet. It was all ours. Even in the midst of my nonstop rebellion I knew the wonder of it and of his relentless pursuit of the goodness in me. He blamed my recalcitrance on my mother as she blamed it on him, but it was caused by them together, by the necessity to both adore and escape them, which I never did, although, for the twenty-four years I was in therapy, I thought I had escaped.

The ranch Daddy bought was called the Double Hitch. He had bought it lock, stock, and barrel, including the furnishings of the house. There was furniture made from Douglas fir and lodge-pole pine. There were Shoshoni rugs and Navajo blankets and a huge geological survey map of the state on the largest wall. All the furniture had been pushed back against the walls, a decor Daddy had begged my mother to embrace for years. Plus, there were two large framed prints of cowboy paintings by Frederic Remington, Daddy's favorite painter. His favorite writer was Louis L'Amour. He would laugh until tears rolled down his cheeks while reading or thinking about cowboys. Exploits on horseback held a delight and satisfaction for him I could never understand until very late in his life he began to tell me about his paternal grandmother, who had ridden to hounds sidesaddle wearing long dresses. This was one of the icons I had never lived up to.

As soon as we put our suitcases in our rooms we went to the map and Daddy began showing us where we were.

"In a few days we'll get in the camper and go exploring," he said. "See this road, Teddy. This is the most beautiful drive I've ever been on. Ten Sleep to Buffalo. They call it the Cloud Peak Skyway. It goes over the southern end of the Bighorns. Powder River Pass, see right here, then Meadowlark, then Ten Sleep Canyon." I was afraid he would start in on God since one of his obsessions was trying to get me to believe in God. I was never convinced he believed in God anyway. I think he believed in authority and chain of command. Anyway, I didn't feel like hearing about it now so I tried to veer him off with a question.

"Why did they call it Ten Sleep?"

"Well, Sweet Sister, why would you think the Shoshoni would name something Ten Sleep? Because it took ten days to get there from somewhere else they camped. They were on horseback and some of them were walking. Well, look here now. We'll go down to Thermopolis and maybe spend the night and take the hot baths, then go find the Wind River and follow that for a while. Change your shoes now. I want to show you the horses."

All this time Valerie had been standing by keeping her mouth shut, something Daddy had never been able to get Mother to do.

"Did you bring the little boy some boots like I told you to?"

"I think so."

"I don't have any, Granddad. I outgrew that pair you bought me the last time I was here. I grew two inches. Can't you tell?"

"You'll get your height. You're just like Uncle Ingersol. He didn't get his until he was sixteen and he kept on growing all the way to college. He grew a couple of inches in his twenties." Daddy turned from the map and went to Teddy and put his arm around him and sized him up. "You'll make a man if I can get you away from that pantywaist city she took you to. Let me see what shoes you have with you."

"Just these. They're the only ones I brought."

"Well, I'll be goddamned. I told you to bring him some practical clothes, Sister. Why didn't you help him pack?"

"I was busy. I barely got away as it was. I was working on the Symphony Benefit for the synagogue. I was helping Eric's mother."

"Never mind. Get your hat, Son. We'll go into town and get you some boots. There's a store that stays open late. Come on. Get your jacket and your cap."

In a moment they were gone and I was left alone with

Valerie. "We have a closet full of boots," she said. "If you need some there might be some that fit you. What size do you wear?"

"I brought some cowboy boots I had made in Dallas. I wear a seven or eight. Let me see what you have. I hate to tramp around in mud in my good boots. They were handmade for me."

We went back into a spare bedroom and there was a closet full of cowboy clothes and plaid shirts and warm jackets and long underwear and extra ski clothes and a row of different kinds of boots. "I like hiking boots when I go off with him," she said. "You never know where he's going to take you. Most of these are things your brothers or their visitors left here. They don't care if you use them."

I picked up a pair of expensive brown leather hiking boots and stuck my foot in one. It fit, so I took the boots to my room and changed into corduroy jeans and a flannel shirt and put on the boots with some socks. I liked the feel of them. I liked being in this strange house with Daddy off buying shoes for someone, his favorite occupation, and Valerie acting like she was a Mexican servant she was so afraid something would go wrong and I would ruin her little love nest. I had a reputation for volatility which I had gained when I drank too much. Sober, I was a different person, but it was going to take my family many years to learn that, and in the meantime the women were still afraid of me. The men weren't afraid of me no matter what I did, but they didn't like me to drink because it was so much trouble. Men don't like trouble. They like maps on the walls and the furniture pushed back out of the way and meals on time and the dream of blow jobs. Men are so simple. That's why I like them.

★   ★   ★

After I changed clothes I went into the kitchen to watch Valerie cook. It was simple country fare, a meat loaf and several pans of cooked vegetables. There was a custard pie on the sideboard. *Tacky* was the main word that kept occurring to me. Tacky, tacky, tacky.

I went into the bedroom and called Mother and gave her a quick report. "She's fat," I reported. "Short and fat. I guess he wants her for a servant. She made a cream pie with meringue. I don't suppose they'll expect me to eat it, will they?"

"Don't be rude to her, Rhoda. She's the grandmother of the girls."

"Alas. That's where they got those hips. Half of them have her hips. You know it's true. Well, I have to go now."

"His mother had those hips. The Cassidys have them."

"Well, thank God I don't."

"Do you want to know about your children?"

"Of course. What are they doing?"

"Eric took Jimmy to a baseball game. Malcolm's spending the night with Clinton Marais."

"That's good. Well, goodbye, Mother. I have to go."

I hung up the phone feeling virtuous. I had made Mother's day. Plus, Malcolm was running around with people from nice families and maybe the worst of the children's taking drugs was over, at least for nice people in New Orleans. I decided to go outside and look at the horses and saddles. Daddy loved saddles and tackle of all kind. It would make him happy if he came back from town and found me out in the barns or sitting on a rail at the corral.

"I made a lemon meringue pie," Valerie said, as I went

through the kitchen. "You can have some if you're hungry. Or I could make you a sandwich. Dudley loves that pie. He wants me to make one every day."

"You just leave it out uncovered like that?"

"There aren't any flies this time of year."

"Okay. Well, I'm going out and look at the horses."

"There are two men who work around the place. Ed and Jack. I never know when they'll be here. They take care of the cattle and the barn. Ed stays back there in that trailer part of the time."

"Okay. I'll look for them."

I went across the small back porch and down the concrete block steps and down across the yard to the outbuildings, which were spread out in a semicircle, with no discernible plan. There was what might have been a bunkhouse. I looked in the window and saw some of Mother's furniture. A cherry dresser sitting on a Persian rug with boxes piled up around it. On top of a pile of boxes sat a mirrored dresser top. It had been in my parents' room all my life. It went on top of Daddy's dresser. There had always been a quotation stuck in the mirror. "Every day the world turns upside down on top of someone who thought he was sitting on top of it." Beside that, a photograph of his father in the fields with his dogs. In the photograph his father is holding a rifle and looking off in the distance. He is wearing a tie and a hunting jacket.

I heard the car coming up the driveway and turned and walked back to the parking spaces. Teddy was beaming. Daddy had bought him some Tony Lama boots, silver and black with a steer's horns worked into the leather. It was starting. The man thing, the big seduction. Teddy was the most wary of my father of all my sons but even he was not immune to the man deal. Even if he ended up being hit with a belt when I wasn't looking he would ride shotgun with my daddy when he got the chance. He would be seventeen years old before he rebelled and jumped out of a moving car to escape the old man. And that was when he was on drugs. Before it cost me twenty thousand dollars to undo the damage a black pusher in Audubon Park and the culture of the decadent South and the hippies and the Vietnam War and bad luck and bad mothering and his father's coldness and his stepfather's spoiling had caused my child. Anyway, I had the money and he got well. But that was all in the future. For now he was a divine twelve-year-old boy and my father adored him and wanted to save him from what was happening in the United States. I wish I had listened to my father. I wish I had let him buy me a bank or a dry-cleaning establishment and stayed out there and tried to save my children with mountains. Except I let Jimmy stay and when he left he went to Alaska and I still haven't gotten him back.

I made the best decisions I could based on the information I had at the time, but the information wasn't good enough because I could never believe my children would take drugs. I never believed it. I couldn't believe anyone would do something I was afraid to do.

We spent two days riding horses and driving around the country and meeting cowboys and bankers and going in the Jeep to follow herds of antelope. Daddy's deed to the ranch included hunting rights to ten thousand acres of adjoining land.

There was an old house on the land that had been the headquarters for the small ranchers who had defended Buffalo against the hired assassins of the big landowners during the Johnson County War. My father got tears in his eyes telling how the small ranchers banded together and formed an army to save their cattle from being confiscated by the absentee landlords of the Wyoming Stock Growers Association.

On the third night we were there he began to pack the camper with the gear we would need for our trip to the Wind River. "It takes two days," Valerie whispered to me. "Don't think you're going to get back in a day." She wasn't going with us. In the first place the camper was a four-wheel-drive truck with a camper built on the back and there was only room for three in the front seat. In the second place she had already been on the river and didn't want to go again. "I'll clean the house," she said. "There are things I want to do while he's gone."

Daddy packed the camper with sleeping bags and food and bottled water and extra coats and boots. Then he put the Grumman canoe into the back and tied it down and tied the paddles to the walls of the camper.

"Put on plenty of clothes," he told Teddy and me. "We'll be up at ten thousand feet part of the way and it's still cold up there. Put on layers like you were going skiing."

"Why don't you take that big truck," I suggested. "That way you could close the back around the canoe."

"Because this is the one you need to climb mountains. Just keep your mouth shut, Sister, and wait and see what happens.

There's never been anything in the world prettier than these mountains. Up at Cloud Peak you can see a hundred miles. It's God's world up here and even you might know it when you get there. Let's get to bed early tonight. I want to be on our way by five or six so we can see the sun rise in the mountains."

We went to bed at eight. At four thirty the next morning he came into my room and woke me. He was already dressed, moving full steam ahead. "Coffee's made," he said. "Don't wake Valerie if you can help it. You get dressed. I'll help the little boy."

At five thirty we were finished with breakfast and out the door and down the concrete block steps. We climbed into the camper and Daddy started driving. The headlights plowed through dense fog. We could barely see ten feet ahead. We turned onto a two-lane highway going due west into the Bighorn Mountains and began to climb. As we climbed upwards, we left the fog behind us. By the time we had gone fifteen miles there was light in the sky and we were in mountains. Another ten miles and we were at the Powder River Pass. We stopped at an overlook and drank coffee from a thermos. To the north and west were snow-covered peaks with rings of clouds around them, like something from another world, something you could never imagine or really tell about, never really photograph or paint. The immensity and stillness enclosed us. It was a thrilling moment and I was thrilled to be there with my father. To be with my daddy in the early morning, in such mountains, so much a part of him and all this beauty. My son with us to make it all complete.

"Who will go ride with Fergus now," I kept thinking. "And pierce the wood's dark woven shade."

My father was Fergus, the great king who renounced it all for freedom. He had escaped and he wanted to help us escape only we didn't want to yet. Each generation has to escape in its own way from its own particular demons. It was Daddy's time now but it was not mine. I was still too caught up in confusion and sexual energy. I was many years away from even the beginnings of wisdom but I longed for it and knew it when I saw it. This escape of my father's was a kind of wisdom and I am glad he had it and sorry that in the end he had to let it go and come back into town.

We got back into the camper and drove to a 9,666-foot pass and stopped again to marvel at the beauty of the morning and the broad alpine meadows and the high peaks of the mountains. "There is rock up here that's three billion years old," Daddy said. "I'll show you Meadowlark when we start down. That's where I'm skiing now. It's the best downhill skiing in Wyoming and they don't want anybody else finding out about it. Jackson Hole and Targhee are about ruined. All that crowd from Vail is coming there now and jacking up the prices."

"Could we stop at their ski store and let me get a pin for my jacket?" Teddy asked.

"I don't think they have pins there," Daddy answered. "This isn't some pantywaist ski resort. There are people up here still skiing on wooden skis they made themselves."

"We can ask and see," Teddy said.

"We'll stop at the lake and walk around," Daddy said. "I can't drive as far as I used to be able to. It hurts my back if I don't get out and walk around."

"Why don't we put the canoe in the lake?" I asked. "That might be fun."

"Because the water's so cold you couldn't live long enough to swim to shore. That water's made of melted snow. In the middle of summer you can die of hypothermia in there. Glaciers cut down through here so many years ago they can't even measure it. A glacier built that lake."

"I thought you didn't believe in plate tectonics and evolution," I said.

"Believing glaciers made the lakes and believing men came from monkeys are two different things, Sweet Sister. Well, let's move on. We have a lot of country to see today."

"I want to collect some rocks," Teddy said. "I want to get a rock from every place we stop."

"Good idea, Ted. Go pick you one. I'll help you write down where they came from. Go see if you can find a piece of granite. It takes granite to stay up this high this long."

Teddy went off and returned in a minute with a piece of gray stone. Daddy declared it was granite and took a pen out of his shirt pocket and gave it to him and Teddy marked the rock. Exhibit one.

When we got back in the car Daddy gave him a notebook and he started his list. Exhibit one. Powder River Pass, Wyoming. 9,666 feet. Seven thirty, June 9, 1975. Piece of granite, 3 billion years old.

*   *   *

We stopped again at Meadowlark Lake and looked at the ski runs. Then we drove the Cloud Peak Skyway past Ponderosa pine and Douglas fir and aspens and lodgepole pine and spruce and alpine fir. It was dazzling all the way. Lush and green and verdant and amazing and clean, so clean I felt I had never had a breath of air before. I kept breathing it in. "We're mighty high up here and the air gets thin," Daddy said. "You and Teddy eat one of those bananas and give me one. You got to keep your strength up in the mountains. There used to be Bighorn sheep up here but they caught diseases from cattle and died off. They're bringing them back, but it's taking a while. There's an auction every year in Sheridan to win two hunting permits for them. Your brothers are both in the pot this year."

"So if they're disappearing why hunt them?"

"To raise money for conservation. They raised three million dollars last year and only shot one sheep. The second man wouldn't shoot his. He just hunted it and then didn't take the shot. These are fine people here, Sister. When you get to know them, you'll see."

"I wouldn't shoot mine," Teddy said. "I'd take it home and let Fleming guard it. He's a sheepdog. He'd really like to have a sheep."

Daddy started laughing. He laughed until tears rolled down his eyes. "Come sit here by me," he said. "Sister, trade places with him. I want to show him how to drive in these mountains."

So I moved over and Daddy stopped the car and put Teddy behind the wheel and started letting him drive the truck. I got a book out of my bag and started reading.

★   ★   ★

Teddy drove for fifteen miles. He drove us down into the Bighorn National Forest, and all the way to the turnoff to the Nature Conservancy Preserve. We stopped there to talk to the forest rangers and look at their maps and then we got back into the camper and drove down Ten Sleep Canyon to the town. The weather was perfect, sixty-five degrees and sunny, the air as clear and clean as spring water. I had gotten interested in the topography at the ranger station and was studying the map as we drove. That made Daddy so happy he was whistling through his teeth. Teddy was trying to whistle with him.

At Ten Sleep I got behind the wheel and drove the twenty-six miles to Worland and the twenty-nine to Thermopolis. Daddy slept most of the way, only waking up every now and then to tell me to slow down. Teddy was reading *The Hobbit*, and kept laughing out loud when he got to good parts.

"Read it to me," I would say, and he would read it for a paragraph or two. We both knew it by heart. We had read it at least six times and the whole trilogy twice. "Escaping dwarves to be caught by goblins" was a saying we had from *The Hobbit*. We could fit it into many situations but so far we had not had to say it on this trip to Wyoming.

At the edge of Thermopolis Daddy made me pull over so we could study the map. "We'll spend the night here and take the hot springs baths," he said. "Then in the morning we're going to try to take these roads that border the Indian reservation. Valerie and I tried it last month but we couldn't get all the way through. We had to go back and go down to Riverton and backtrack. It ought to be clear by now. The land gets poor and arid here. See, here's the west fork of the Wind River and here's the main branch and they come together here and go under the mountain and come out on the other side as the Bighorn River. This river was here before the mountains rose, Ted. Which is why it keeps its course straight through instead of going around like most rivers do. It stays its course."

"It's hard to see it on this map," Teddy said. "It keeps disappearing, then showing up again."

"Well, look here." Daddy fished a small magnifying glass out of the glove compartment and spread the map on Teddy's knees. He took a pencil out of his shirt pocket and traced the river on the map, how one fork came down from Meeteetse and another from Thermopolis and how it came out of the mountains and flowed north as the Bighorn. It was beautiful to imagine. "You'll be on it through a valley," Daddy said. "Not a bug on it, Sister. You can go for miles, not a mosquito, not a fly, nothing but the beauty God made."

"God made bugs," Teddy put in, then looked at Daddy and backtracked. "But I guess he wanted the birds to have something to eat. We like the birds, don't we, Granddad?"

"Yes, Son, we do. We like it all."

Daddy got in the driver's seat and turned on the motor and we drove into town and got rooms at an old hotel. We put our bags in our rooms and then went down on an elevator to the basement and the hot tubs. I went to the women's side and was given towels and a robe. I undressed, put on the robe, and was led to a table where I was massaged with lots of oil and then led to a huge canvas-lined tub of hot spring-fed water. I let myself down into it and lay there for a long time, thinking of the mountains and the hot middle of the earth and the moment I had stood on the pass with my father and known that the world was too beautiful to be believed. The world and what man has done with it, the roads we have built and dams and vehicles and hotels and hot tubs, the food we have grown and the horses we have tamed and skis and houses and shelter of any kind, lean-tos and tents and painted caves. Man and nature, nature and man. Wonders, wonders.

I sank down into the water and tried to remember the moment I had stood beside him at the pass barely able to breathe for wonder. The moment when I had known it was enough to be here on this planet and that wonder was enough, was what men called God. "Oh, thin men of Haddam, why do you imagine golden birds? Do you not see how the blackbird walks around the feet of the women about you?"

When we had finished with the baths we dressed and met for supper in the hotel dining room. "That hot water comes out of the middle of the earth," Teddy said. "Momma, it's coming straight up from the middle. It goes past molten rocks and gets heated and shoots on up. Think about it!"

"I was thinking about it. Did you get a massage too?"

"Of course not, Sweet Sister," my father said. "What are you talking about?"

For dinner we had thick steaks and fried potatoes and huge pieces of buttered bread and then we walked around the town and looked at the buildings and got lectured on the thickness of the wood they were made of and the history of logging in

Wyoming. Then Daddy went to bed to read and Teddy and I went to a local movie house that was showing old cowboy films. We saw *Across the Wide Missouri*. It was no surprise to him. Daddy had been letting my sons ride horses across ponds since they were five years old. He had made me ride a lot of horses across a lot of different country when I was little but he had not had any ponds to make me ride across until my sons came along. I was thirty-two before he made me swim a horse across a pond.

Before dawn the next day Daddy woke us and we got up and ate breakfast and packed the car and continued on our way. We were taking roads that skirted the boundaries of the Wind River Indian Reservation. "Some of the roads are asphalt," Daddy said. "And some are gravel but they maintain them good when the snow melts. I talked to the hotel owner and he said he drove it a week ago and everything's hunky-dory now. That's why we're in this truck. It's better on gravel than the big one and we've got the hitch on the front if we need it."

"Granddaddy and I pulled ourselves across a creek with the hitch last summer," Teddy said. "Water came up to our feet but we just went right across."

"What?" I asked. "What are you talking about?"

"Don't worry about it, Sister," Daddy answered. "We don't have to ford any creeks today."

We turned off the highway onto the first of several straight, narrow roads. It was beautiful country but arid and almost desert-like. We went due east, then turned south and ended up in the town of Wind River. We stopped at a filling station and got gas and Daddy bought a loaf of whole-wheat bread and a package of cheese and a gallon of water in a plastic bottle. "Supplies," he said. "You'll be on the river for a while. I'm going to put you in where Valerie and I put in last month. It could get cold, so take your jackets. There's an extra paddle. I'll put you in and the current will take you down. When you see me on the shore, stop. You got all that straight, Sister?"

"Sure, Daddy. Except I have no idea where I am."

"Just look at the map, Sister. You're on the west fork of the Wind River. There are bluffs a few miles up and the trees you see are mostly willow and cottonwoods. You might see wildlife if you keep a sharp eye."

We drove two miles north of town and down a small dirt road to the banks of the river. Daddy unloaded the canoe and put us in, me in the bow, Teddy in the stern. He handed us the supplies and the paddles and stood for a moment holding the line. "Here, Teddy," he said. "Take these." He fished a container of matches and a pocket knife out of his pocket and handed them to Teddy. Then he started pushing us out. "It would be better to start out in the early morning," he added. "But I haven't figured that out yet. The river meanders, Sister, but it knows where it's going." He let go of the line and tossed it to Teddy.

"How will we know where to find you?" I asked.

"I'll be watching for you. Keep the little boy in the back. Let him steer." He moved back up the bank. "It's easy going," he called out. "All you have to do is steer."

He was right. The current was so strong it was like a motor. All you needed paddles for was to keep the boat away from the banks.

We drifted away. Behind us Daddy stood by the camper until we were out of sight. *It never occurred to us not to go,* Teddy told me many years later. *It never occurred to either of us that it was an unusual thing to do.*

Two and a half hours later I began to worry. "What time did we leave?" I started asking Teddy.

"I don't know. I didn't look at my watch."

"What time is it now?"

"Two thirty."

"Shit. Look at the sun. We must have been out here three hours. I know we got to Wind River before noon. It wasn't twelve o'clock when we were at that store."

"Let's eat the bread and cheese. You fix me some. There are some potato chips. I put them in."

I opened the sack and took out the cheese and borrowed the knife and made him a sandwich. Then I moved to the back of the canoe and steered while he sat in the bow and ate. When he was finished we changed places again and I ate while he steered.

"Let's use my paddle and the beach towel to make a sail," I suggested. "I'm getting tired of this, aren't you?"

"I guess so. Give me back the knife. He'll get mad if you lose it. It's his lucky knife he had when he built levees. It saved his life one time."

I didn't question the story. I just cleaned off the knife and dried it on the towel and handed it to him. He put it back in his pocket.

"Steer over to the side. I'm going to fix this towel for a sail.

All I need to do is find something to hold up the oar. There's got to be a beach somewhere where we can stop. Some sort of bank."

"There aren't any, Momma. This water is deep. It's real deep. It's cut a deep deep channel."

"It's melted snow. I guess we could drink it if we had to. But look, pull over to those willows on the side. You can hold on to them while I fix the sail."

"Okay, you paddle on the other side. I'll try to get us over there. It's hard to. This current's fast."

Teddy began to steer the canoe toward the trees. As we moved out of the main current I looked up and saw a huge moose standing in the mixed sunlight and shade of a grove of trees. Beside her was a calf. It was so beautiful and unexpected I lost my breath. We were in the middle of nowhere and we were not alone.

"Did you see her?" Teddy whispered. "Did you see it?"

"Yes." But she was gone now, disappeared into the trees as if she had never been. "Get back in the middle. If there are moose, there could be bears. I don't think we should stop out here. Where do you think he is, Teddy? How far do you think he's planning on us going?"

"You can't tell with Granddaddy. He never tells you where you're going until you get there."

"He's out of the old school. God, he's a crazy man."

"Eric wants to come out here with him. Eric says he's the smartest man he knows. Eric said he wants to get a ranch here too."

"Eric's never even been here."

"He's been to the West a lot. It's weird having Granddaddy out here with Lacy Leigh's and Carla's grandmother, isn't it? But she's nice to us. She helped me put boot wax on my new boots the other night."

"Well, you and I sure can't do anything about that situation. Listen, as soon as we get back in the middle where the current's strong, I'll just hold the towel up on my oar. We need to go faster."

"When is the river going under the mountain?"

"I don't know. No. He's not that crazy. He wouldn't send us down rapids or under a mountain without telling us."

"Maybe we ought to put on those life preserver belts."

"They aren't any good. The one up here doesn't even have a buckle." I pulled out the old life belt and examined it. "We could hold on to the canoe. Besides, we can both swim and I used to be a Red Cross lifesaver. I could save us if I had to."

"The river's starting to curve a lot. We better put them on. Just tie yours on any way you can." He reached under his seat and pulled out the old life belt and tied it around his waist, his beautiful, strong, scrawny arms working fast and steering at the same time. Suddenly I loved him so much I could not bear it. More, I knew that if the canoe turned over I would save him if it killed me. I would kill or die for him as Daddy would kill or die for any of us and would like the opportunity to try.

More. For a moment I understood that what passes between the generations is beyond words or human understanding. More, I knew what it meant to be on this river in the middle of a wilderness and have no real fear because somewhere at the end of it was a man who had measured us and wanted the full measure manifested in our lives as his was in his. Who would not give up on us or ever stop trying to teach us what he knew until we gave in or he died.

At my father's deathbed I was afraid to go in the room and so was my older brother. Not afraid of the horror of watching our father doped up on morphine by the hospice bullshitters or of him dying, but for fear he would say one last true thing to us about how we had wasted our lives and what we could do to change it if we tried and kept on trying.

In the deep shade of the willow trees, on the soft, lush bank, the moose had stood with her calf and looked at me from the sweet clear wisdom of a world where bullshit was only used as fertilizer and was not the main ingredient. It had worked. The old man's seduction was complete. Just because it would be years before I could find and complete a Wyoming of my own didn't mean I wasn't on my way. I would find a place where I rose with the sun and went to sleep when it set and lived in peace and didn't have to tell a lie of any kind to anyone in thought, word, or deed because I stayed away from people who had to be lied to. I was on my way to this good place anytime I was in the presence of the old man. I only hope somehow he knew I was learning something. I hope he knew the messages were being delivered, would be waiting when I needed them.

Teddy turned around on the seat and held the paddle with his knees while he tied the life belt tighter around his waist.

"I guess we're in the middle of nowhere," he said.

"I guess we are."

"You know what? I haven't heard any birds out here. Maybe they don't have birds in Wyoming. You know those birds that stand by the cattle at home and eat the seeds they drop?"

"Egrets. White egrets."

"Well, these cows don't have any. I asked Granddaddy about it when we went riding the other day, and he said he'd never thought about it and he'd ask around."

"Tell me about the cowboy he took you to see last summer when you were in Casper with him."

"He was just this old cowboy. That's when he was looking for a ranch to buy and he kept going out and asking people where to get one."

"So what did you do with the cowboy?"

"Nothing. He didn't talk much. They were talking about Granddaddy buying some horses and then about the government and the Communists and Jews and all that."

"Eric is a Jewish man and all his family but they don't like it when people call them Jews. Also, Granddaddy adores Eric so how do you think that fits in with his saying Jews are with the Communists?"

"He says Eric is a good Jew because he's Republican. But you're not a Republican anymore, are you?"

"I don't know, honey. I'm trying to learn how to be a good person. I don't know all about it yet but I hated the Vietnam War and thought it was a mistake. You know that."

"Yeah, like when you and Crystal went on the marches down Saint Charles."

"I'm glad you remember that. Well, what do you think we

are going to do, Teddy? You think that son-of-a-bitch is going to make us float down this river until night?"

"No. We'll see him in a while. He just wants us to have adventures and find out what we're made of. That's why he made me drive home when we went to see the cowboy."

"Drive home? From where?"

"From up on some road. It was really dark and he got drunk drinking with the cowboy so I had to drive. I was scared at first but he kept yelling at me and telling me what to do and finally I got us home."

"I don't believe he got drunk. He never gets drunk."

"He got drunk that time. That old cowboy got him drunk on rotgut."

"Jesus. Why didn't you tell me about it?"

"I don't know. I forgot. You want me to get up there awhile? I can paddle better than you. We might go faster."

"Sure. Wait a minute. Wait until the river straightens out."

We were at a place where the river snakes along, taking turns every thirty feet. In a while it straightened out and I climbed to the stern and took the steering paddle while Teddy went up to the bow and began to paddle. His little arms worked the paddle like a man.

I kept falling into states where I didn't care when we found Daddy, then it would fade and I would be mad at him for leaving us on the water so long. It was a nice metaphor for my relationship with him. Glad and mad, glad and mad, glad and mad.

We moved down the river as the water became faster and the river more narrow and mesmerizing in its beauty and perfection. When I had given up caring where we were or why we were there we came down a long straight stretch and there at the end was Daddy, standing on a small bank waving his arms and grinning. "There he is," I yelled at Teddy. "Steer for the bank."

At two o'clock that morning we arrived back at the ranch. I had driven from Worland to Ten Sleep, then gone to sleep with my head on the window. Teddy had made a bed for himself in the back of the camper. Daddy had kept himself awake on Hershey bars, bananas, and finally, on the road from Ten Sleep to Buffalo, on Scotch whiskey.

What a man. What a river. What a moose.

I wonder if I ever thanked him for it. Or if he knew that some-day I would know what I had been given. Maybe he didn't care what I thought about his gifts as long as he could figure out a way to give them. Around all my craziness and confusion and de-sire for a different kind of love, he had kept on giving me what he himself would have wanted, if he were me, because he is me, world without end. Amen.

The Golden
Bough

IT WAS CHRISTMAS WEEK and my family were all
down on the coast going quail hunting or having parties or
buying extravagant presents for each other. I have a house down
there and usually I join in their celebrations, but this year I had
decided to stay home and talk to them on the phone.

My sons are in their forties now. They have lives of their
own. Even my grandchildren are getting too old to need me,
with the exception of a three-year-old named Isabella who likes
me so much she wakes from naps swearing she hears my voice
downstairs. I was sorry not to be there for her but I would make
it up in February. She'll be four in February. I'll be sixty-four.

So I was staying home for Christmas, right here in my stone-
and-glass house on a small mountain overlooking the small town
of Fayetteville, Arkansas. I wanted two things for Christmas, a
red down vest from The Gap and a Christmas week where no

one got drunk in my presence. I already had the vest. Now all I had to do was stay away from places where people were drinking wine. "And much as wine has played the infidel and robbed me of my robe of honor . . ." Once it had robbed me of mine but no more. It was thirty years since I quit drinking and in those years my tolerance for people who drink had diminished to zero. I hate the bloody stuff. Most of all I hate talking to people when they are drinking. Most of my children have quit too, but I didn't feel like spending Christmas dodging the ones that still do.

So I was home for Christmas with one string of lights on my mailbox and my vest. It was cold and threatening snow and I had plenty of books to read and the unending Presidential Vote Count on the television and I was happy. I even had a Yuletide epiphany. I was driving down Dickson Street and saw a beautiful sight. A little fat man in a baseball cap stretched out on the flat roof of the post office with the American flag waving in the background. He was lying on his stomach at the very edge of the roof tacking up a string of lights that had fallen.

On the seat beside me I had a camera I had used the week before to photograph my undergraduate creative writing class. I threw on the brakes, jumped out of the car, and snapped a photograph of the man on the roof. He was my Santa Claus, in his dirty green coat and fingerless gloves and his dedication to the integrity of the post office lights.

I drove straight to the One Hour Photo lab and had the roll developed and an enlargement made of the photo of the man on the roof. I took it home and put it on the music stand of the piano and looked at it while I played Satie.

I'm a loner at heart. Three sons, three daughters-in-law, and fifteen grandchildren have not altered my recurrent desire to be alone for long periods of time. Even as a child in a house full of people I had hideouts and forts where I hid for hours. My family understands this and knows it has nothing to do with them. Besides, they are glad when I'm not around for the holidays. They are young and love excess. Why should they waste their time justifying their lives to me?

So I was alone on Christmas Eve and ecstatic to be. I was reading *The Journey of the Magi* by T. S. Eliot with its brilliant opening lines by the sixteenth-century cleric Lancelot Andrews. "A cold coming we had of it, just the worst time of the year, for a journey, and such a long journey: the ways deep and the weather sharp, the very dead of winter. . . ."

I stood in the long windows looking out on the mountains. Then I put on my down jacket and started out for a walk. I live on the south part of the mountain, with the windows of the house facing west. If I go up a steep, winding road for half a mile I come to a circular drive which has been used as a walking path for fifty years. Usually I see several people I know on the path, but this day it was empty. I had it to myself and I liked it that way. I walked for a long time, circling the mountain twice.

I don't know when I got the idea to walk down to the cave. I hadn't been there in years. It's not much of a cave, just a long, narrow limestone opening with shrub pine and cedar trees around it. Cedar becomes fragrant in December and I was thinking about exploring the cave with my boyfriend in winter, when I was young and in love. I wasn't thinking about my daddy. I was thinking about poetry and love and how I had definitely had my share of those things.

I had, however, been thinking about Daddy a lot in the past few months. He had died three years before, and for the first two years I wouldn't admit he was dead. I had taken all the photographs of him out of my house and anything that reminded me of him. Then, slowly, in the past year I had begun to get things back out. His plumb bob. A pair of gray cotton socks I had taken from his room after the funeral. Photographs of him when he was a child. Finally, a photograph of us together, standing in a field on the farm. I had admitted he was gone and I guessed this Christmas was part of that concession.

My daddy hated people wasting money and getting drunk more than I could ever hate it. It was his money we were wasting and he let us do it but he didn't join in.

Now that it was my turn to be a matriarch I usually went along with the hilarity and shelled out money left and right and bought expensive gifts for everyone and pretended to let the good times roll. But I was taking the year off this year.

So I was already with my daddy in spirit as I walked around the mountain and started thinking about hiking to the cave. The path to the cave begins below my backyard, so I stopped at my house to get some supplies. I stuck a tarpaulin and some cookies in a backpack and put it on. Then I grabbed a small book and put it in my pocket. The book I grabbed, and there are no accidents, as we all know, was Seamus Heaney's *Seeing Things*, with its wonderful opening translation from the *Aeneid*, the long passage about the Golden Bough. I was reciting it as I passed through the back gate and moved down the path into the woods.

". . . But one thing I pray for especially: since they say it is here that the King of the Underworld's gateway is to be found, . . . I pray for one look, one face-to-face meeting with my dear father. Teach me the way and open the holy doors wide."

I moved down the rocky path, holding on to saplings when it was necessary, coming at last to a wide curve where the path started back up the hill. I stopped there to listen to the woods. I leaned against an oak, looking up into a stand of hickory trees. Most of their golden leaves had fallen, but high in the boughs of one was a thick branch the wind had not been able to reach. The sun caught the yellow leaves and turned them into gold and I imagined Aeneas seeing a similar sight. ". . . Hidden in the thick of a tree is a bough made of gold and its leaves and pliable twigs are made of it too. It is sacred to underworld Juno, who is its patron, and it is roofed in by a grove, where deep shadows mass along far wooded valleys. No one is ever permitted to go down to earth's hidden places unless he has first plucked the golden-fledged growth out of its tree and handed it over to fair Proserpina, to whom it belongs by decree. . . .

". . . Take hold of it boldly and duly. If fate has called you, the bough will come away easily, of its own accord. Otherwise, no matter how much strength you muster, you will never manage to quell it or cut it down with the toughest of blades."

I have always been a climber of trees, a builder of tree houses, a girl who doesn't mind nailing boards into a tree trunk if the branches are too high. I looked up into the tree and watched the branch of yellow leaves. The sun caught it at an angle and it glowed. Oh, gods, I thought. I have found the source of Aeneas's dream. It was fall leaves left in a tree after winter had come. The sun caught the yellow leaves and Aeneas thought they were gold. What does the *Aeneid* say? *Hidden in the thick of a tree.* The thick of the tree where they are safe.

But first you must go to the cave and speak to the sibyl. But I already knew what the sibyl would say. It's easy to go down and chat up your daddy one last time but the hard part is getting back.

I opened my backpack and got out a cookie and ate it. I better mark this tree, I decided. It might be hard to find when I come back. I took off my long red scarf and attempted to tie it around the trunk but it was too short and wouldn't reach so I threw it over a branch and let it hang there. It looked wonderful. A Christmas flag in the middle of the dark woods. It wasn't a valuable scarf but I liked it and had worn it through nine or ten Christmas seasons. I can't lose it, I decided. There's only one path. I can't get lost.

I was into my fantasy now. I hiked up the path in the direction of the cave, completely happy with the Christmas I was making, my little game.

The cave surprised me. I had forgotten how small and unobtrusive the entrance was. If you didn't know it was there, you would never notice it. You turn a corner on the path and there it is, a small opening covered by vines. Above it, a holly tree with berries. I took my Swiss Army knife out of my backpack and cut the vines away. Then I spread the tarpaulin in the entrance and sat on it and thought about my daddy.

I liked my father better than any human being I have ever known. I liked to talk to him and I loved to argue with him and in my late middle age I was becoming so much like him it was uncanny. When I was small I was the only one in the house who got up as early as he did. No matter how early I woke he was always awake before me, full of ideas, running full throttle. If it was winter he would have fires going in the living room and kitchen, coffee perking, and water boiling for poached eggs. In his seventies and eighties he would be on the den floor doing back exercises or at his desk writing letters to Pat Buchanan.

But the father I wanted to talk to now was the one who had been there when I was a child. My daddy, who woke each morning full of ideas, excitement, life. He was the best person to talk to in the morning I have ever known, and I wanted to talk to him again.

So, therefore, Vestal, I beseech you take pity
on a son and a father, for nothing is out of your power
Whom Hecate appointed the keeper of wooded Avernus.
If Orpheus could call back the shade of a wife through his faith
In the loudly plucked strings of his Thracian lyre,
If Pollux could redeem a brother by going in turns
Backwards and forwards so often to the land of the dead,
And if Theseus too, and great Hercules . . . but why speak of them?
I myself am of highest birth, a descendent of Jove.

I was reading the passage out loud when a flock of crows came flying in and landed on a grove of wild cherry trees. "Caw, Caw, Caw," they came crying and didn't show a blush of fear of me. I hate crows and usually run them off when I catch them in my yard, but now I sat very still and whispered to them under my breath. "I pray for one look, one face-to-face meeting with my dear father. Teach me the way and open the holy doors wide."

The crows set up a raucous row. They flew from tree to tree yelling at me. They attacked the boughs of the cherry trees, looking for anything left to eat, then they spread their wings and took off for less barren pickings.

"Hidden in the thick of a tree is a bough made of gold. . . . No one is ever permitted to go down to earth's hidden places unless he has first plucked this golden-fledged growth out of its tree . . ."

I know what to do, I decided, so I'll do it. I packed up my things and climbed the path to where it came out in my neighbors' yard. Two of their children were playing on the trampoline, William, age eleven, and John Tucker, age eight. "Merry Christmas, Miss Rhoda," they called out to me.

"Merry Christmas, John Tucker," I called back. "Merry Christmas, William."

John Tucker and William were my sometimes highly paid leaf blower operators and heavy object movers. I had ruined the neighborhood pay scale with them to such an extent they wouldn't work for anyone else.

I walked over to the trampoline and stuck my hands in my

pockets. "You want to make ten dollars each for helping me with something that won't take an hour?" I asked.

"Sure," William said, jumping down off the trampoline and coming to stand beside me. John Tucker took one last high bounce and joined us.

"What do you want us to do?" he asked.

"Help me carry a ladder and some boards down into the woods about a quarter-mile from here. I'll give you fifteen if it takes more than an hour."

"We will," William said. "Let me go ask Momma."

"Sure. Meet us by my storage shed. John Tucker, you come with me."

John Tucker walked along beside me. I had been there when he was in his momma's tummy. I had been there when he was born. He was as dear to me as my own grandchildren, and I gave him a big hug and asked him what he wanted for Christmas.

"A trick scooter," he answered.

"Oh, no," I screamed. "They are too dangerous. Don't get that."

He laughed. He loved it when I pretended that everything he did was fraught with danger. It was a game we had been playing since he was small.

"What're you going to do?" he asked.

"Wait and see," I answered. "It's something in a tree I want to get down."

"What kind of tree?"

"A big one. We're going to need the stepladder if we can carry it down there and some boards to nail on the tree for steps."

We were collecting boards when William came up and told us his mother said it was okay.

"She's going to climb a tree," John Tucker told him. "You think we can carry a ladder down the path to where the cave is?"

"We can carry the little one." William picked up my four-foot ladder and lifted it over his head. He loved to show off for me.

"Okay," I said. "Let's go. You want any cookies before we leave? They're in the kitchen on the table."

"Sure," William said. He put down the ladder and ran into the house and returned with both hands full of cookies. He handed two to John Tucker and stuck the rest in the pocket of his jacket. Then, carrying our tools, we started down across my lot and on down to the path to the woods.

At the tree we stopped and ate some cookies and decided what to do. We had five short boards, so William thought we could just forget the ladder, but John Tucker and I thought we should make the steps closer together in case anyone with short legs wanted to use it later. "'Going up is easy,'" I said mysteriously. "'But to retrace your steps and get back to the upper air, This is the real task and the real undertaking. . . .' John Tucker, you and William hold the ladder and I'll nail the boards. See that branch of leaves up there, that's what I'm trying to get."

"What for?" William asked. The sun had changed its direction now and without sunlight the leaves looked like what they were, a thick branch of yellow hickory leaves.

"I need them," I said. "To give to a girl named Spring."

"Okay," William said and began to move the ladder around in the roots of the tree, trying to find stable footing for it.

William was a reasonable child, dependable and smart, and I didn't give him advice, just stood back and let him work.

When he was satisfied, John Tucker came over to hold the other side and I climbed up carrying a board, some nails, and a hammer.

I got the first board nailed in easily and began on the second. I ruined three nails getting that one to stay.

"You're nailing in a knot," William called up. "Move it over a little bit."

"Give me some nails." I leaned down to wait for the nails.

William left his post and returned with the nails. He climbed up and handed them to me and I added a nail to the second board in a spot to the side of the knot. Then I nailed in the third and fourth boards and tested them with my hands. I was off the ladder now but they were still standing beside it.

"Go on up," William advised. "You can get up now. You want me to do it?"

"No, I have to pick the leaves myself. That's how it's written." I pushed off from the last board and pulled myself up into the fork of the tree. Above and to my right was the branch of leaves. I reached for it and pulled. It came away easily, as the sibyl said it must. "Fate has chosen me," I said. "But I knew that already."

"She's got it," John Tucker called out.

"You coming down?" William asked, positioning himself by the ladder.

"I guess so," I said. "It's really nice up here. I haven't been up in a tree in a long, long time."

I looked out over the woods to the houses on a far hill.

Smoke was rising from their chimneys. Christmas Eve, so magical, so new.

I moved down to the top step and put my foot on it, holding the branch with my left hand and climbing with my right. I put a foot on the third board and transferred the branch to my right hand so I could hand it to William. Then I stepped onto the second board. I felt it splinter before it began to fall. My only thought was that it would fall on William's head. Then I was falling too but I can barely remember that.

I woke to the sound of my granddaughter, Isabella's, voice. "Ma Rhoda," she was saying. "I come here for you." They were all around me, two of my sons, two of my daughters-in-law, at least three of my grandchildren, including the oldest one, the one I love as much as I did my father. It was Isabella's voice I heard but it was Garth's face I saw. "We thought we had lost you," he said. "Merry Christmas, Grandmother. Thanks for staying here."

Later that night I asked what day it was. "December twenty-sixth," Garth said. He had not left my side all day. The others had been coming and going but he had stayed there. He was a second-year medical student and he thought he understood everything that was going on. "We thought you had severed the spinal cord," he told me. "When I got on the plane I thought you would be dead."

"What were you doing in a tree?" his father asked. "Momma, what were you doing up in a tree?"

"I was trying to pick a golden bough," I answered, looking at

Garth. I had taught him to read and guided his reading when he was young. "I was going to talk to my daddy."

"Well, you almost got to," my son said. "I don't know why you have to live up here all alone for anyway. It's time for you to come on down to the coast where we are and stay there. It cost me three thousand dollars to fly everyone up here, in case you're interested in that. I can afford it, but what if you had died? What if we hadn't gotten here in time?"

"Where are John Tucker and William?" I asked. "Are they all right? Did they carry me? What happened?"

"They got their mom and dad. They called 911. If they had picked you up you would be dead."

"What am I? Am I okay?"

"You will be," Garth said. "You won't be crippled or anything, Grandmother. So what happened then? Did you get to talk to him?"

"Come here. Get closer." He leaned down so I could whisper to him. "Yes," I whispered. "He said to tell you hello."

Then the nurse came in with a shot of Demerol, and after she gave it to me they said I blabbed a lot about how to divide up my jewelry but I don't remember that. I remember holding Garth's hand while I went back to the place where only the ones whom fate has chosen get to go, the place where only the bravest visit.

"It would do you good to listen to people who know more than you do sometime, Sister," my father was saying. He was sitting on a straight chair with his back to the river. Behind him were cliffs and forests covered with mist. In the distance was a great, gray lake, opaque and still.

My father looked just like himself. He had on his khaki pants and white shirt and his work boots. His pencils were in his pocket with the folded envelope he used for a notebook when he was in the field. I walked toward him and stood waiting. His voice was low and still, his reasonable mode. He never raised his voice until someone started arguing with him.

"You are well educated in many things," he continued. "But please quit thinking you know everything about the world and its True History and God's prophecies concerning it."

"I don't believe any of this," I answered. "But I am so glad to hear your voice. Keep talking to me, Daddy. Tell me about rivers. Tell me about rivers you tamed."

"I didn't tame any rivers, Sister, no man can. All I did was pile up some dirt to keep it back another fifty years."

"Tell me about the Delta before I was born, talk to me, Daddy. Keep on talking." I was weeping then and he took pity on me and reached out his hand as though to touch me, but of course he could not do that so he began to tell me what I wanted to know.

"Some rivers I have known," he began, and I spread out my coat on the ground before his chair and lay down with my hands on my chin and listened to my daddy tell his story.

"The White River in Arkansas begins near Pettigrew, Arkansas, and runs north by Fayetteville and on up into Missouri through

Table Rock Lake and southeast to near Magness, Arkansas, where it joins the Black River and then flows south to the Arkansas River just before the Arkansas River runs into the Mississippi River across from Rosedale, Mississippi."

"The Missouri River starts in the big Rocky Mountains near Butte, Montana, and runs north and northeast to Fort Peck Dam and on into North Dakota, where it picks up the north-running Yellowstone River and the north-running Little Missouri River, and then it turns south to Kansas City and then east across Missouri to the Mississippi River near St. Charles (just across from St. Louis)."

"The Bighorn River in Wyoming runs north to the Yellowstone River and then they both (as the Yellowstone) run northeast into the Missouri River."

"The Tennessee River starts up above Knoxville, Tennessee, in the Great Smoky Mountains and runs southwest to north Alabama, thence north across the state of Tennessee to go into the Ohio River near Paducah, Kentucky."

I sat at his feet and imagined the rivers as he painted them for me. I forgot the long days of his death and the sadness buried deep in my heart and the mist that was drawing near to the river I must cross again soon.

There were no souls in pain where my daddy was sitting on his straight chair telling me about rivers. It was just my daddy being sweet while I loved him. Then I heard Garth's voice calling to me and woke to the sight of my progeny. What would they dream I was saying when it was their turn to mourn? I'd better quit fussing at them while I could, I decided. I'd better start trying to teach them what I know. Every generation has things that will never be known again unless it is told or written down.

Götterdämmerung,
In Which
Nora Jane and
Freddy Harwood
Confront Evil
in a World
They Never Made

I

NEW YORK CITY, NEW YORK, September 13, 2000. The inhabitants of a building on the upper left-hand corner of 92nd Street and Park Avenue were experiencing a disturbance of the first order. Music had begun blaring out of an apartment on the fifth floor at all hours of the night and day. Loud, crazy music played on Mittenwald zithers, or worse, Wagner: Brunhilde, the Valkyries, Siegfried, Götterdämmerung. The music was coming from the opened windows of the largest apartment in the building. The apartment had been empty for many months. It had belonged once to Emily Post, then to Alice Walton, then to a diplomat from Jamaica, and finally, mistakenly it was turning out, to a couple from London no one had ever seen. The couple's résumé had seemed perfect. He was a London stockbroker, she was a photographer. They had no children, no dogs, and the real estate agent told the condominium association the couple only planned to use the apartment a few months each year. There were recommendations from people members of the association knew, if not well, at least well enough to speak to at cocktail parties. Because the résumé had seemed so stellar, the association voted to allow the sale without a personal interview. The buyers were in London, the association was told, and didn't plan on coming to New York for many months.

There were three empty apartments in the building and several more for sale. Four occupants were in arrears in their condo fees. It was not a year in which 92nd and Park could afford to turn down a cash sale that included a year's condo fees paid in advance.

The sale went through, a yellow van came and stripped the apartment of the Jamaican's possessions, painters arrived and painted the rooms, a flooring company came in and pulled out the carpets and installed oak floors, mirrored walls were dismantled and replaced with wallpaper. Then, nothing for six months. Before the first year was up, a check arrived to cover the condo fees for the second year. "Apartment 17, the cash cow," became a joke at association meetings. "Let's get some more London brokers here. What a deal."

Then, suddenly, in late July of 2000, several tall, unpleasant-looking Middle Eastern men began to leave and enter the apartment at all hours of the day and night and the music began to blare out of the open windows. *The Ring of the Nibelung,* and, even louder and worse, music played on zithers.

This activity would go on for several days, then nothing, then begin again.

A retired orthopedic surgeon named Carlton Rivers was the new president of the condominium association. He thought it was just his luck that this situation should develop the month he took office. He had run for the unpaid job because he had it in for the building supervisor and was planning on firing him soon. Instead, this blaring music, coupled with the sleazy-looking Middle Eastern men. Carlton wasn't Jewish but his college girl-friend had been, and he felt a deep empathy and connection with Israel, to which she had disappeared the day after their college graduation. Her name was Judith and she had given Carlton the greatest sexual experiences of his life. He had let her go, thinking he could reproduce those experiences elsewhere in the world. It had not proved to be true. It had been his initiation into sex and it had proved unbeatable. For years after she was gone he would drift off in the middle of an operation and remember her teeth or mouth or hair and sigh deeply for the paradise he had lost.

When he began to make money, his main charity was a re-search hospital in Haifa. He thought of going there to find her but he never did. He was busy in medical school, then as an in-tern, then establishing a practice. Finally he married a dark-haired nurse who gave great blow jobs and went on with his life. There were no children of this union and Carlton was secretly glad of that. He was not a man who could tolerate much dis-order.

★   ★   ★

His wife died the year after he retired. When he recovered he threw himself into campaigning to become president of the condominium association. He had barely had time to enjoy his success and begin his campaign to rejuvenate the place when the goddamn Arabs started coming into the building and blaring out Wagner at all hours of the day and night.

He called the condominium lawyers and they wrote letters to the owners in London. There were no answers to the letters. Phone calls were made to the phone numbers in the records of the condominium association and those at the real estate firm which had handled the two-million-dollar sale. A call was placed to the brokerage firm the owner was supposedly associated with. All these telephone calls were answered by machines. Mr. and Mrs. Alterman were out of the country and could not be reached was the information supplied by the machines.

Carlton was going ballistic when, as suddenly as it began, the music stopped and did not start up again. No one entered or left the apartment. There was no mail. The apartment phones rang but were not even answered by machines.

Three weeks of silence went by. Then, on September 13, there was a meeting of the association and the first order of business was what was going on in 17 and what should they do about it, if anything.

"Apartment seventeen," Carlton began. "We allowed the sale to a couple we had never met. That's done. They never set foot in the building. Nothing wrong there. Wealthy people buy things they never use. Then, suddenly, there are Middle Easterners coming and going at all hours and music waking up eighteen, nineteen, twenty, fifteen, and the people on the fifth floor of 988. Our lawyers write the owners and get no reply. We call all the numbers left by the owners with us, the Realtor who sold the place and the brokerage firm where he supposedly worked at the time of the purchase, but they say he is no longer with them. So what are we to make of this? And what should we do?"

"Nothing," Mrs. Bloodworth answered. She was the vice president of the association and still had her nose out of joint because Carlton had been chosen over her for first in command. She was a stout matron with iron gray hair who wore old-fashioned suits made by a tailor on the Upper West Side. She had taught chemistry at Harvard and never let anyone forget it. "We called this meeting to talk about raising the condo fee three hundred dollars a month to make up for the shortfall of unpaid dues on empty apartments. That, coupled with the seven-hundred-dollar raise in insurance premiums, has put many owners in distress. The last thing we want to do at this point is create a problem with seventeen. Seventeen is paid in advance for the next fourteen months. The problem has ceased. We should forget it and get on with the business of finding someone to work on the eaves and roof."

"You're prejudiced against Middle Easterners, Carlton," a man named Herman put in. "You wouldn't vote for that nice Saudi woman two years ago. She was an internist."

"With a degree from a medical school in Guadalajara, Herman. Don't talk about things you don't understand. It was on the basis of her so-called education that I voted against her."

"And now that apartment's empty too. You can afford to pay these ever-higher fees but some of us can't. . . ."

"Please, ladies and gentlemen." Mrs. Bloodworth stood up. "Please. Order in the room. Order."

"They were advance men for a decorating firm," Herman said. "One of them told the supervisor that. I don't understand this constant prejudice we encounter in this group at every step."

"Bleeding hearts," Carlton snapped. "I'd have an easier time believing they were making a nuclear device. The music was to cover up conversation. That's what people do when they don't want to take a chance on being taped. High decibels render even very sophisticated listening devices mute. I saw that on 20/20 last year."

"Oh, please," Mrs. Bloodworth said. "Let's move on, may we?"

The meeting broke up after a vote on raising the condo fees to cover the cost of the roofing problems, and everyone went back to their apartments muttering about ineptness and the cost of life in the city.

That night Carlton decided to take matters into his own hands. He had a key to the back door of 17 that one of the former tenants had left in his care. He could have used the keys the maintenance crew kept in the basement, but those had to be checked out. After dinner he drank a couple of brandies, found a flashlight, and went up the back stairs to 17. The key worked. No one had bothered to change that lock. He let himself in and, using only his flashlight, began to search.

After an hour of poking around in empty drawers and closets he found the first piece of handwriting he had come across in the whole apartment. It was in the drawer of a bedside table near a phone. It was a list of names.

> Frederick Sydney Harwood, Berkeley, California
> Joseph Leister, Madison, Wisconsin
> Holly Knight, Eureka Springs, Arkansas

Carlton copied down the names and carefully replaced the paper in the drawer. He wrote down the serial numbers of the expensive Bose CD player and the television set. Then he left and went back down to his apartment and called a private detective he knew named Lynn Fadiman and asked to have someone come and get fingerprints from the doorknobs and glass surfaces. "Possible," his friend answered. "But very expensive."

"I'm rich," Carlton said. "Do it tomorrow night. In the meantime, if I give you the names of three people can you get dossiers on them and tell me what they have in common?"

"You could probably do it on the Internet. Have you tried?"

"I don't have a computer. I'm a Luddite."

"Okay. Tell them to me."

Fifteen minutes later Lynn Fadiman called Carlton back. "I've got data on all three. Easy. You do have a fax machine, don't you?"

"No. But there's one at the all-night drugstore down the street. Here's the number. 212-555-2345. You got it?"

"They're booksellers."

"What?"

"The three names. They sell books. All three of them are big shots in the Independent Booksellers Association."

"My God!"

"Maybe your music man was a budding author."

"I don't think so. Can you get the prints tomorrow night?"

"I told you I would. You're sure I won't be caught?"

"I'll go down and talk to the night watchman while you're in there. He loves to talk. I'll pretend I'm having a fight with one of the tenants. I am having a fight with one. I'll stay with him. He's the only person who might go in."

At nine the next morning Lynn called Carlton on his cell phone. "Go to a pay phone and call me now. I don't like this. Call me now."

Carlton put on a coat and shoes and went out of the building and over to the drugstore where he had collected the facsimiles the night before. He called Lynn Fadiman. The phone rang once.

"Holly Knight died last night in an accident on a remote highway. She was alone in a car and the car went off the road and into a lake. She was a fifty-seven-year-old woman who never went anywhere at night and at eleven at night she drove a Pontiac off a bridge into Beaver Lake near Rogers, Arkansas. It's a hit list, Carlton, and it's time to take this to the police."

11

A FIVE POINT TWO AT TEN A.M. in the locker room. Nora Jane Harwood was in the ladies locker room of the Berkeley Athletic Club trying to get Little Freddy to put on his new swimming trunks when the earthquake moved beneath San Francisco. It began in the sea and roiled its way inland, moving and shaking and being mean. Moved by forces beyond our control, Freddy Harwood was always saying for a joke and it sure fitted earthquakes. If the metaphor fits, wear it, was a private joke between his twin daughters.

"He's going metaphor," Tammili would say.

"He's close. He's almost there," Lydia would answer.

"It itches me," Little Freddy was complaining as Nora Jane tried to get him to put his fat legs into the denim bathing suit Lydia had ordered him from Land's End. Little Freddy wanted to wear his old red trunks with the torn inner lining and the small, thick elephant sewn on the side. He was immune to arguments that the red trunks were too small. He wanted to take the elephant into the water, where it wanted to be. He was fascinated by two things in the waning months of his third year on the planet Earth. Elephants and *The Wizard of Oz. Elephants of the World* was his favorite book. *Horton Hears a Who* and *Horton Hatches the Egg* were his second favorite books, and his favorite garment was his red bathing suit with the elephant on the side and he wanted to take it into the water and let it swim. Besides, it kept him from getting drowned.

Little Freddy hated his swimming class and the big, bossy girl who was always making him put his head under the water or wait his turn to practice on the kickboard. The longer he put off stepping into the new denim trunks the longer it was going to be before Nora Jane took him out to the pool.

"If you just wear it this one time we'll go out to the mall and get you another one like the red one," she was saying. "The red one is too tight for you. It pinches your little tally-wacker."

"Tally-wacker," Little Freddy replied, moving away from her

and climbing up on a bench where a woman the age of his grandmother was putting on her running shoes. "Me don't have any tally-wacker." He paused, while his mother recovered and the older woman began to giggle. "If you gimme that PowerBar, I'll put them on."

The older woman was really laughing now. Her name was Sylvia Kullman and she was in charge of fund-raising for Marin County Planned Parenthood. Nora Jane had seen her on television and admired her brilliance in debate and also her fabulous designer clothes. All the famous designers liked to dress Sylvia for her debates. She was always at the athletic club. She worked out four days a week and it showed. She was past seventy years old and still as trim and supple as a girl.

Little Freddy eyed Nora Jane while she considered his offer. "Okay," she said at last. "You can have part of the PowerBar but not all of it. You can have one third of it now and the rest when you finish your class." She pulled the PowerBar out of her bag and showed him how much she would break off if he agreed to the deal. He climbed down from the bench and went to her and began to step into the denim trunks. Sylvia finished tying her shoes, still laughing and smiling at Nora Jane.

"Enjoy them while you can," she said. "They grow up so fast. Then they're gone and you have to pretend you don't miss them."

Then Berkeley moved. Not just the concrete slab that held the athletic club but the whole town moved, slanting to the east, and then it moved again and then it stopped. Nora Jane grabbed Little Freddy and pulled him to the floor. Sylvia dove beneath a sink. The other women in the dressing room began to moan. A group of three women beside the private lockers were moaning as a group.

"That's a big one," Little Freddy said. "I want my PowerBar. You said I could have it. It's bad to break your promise."

Nora Jane sat up and handed him the bar. "Are you all right?" she asked Sylvia.

"I'm okay. Should we stay here or go out in the main area? I mean, aftershocks."

"There're no windows in here. Not much to fall."

"But the lockers," a woman called out. "Could they fall?"

"They didn't," Nora Jane answered.

"It was built to specs," Sylvia said. She stood up and began to take charge. "We're okay. That wasn't a big one. We're all right here. Let's just stay here a few minutes and not panic. Does anyone have a phone?"

Nora Jane got one out of her bag. "Let me call my husband, then I'll give it to you. I have two girls at school. Surely they're okay." She pushed a button and Freddy Harwood answered at the bookstore. "I'm okay here," she said. "I'm at the club. Call about the girls. I need to let other people use the phone. Call me back when you can."

"What are you doing?"

"I'm in the locker room. We're going to stay here for a while. I won't leave."

She handed the phone to Sylvia, who called her husband, then handed the phone to the other ladies and they made calls but none of their calls went through. The lines were getting jammed.

Little Freddy was sitting on the floor eating the PowerBar.

Nora Jane got another one out of her bag and offered it to Sylvia.

"Half," Sylvia said. "He's making me hungry. What's his name?"

"Frederick Sydney Harwood. I'm Nora Jane. We own Clara Books. On Telegraph Avenue."

"I go there all the time. Sylvia Kullman. I'm glad to know you. I see you working out although why you bother with your body, I don't know."

"To be healthy," Nora Jane replied. "I like to do it. It feels good. I think about all the carpenters and cowboys and people who do real work and how fine and strong their bodies always are, compared to people who sit at desks all day and screw up their minds with thinking and selling things."

"I'm afraid it's vanity with me," Sylvia replied. "My mother was injured in a face-lift situation so I won't do any surgery. I have to do it with exercise and so I do. Sometimes I like it but I think it's mostly vanity."

One of the three moaning women had gone around the corner to the sofas where the young women nursed their babies and had opened the door to the main room of the club. A woman was screaming in a distant room. Screaming her head off. Screaming like there was no tomorrow.

Then the second shock shook the building and the woman began to scream even louder.

"An hysteric," Sylvia said. "It doesn't sound like pain."

"We should go home now," Little Freddy said. "I want to go to my own house."

"Let's get on your shoes," Nora Jane answered. "There could be broken glass anywhere. You have to wear your shoes."

"Let's make our way to the lobby," Sylvia suggested. "At least let's move to the nursing sofas and get near the door to the lobby. There's nothing in that area to fall, is there?"

"The glass table with the flower arrangement."

"Let's move it." Sylvia led the way around the corner to the nursing alcove, which was near the door to the main lobby. The others followed. There was a glass-topped table on a thick pedestal near the door. Nora Jane and Sylvia moved the flower arrangement, then picked up the glass top and set it on the floor. "Upper-body strength," Sylvia said. "I told my husband it would come in handy. He thinks I'm nuts to work out all the time. He's jealous." They shoved the beveled glass tabletop underneath the coatracks, and Nora Jane dumped a basket of wet towels on top of it. They moved past the nursing sofas and pushed open the door to the lobby. It adjoined the racquetball courts and the basketball court and the aerobics and yoga rooms. Men and women were herded into small groups in the lobby. The glass walls of the racquetball courts were intact, and two of the trainers were passing out bottles of Gatorade and trays of health food snacks, Luna Bars, Power-Bars, peanut butter bars, and homemade raisin cakes. People were talking on cell phones and looking subdued. Two young women were nursing babies on a large flowered sofa. Little Freddy made a beeline for that activity. "Titties," he whispered to Nora Jane. "Titty babies. Them not big like me." He burrowed his head in her legs and she sat down and took him into her arms. Weaning had been very hard on Little Freddy. Just the thought of titties drove him wild with deprivation. There was nothing on earth he liked as much as sinking his mouth onto his mother's sweet, milk-filled teats. His lost paradise, his Shangri-la.

"You're a big boy now," Nora Jane told him. "You have chocolate milk in a paper carton with a straw."

"Yes," he said mournfully. "That's what I do."

A young trainer, one of the fifteen or sixteen men at the club who was in love with Nora Jane, that is, deeply smitten, not just in constant appreciation of her startling, luminous beauty, stopped beside the sofa to ask if she was all right.

"Who was that screaming?" Nora Jane asked. "Was someone hurt?"

"A woman fell on one of the treadmills. She skinned her knee. Jay Holland, the eye doctor, was up there and took care of her. He's got her in Beau's office. There were three doctors on the machines, a radiologist, an eye surgeon, and an internist. I guess this is the place to be if an earthquake hits. The little guy seems happy. He didn't cry?"

"He was eating a PowerBar. He loves to eat."

"Did you see that demonstration at the Democratic convention? With those nuts protesting breast-feeding? They said it caused unhealthy oral fixations. I thought it was a joke, but then the cops arrested some of them."

"I didn't see it. I guess we have enough crazies in California now. I guess we've reached our limit."

"There is no limit. They keep coming. Anyway, I thought of you when I saw that on television. I thought you'd get a kick out of it."

*   *   *

The owner of the club had come out into the center of the lobby and was holding up his hands. "There could be other aftershocks. The police have asked us to stay here for another hour or so. Traffic is going to be horrific everywhere anyway. You can take mats into the aerobics or yoga rooms and do stretches, none of you stretch enough, admit it, or you can use the basketball court but we don't want anyone upstairs near the machines. Snacks and drinks are on the house. Jeff will get a television going in the snack bar if you want to see it on television. We think there are forty-six people in the club and fourteen three- to four-year-olds. If your children are okay, take them into the playrooms and let them play together. No one was in the pool. There was only one injury and it's being treated. Let the trainers know if you need help. It's ten forty-five. Let's shoot for staying in the building another hour."

People began to wander off into various activities. Sylvia invited Nora Jane to stretch with her in the yoga room and Little Freddy agreed to go into the nursery to play with the other children.

The third shock hit just as Little Freddy was settling down with a Lego game. His friend Arthur was sitting beside him. When they felt the floor and table move they started laughing so hard they couldn't stop. "It's a big one," Little Freddy yelled. "Get on the floor."

"Titty babies," he whispered to Arthur to make him even more hysterical with laughter. "Them are titty babies."

Nora Jane and Sylvia had just unrolled their mats when they felt the third shock and they felt it roll and took it. Then they got up and went to the nursery to see if Little Freddy was all right. He and Arthur were still sitting at the table laughing their heads off.

"We could learn from that," Sylvia said.

"I do," Nora Jane replied. "It's a new world. I never had a boy."

"You sing opera, don't you?" Sylvia asked. It was an hour later. People were beginning to fan out into the parking lot to find their cars. "I know Anna Hilman, the director at San Francisco Place. She told me about your voice. She heard you sing last year at the benefit. She said it was divine. I wish I'd been there. The reason I'm bringing it up is that we are having a fund-raiser in December and I wondered if we might persuade you to sing for us. It's national. I mean, you'd have to go to New York. It's going to be in the Metropolitan Opera House. We want to take San Francisco talent with us so it won't be all East Coast. Would you even consider doing it? We'd pay your expenses, with your husband, of course. I have a house on Park Avenue, actually. You could stay with us if you don't have a hotel you like."

Nora Jane wasn't answering, so Sylvia went on. "I don't mean to ask you on a day like this but I thought you might want to do it. It will be on C-Span. I don't even know if you are interested in Planned Parenthood."

"Of course I am. I just never sing in public. It just isn't something I enjoy doing. I've done it five or six times in the last few years, but proving I can do it doesn't make me like it. My grandmother was a diva. She taught me, years ago in New Orleans.

Somehow it has always been part of my love for her, not something I want the world to hear."

"Anna said you sing like an angel. She said you had a really astounding range."

"I do. It's a gift. I've almost never studied or used it. I took from Delaney Hawk for two years. Sometimes I go over and sing with her for a month or two, but that's about it. I like being a housewife and a mother."

"That's lovely, Nora Jane. Commendable in this day and age. Well, think about my offer. I might even be able to get an honorarium. If you get interested, call me." Sylvia handed her a card and smiled and left and Nora Jane took Little Freddy by the hand and walked out to her Volvo and put him in the back in his car seat and got into the driver's seat and started driving. She had been in a fine mood, glad the earthquake was a small one, glad to spend time with a star like Sylvia, feeling good, and now she was feeling bad. The world was always reaching out and wanting things from her that she didn't want to give.

There had been no home for Nora Jane when she was young. Her father was dead and her mother drank. Only when she was at her grandmother Lydia's house was life beautiful and quiet. All Nora Jane wanted in the world was to keep the world quiet and good for her children. She didn't want fame, she didn't want applause, she didn't want half the money Freddy gave her and put in her name and put in bonds and stocks and accounts for her. All she wanted was for the days to pass in peace and the people she loved to be safe.

Is there no way they'll let me alone? she thought. All I ever wanted was to keep this one thing to myself, this music Lydia gave to me, the Bach and Scarlatti and, oh, the Puccini. She began to sing an aria from *Tosca* and Little Freddy raised his voice and sang with her, screaming at the top of his lungs to match her high notes and beating his legs on the car seat with power and joy.

Five days went by and Nora Jane avoided the weight room at the club because she didn't want to run into Sylvia. Once or twice she brought up the subject of the offer to her husband, Freddy, or her daughters, but they were busy with their own thoughts and didn't seem to want to discuss her quandary at any length.

"It's up to you," Freddy kept saying. "If you want to do it, I'll go with you and support you in any way I can. If you don't want to, just tell her so."

Then a letter came in the mail from the national office of Planned Parenthood inviting her formally to participate in the program and offering her five thousand dollars and her expenses and a dress designed especially for her by Geoffrey Beene. He would send someone to take measurements and consult with her about her taste in color and fabric.

"I'm going to do it," Nora Jane declared and put the letter in front of Freddy at the breakfast table. "I am doing it for Planned Parenthood and for the dress. I'll give back all the money I don't spend. I might have to spend some on lessons with Delaney for a few months. I want to work something up. A tenor from the Met will be there and they think Christopher Parkening. I have to do this, Freddy. I can't turn this down. This fell in my lap.

Grandmother would want me to do this. She would want me to sing at Lincoln Center."

"Are you sure? Absolutely sure?"

"Yes, I think I am." She stood in the light from the windows, with her beautiful face screwed up into a terrible imitation of courage and Freddy loved her so much he could not breathe.

"Then say yes. When is the performance?"

"On December the eleventh."

"We'll take the kids and spend a week and do Christmas things."

III

IN 1996 THE GROUP LED BY ABU SAAD had killed a writer named Adrien Searle as part of the cleansing that surrounded the Salman Rushdie shame. Now more killing must be done. Blood revenge, blood for blood, life for life. If blood doesn't flow, men never learn.

The new cleansing was supposed to take place on the three days covering the anniversary of the day the three men who killed Adrien Searle were locked away in a prison that was worse than death.

September 13, Holly Knight. September 14, Freddy Harwood. September 15, Joseph Leister. The paladins would move from Arkansas to California, then to Wisconsin.

It would be a full moon, the brightest moon of the year, a lunar shadow, three victims, three assassins, a car wreck, a throat slit, a fire, and they were done and the message was delivered that Fire From Heaven takes vengeance on the ones who helped the one who broke the sacred vows that knit the souls of the faithful together for all time. Amen.

But no one could have predicted an earthquake that would not let the 747 land in San Francisco and took the protectors of the faith to Las Vegas, Nevada, instead, into a hell of iniquity and disgust, unclean past all imagining.

They spread out to stay in three different hotels. They waited for orders but none came. Nothing could be depended upon for several days.

"Allah is good. Blessed be his name," Abu said. "Order things from room service. Maintain yourselves in patience. We have to wait until he returns to his routine. It won't be long."

"Then we go to Wisconsin and do the third act."

"No, it must be in sequence. The president, the vice president, the secretary-treasurer of their organization, this bookseller's group. His holiness wants it that way. Do not question things, Davi. Say your prayers, eat food, rest, amuse yourself. In good time."

Abu hung up the phone and settled himself on the bed to study his French grammar. He was no longer a young man with fire in his blood and was glad that he was not. Every year his study and learning made him a more valuable man to the God he worshiped, and in that knowledge lay all his happiness. He had learned four languages in ten years. French would be his fifth. He needed no praise for his work. He was his own praise. He thought of his father in heaven thinking of him and his begetting and he was glad.

★   ★   ★

Nora Jane dropped Little Freddy at his playschool and started off for Delaney Hawk's studio on Euclid Street. When the Presidio became the place to be, Delaney had sold her house in Marin and moved back into town. It was a typical Delaney move. A sixty-four-year-old woman selling her house and all her furniture and starting over in a Bauhaus world of bleached wood floors, stark white walls, uncurtained windows, and Pensi and Mies van der Rohe copies. The piano had a room to itself. The only other furniture was three Wassily chairs and an Axis table.

Nora Jane had not seen Delaney since the move, and it added to the strangeness of her decision to sing in New York to have to seek out and find her teacher in a neighborhood she knew nothing about.

Delaney was waiting on the front sidewalk, watching for her. It might be a new neighborhood but it was the same old Delaney, dressed in a long skirt, an orange linen blouse, and a gray cashmere sweater that had belonged to Nabokov when she had known him in London. She always wore the sweater around her shoulders. She wore it summer and winter. The sight of it reminded Nora Jane of whom she was dealing with and made her humble. Delaney Hawk had walked with gods and she did not forget.

Delaney tied the arms of the sweater into a knot and began to direct Nora Jane to a parking place in what anyone would have thought was the front yard. When Nora Jane had turned off the motor, Delaney came around to the driver's side and opened the door and held it for her while she got out. Delaney was smiling her professional, no-nonsense smile. It was her main smile at this time in her life.

"I'm glad you want to get back to work," she said. "I need money to get a driveway poured and tear off this porch. Come on in. See the new place." She led the way to the fated porch and up the stairs and opened the front door and held it while Nora Jane moved into the living room. Four Mies chairs sat in a square around a marble table holding a vase of yellow tulips.

"It makes me want to sing right now." Nora Jane was laughing. "My God, I bet the acoustics are wonderful."

"You bet they are. The floors are synthetic wood, they're made of oil, they contain liquid, not that everything doesn't although we forget that. Well, let's get started. What do you want to sing?"

"The *Ave Maria* by Schubert. Handel, *Let the Bright Seraphim.* And a modern piece. The girls want me to sing *O Holy Night.*"

"Oh, God. The Schubert's tricky. If you have the slightest cold, anything can ruin it. Well, we can do it. This is some turn you've taken. What are they paying you?"

"Geoffrey Beene's designing the dress. I get to keep it. Oh, it isn't that. It's for my grandmother Lydia. I might sing Puccini. We'll see."

"Which Puccini?"

"*Vissi d'arte.*"

"I see." Delaney went to the piano bench and sat down on it facing the piano. She played several notes of the Puccini. "Well, why not. You can do it."

"It was what Lydia was listening to when she died. When she sang it she wore a blue velvet dress and that is what I'm going to ask Mr. Beene to make for me. I have never sung it out loud since she died. Only in my heart, but I know it better than I know any music in the world." Nora Jane was crying. Standing in the beautiful, pristine room crying without moving or making a sound. "This is for her. She was the most important person in my life and I have to quit being in denial about what her death did to me and celebrate what I knew."

"Oh, God." Delaney was crying also. She had not sung and taught grand opera all her life to back away from the heart and breath of life.

"Then let's begin," Delaney said. "There's water in the pitcher on the table. Have a sip. Come over here. Maybe I'll go to New York with you if you do this thing. My sister lives there, on the Upper West Side. Yes, if you do this, I'll go with you. I haven't been in several years. It's time to go."

"Yes," Nora Jane answered. "Yes, yes, yes."

She went to the table and poured the water and drank a small amount and walked over to the piano and waited while Delaney looked for the music in a Treviso bookshelf filled with scores and sheet music.

"Do scales," Delaney ordered. "Start warming up." She moved back to the piano and struck one note, a C, and Nora Jane picked it up and began to move her voice up and down her incredible range. Delaney shivered, then straightened her shoulders and went back to the bookshelf and began to take out music.

I didn't forget how, Nora Jane would decide later. You don't forget. It's like skating or skiing, balance sports. No, it's like looking at my children, like love, because it is love and I have not forgotten. My body can still do this thing I love so much, this clear happiness my grandmother gave to me so long ago when there was nothing else I had but this and her and it was enough and I survived and lived to find Freddy and have Lydia and Tammili and Little Freddy and become a person who is going to sing Puccini at the Metropolitan Opera and not be afraid.

That coming weekend, Nora Jane's twin daughters, Lydia and Tammili, were planning on being gone for two nights to a Girl Scout retreat that included a tour of the California Academy of Sciences in Golden Gate Park.

"Let's take Little Freddy and go up to Willits," Freddy suggested. "I have a huge desire to get out of town. Please say yes. You can rest and I'll take care of him. I want to take him. He never gets to be there alone."

"If you're absolutely sure the power is going to be high enough to pump water."

"The cells are full. No one's been in months. I'll call and have Deesha go out and clean it up and check. Then you'll go Friday afternoon, as soon as the girls leave?"

"Okay. I'll go. I love the house at Willits. I just like to think I can take a bath if I want to. Yes, yes, I'll go."

"You're in a good mood lately. I would have hired Geoffrey Beene myself if I'd known that's what you wanted."

"It isn't that. And it isn't about singing either. It's about my grandmother. I haven't finished figuring it out yet. It's about who she was and being part of that. She used to polish my shoes twice a day when I stayed with her. It's about having had her and remembering it and being grateful."

Little Freddy pushed open the door and came into the room.

He had his hands folded across his chest as if to begin complaining about something.

Freddy picked him up and carried him to the bed and sat him on his knee. "We're going to see a mountain lion, son of mine. We're on our way to Willits to feed the lion."

"That is not the way to get me to Willits."

"I'm teasing. I'll let him look through the binoculars. I won't take him where there's any danger. You know that. I wouldn't take him down to the woods unless I knew it was safe for him to go."

"He doesn't need to see a mountain lion. He's only three years old. He can look at pictures of wild animals or see them at the zoo."

Abu, Davi, and Petraea moved into a suite at the Sands on the third day of waiting. On the fourth day a message was delivered by a room service waiter. It was in a dialect only Abu read, so he interpreted it for the others.

"On Saturday we go to Berkeley and wait until he closes the store. He is having a book signing for a famous person from New Orleans. He must be there. He parks his car a block from the store beside a shoe store called Intelligent Feet. We can follow him home or we can take him on the street. We will have to use a sedating shot because of the public place. Everything cannot be perfect now. We will leave him in the alleyway between the shoe shop and a ladies' clothing store. Then we go to the airport, give the car to a messenger who will meet us, board airplanes, and go to Wisconsin by three different routes. All luggage will be checked. Anything we need for the work will be supplied when we get there. Leave only clothes in the suitcases. Nothing else of any kind. The messenger will try to return your things later."

"It has been a long wait," Davi said. "Allah be praised."

"Amen," Petraea added.

It was Thursday afternoon when Freddy remembered that the Neville Brothers were going to sign their book in the shop on Saturday night. "There's nothing I can do about it now," he told his secretary, Francis. "Tell them I got sick. No, just say I'm sorry. They don't know me. They aren't going to get their feelings hurt."

"Okay. Okay. We can handle it. I just wish you wouldn't schedule these things if you aren't going to be here to help. We could have two thousand people, for God's sake. I'll be awake for nights thinking about it. They'll tear up the store."

"We can straighten the store. We sell books for a living, Francis. We can't afford to sell only ones we wish people will read. Don't be a snob."

"I like their music, some of it."

"Well, there you are. I'm taking Little Freddy to Willits, Francis. He never gets to go without the girls so he never gets to be there in peace and quiet."

"He's three years old. Three-year-olds don't want peace and quiet."

"He might if he ever knew what it was like."

In New York City Carlton Rivers was arguing with Lynn Fadiman. They were in a bar on Third Avenue drinking martinis.

It was past two o'clock in the afternoon and they had been arguing for two hours. "Don't drink any more of that," Lynn said. "We've got to be sober when we talk to the police."

"We're going to drag the condominium into this before it's over. I know we will. It will get out, Lynn. It will be in the papers."

"What about me? I've been snooping through someone's apartment. But I'm taking my chances. This is duty, plain and simple. That's it. Let's eat something and go on over there and tell them what we know."

Carlton got up from the bar stool and left his third martini untouched on the bar. They walked off to a table a waiter had ready for them. Carlton went back to the bar and retrieved the martini just before the waiter wasted it. "I'm drinking this," he told Lynn. "Goddammit, Lynn, I'm not a lush. You're right, civic duty is the price we pay and I was raised to honor that. We're going. Order something fast. Let's get a steak. Let's have some ballast. They could keep us there all afternoon."

An hour and a half later they were in the office of an assistant district attorney for upper Manhattan talking to a man who was listening very carefully. He was not acting like they were crazy. He was not interested in why they took prints or anything else. As soon as he saw Freddy Harwood's name on the list he began to fit the pieces into place. He had been part of the team that tracked down the writer Adrien Searle's killers. They had killed her by mistake while trying to get to Salman Rushdie's American publisher. The district attorney even recognized the date of Holly Knight's accident in Arkansas as the date when the murderers were finally locked away in a maximum-security prison.

"I'm sending a team over to dust this apartment seventeen," he told Carlton. "I don't want any fuss. The quieter the better. Can you trust the doormen? The supervisor? How long have you known them? We'll have to do background checks on them, but until we do I don't want them to know anything. Can you get my men in without anyone knowing they're there?"

"Sure," Carlton said. "When do you want to leave?"

"We have to hope they'll come back. You understand that. That's why the secrecy."

"What about the owners? Can you find out who they are?" While Carlton was speaking, a secretary came in and handed the assistant district attorney a note.

"They don't exist," he said to Carlton. "You guys were had. They aren't there. Just the money, being paid from Swiss accounts. By next month it will be gone, like smoke, no more condo fees, I'm afraid."

"Mr. Rivers's sister is married to an Arab," Lynn put in. "You'll come across that. She married a wealthy Saudi and they raise Thoroughbred horses in Virginia, when they're in the United States. We discussed it coming over here and decided we'd better tell you about that."

"Is this relevant?"

"They don't speak to each other. Mr. Rivers tried to prevent the marriage. The sister's fifteen years younger. He was trustee of her estate. If this concerns Saudi Arabians, he thinks he might also be a target. It's just an idea."

"This has nothing to do with Saudi Arabia. This is about Iran.

It's part of an ongoing problem. Maybe a group called Medina or Fire From Heaven. They're enforcers. They killed a woman writer four years ago, by mistake. Got the wrong target. They were after the man who published Salman Rushdie in the United States and killed his girlfriend instead. We caught those bastards, some of them, and threw their butts in a federal prison. I can't believe we couldn't get a death sentence. Chickenshit judges, covering their asses. People are afraid of these guys, Lynn, and with good cause. Here's the other thing. One of the people on the list you found is the owner of the bookstore that the publisher and the writer they killed, this Adrien Searle, had just been visiting. He had just had dinner with them. The bookstore owner, Freddy Harwood, is an heir to the Sears Roebuck fortune. He had his store bombed when *Satanic Verses* was published and the death decree went down. So he's been in this all along. He's always been a target. This is a list of the officers of the Independent Bookseller's Association. They've already killed one of them, Holly Knight, the president of the group. Well, they won't kill the others. Okay, let's get cracking. How can you get two or three men inside the apartment in the quietest way?"

"Have them come to my apartment as electricians, workers, and we'll go up the back stairs. I have a key an ex-owner gave me. The locks haven't been changed on the back."

"What about the hit list?" Lynn asked. "Are you going to talk to the other two people on the list?"

"The CIA and FBI are already on it. It's the first thing I did. You both are considered sworn to secrecy. Don't tell this at a cocktail party tonight."

*   *   *

The FBI put four men on Freddy Harwood and even considered warning him, but decided against it. If they could catch the killers trying to make the hit it would be better. Warning people did no good. They always tipped off the assassins. No one can act normally when they think they've been targeted.

The helicopter that passed over the house at Willits and scared all the wildlife away was not looking for marijuana.

Saturday, September 23, dawned clear and cold all across the American West. In Las Vegas the men who had set out to kill Freddy were in a happier frame of mind. They had been taken by limousine to a ranch sixty miles from town and were being treated as honored guests by a Medina sympathizer and former Olympic boxer who had retired to raise cutting horses in the desert. Their host was an elegant, vicious man who had seen to it that everything they wanted was within their reach, including several young blond girls who were working their way through modeling school in Vegas. Davi and Petraea took advantage of these gifts, but Abu asked only to go riding in the desert. He woke before the sun rose and said his prayers and went to the stables where a groom was waiting with a big, gray stallion. By the time he was in the saddle, the owner rode up to join him. The groom ran ahead opening the gates, and they rode out into the beautiful morning.

"You are sad that it could not be on the perfect day, but Allah knows what he is doing, Abu. Your prey is waiting. It will not be taken from you. Blessed be the name of Allah. Allah be praised."

"What time does our plane leave this afternoon?"

"At two. We'll get you there. When we return we will eat and then leave. I wish I could go with you. I would like to be the one to draw the knife across his throat. This one is the Jew?"

"We hack away at the legs while the true infidel sits in splendor in London being idolized by dogs."

"Come, let's ride down into the arroyo. This is beautiful country, Abu. I am honored to show it to you."

In Berkeley, Nora Jane and Freddy were putting Tammili and Lydia's gear into the Volvo while Little Freddy sat in the car seat complaining.

"I'm hot," he kept saying. "Where them going to?"

"We're going to a Girl Scout Jamboree because we are junior counselors. We help the little girls learn things they have to know." Tammili climbed in the back seat beside him and gave him a big kiss on the cheek. "You have to do without us for two days."

"You all don't have to take us," Lydia said. "We aren't going very far. Why are all three of you taking us to Golden Gate Park?"

"Because we're going on to Willits. We've got our gear in the back."

Freddy locked the front door and got into the driver's seat and started down the driveway. "I forgot the stuff in the refrigerator," Nora Jane said. Freddy stopped the car and waited while she ran back into the house and got the milk and lunch she had packed. He was so accustomed to waiting on women he didn't even sigh. He looked out across the street and examined the neighbors' yards. He was learning patience. If there was a heaven he was a shoo-in, he was always telling his best friend, Nieman. A man who lives with three women is a humble man.

So he was watching as the BMW 750 came down the street going ten miles an hour and turned into the Musselmans' driveway and stopped. Since the Musselmans were in Europe for the fall, Freddy thought that was out of whack and picked up the phone and called the Neighborhood Watch and reported it. He picked out the first three numbers of the license plate as he drove by a few minutes later and called that in also. There were three men in the car. Just sitting in the driveway. Not good, Freddy decided. Doesn't make sense.

Information was going everywhere. The Neighborhood Watch alerted the police who told the FBI within minutes. The men in the BMW called Abu while they were waiting for Freddy to leave his driveway.

The Harwood family drove off in the beautiful morning light. Little Freddy had figured out that Lydia and Tammili were leaving him and he was in a bad mood about that. Lydia slipped him a handful of Teddy Grahams and that cheered him up some but not completely. They always went off and left him. He couldn't figure out what he was doing wrong.

"Would you make me a baby coffee?" he asked in a pitiful little voice. Baby coffee was his name for chocolate milk in a baby bottle.

"Not now, sweetie pie," Lydia said. "We're going to Jamboree. Can I make baby coffee in the car? Think about it. Do you see a refrigerator in here?"

"Momma has some. She's got some."

"He needs to stop drinking so much chocolate milk," Tammili declared. "He's getting too fat. He's outgrown all his clothes. We need to start giving him juices and water. He never drinks water."

When Abu and the owner got back to the ranch, the plans had been changed. "They're sending a plane to take you sooner," the owner told Abu after he read a long e-mail. "You need to get ready. The Jew has left town. They are following him. Wake the others and tell them to get packed."

Many things were happening in and around the house in Willits. The ground was still shifting due to the five point two that had rocked San Francisco the week before. Because of that, the doors and windows in the house were getting out of alignment. Not badly, just enough so it was difficult to raise and lower the screens or to lock the sliding glass doors.

In a ravine a mile from the house an FBI truck was setting up for business. In nearby Fort Bragg, California, two helicopters and their crews were on standby. A third helicopter was already taking reconnaissance photographs.

A satellite was also filming the area.

Seven men were now in charge of Freddy's safety. Three were watching the house at Willits and the remaining four were following him in two vehicles. One vehicle was staying within sight of Freddy and his family. The other was three miles ahead.

Abu and Davi and Petraea were in a Ford Explorer driving behind the FBI men but they did not know that was what they were doing. They thought they were alternately following and being followed by a group of gay men and it enraged Davi, who was driving, to have to keep changing lanes with the Chevrolet carrying the FBI people. The FBI men had taken off their coats and loosened their ties in order to seem inconspicuous. Something about the closeness and quietness of the men drove Davi to decide they were gay. He was still in a heightened sexual state due to his days on the ranch. He had also caught a sexually transmitted disease but he wouldn't know that for several weeks. "I can't stand to see them," he told Petraea. "This country is so foul. All foul things are here and nothing is done to stop them."

"How long have you been here now?" Petraea asked.

"Fifteen years. Only twice did I go home and see my family. Allah is great. He has given me this to do in his service. I do not complain about my exile."

"Do not look at them," Abu said from the backseat. "It looks suspicious to stare at other motorists. The police will stop us thinking we are in road rage. And don't break the speed limit. There are weapons with us now."

Davi slowed down and let the FBI get ahead. "But they will get ahead and we can't find them."

"Sensors are on the car. I can pick them up. Besides, we know where they are going. The man has a shack up in the hills where

he goes sometimes on weekends. We are sure that's their destination. We have a man up there watching for us."

The fourth Iranian was parked at a small filling station and grocery store at the turn-off from the highway up into the sandy dirt
roads that led to Freddy's house. He had already been waiting
long enough to read three newspapers and begin on a magazine.
He had told the store owner he had to wait until his engine
cooled down. But this was taking too long. He read two articles
in the magazine, went in and thanked the owner and bought
some potato chips and went back to his car and began to drive
slowly up the dirt road. When he was half a mile from the FBI
truck he pulled the car behind a large outcrop and turned off the
motor and went to sleep. He set an alarm on his watch for
twenty minutes. He was very tired. He had not slept the night
before. It was difficult work and he did not like not knowing
what it was about.

Freddy speeded up to seventy and reached across and patted
Nora Jane on the knee. Little Freddy was asleep in the backseat.
They were on a two-lane highway that Freddy loved to drive. It
had curves and wonderful cuts through the mountains and you
could see the history of the land laid bare. He knew it bored
Nora Jane to be lectured on geology so he spared her that and
told the story to himself. When it was my best friend, Nieman,
and myself, we could stop and look at rocks, he thought, but
those days are gone. We are married men with lives. He sighed,
remembering the year when they built the house, driving up

from Berkeley on the weekends in a pickup truck, sleeping in a tent, building fires, seeing stars, studying rocks.

The FBI men had dropped way back. The helicopter had them now and the point man was in place. They could take their time.

In the Explorer Abu was going over their plans. "I want to make sure of the destination," he said. "Although it could be no place else now that he's on this road. He's a creature of habit. Then we will circle around on a connecting road that leads to the house. Then we wait until dark. We go in after midnight and take him without hurting the others. All communication lines will be cut and the car disabled. We leave him in the meadow below the house and walk back to the car and drive to an airport near Fort Bragg. A plane is there already on the ground, waiting. It will take us to catch the planes to Wisconsin."

"Allah calls for blood," Davi muttered. "Allah is thirsty for the blood of infidels."

"Don't preach, Davi," Abu answered. "We have not become Baptists yet. You should not watch those preachers on television so much or listen to them on the radio stations. I have been meaning to talk to you about that. You must keep your mind clean to do your work. Also, it is bad for your English and makes you say strange things. It is not good to call attention to yourself. They do not like us here."

Freddy turned onto the gravel and dirt road that led to his house. The bumping woke Little Freddy and Nora Jane gave him his bottle of baby coffee to get him back to sleep.

When they arrived at the house, they began to unpack the car. The helicopter had its camera trained on them and missed the two minutes it took Davi, Petraea, and Abu to get out of their car and start on foot down into a dry riverbed and begin to walk the back way to Freddy's house. There was still foliage on the trees near the dry river. It had been a wet summer and the river had been full for months. The trees had had a banner year. Now they waved their leaves above the assassins and hid them from every camera.

"We've lost the ragheads," the FBI agent in charge yelled. "Speed it up. They're gone. The goddamn sand niggers have fucking disappeared. Let's go. Let's get to the house."

By the time Freddy and Nora Jane had unpacked the car and opened the house and turned on the solar fans and started running water to clear the pipes there were men hidden all around them. Abu, Davi, and Petraea were in a stand of Douglas fir and madrone trees below the house. They were only thirty feet from the mountain lion's den but they did not know that. The lion had been gone all day foraging near the falls to the west of the riverbed.

The FBI men were out of their car and spread out in a fan along the front of the house. The FBI helicopter was frantically trying to find the men it had lost but was only coming up with the man asleep in his car.

The satellite picked up the lion and got some really good footage of him crossing a sump below the falls, heading for home.

★   ★   ★

Little Freddy was playing on the back stairs while Freddy watched. Nora Jane was putting groceries away and wondering how the girls were getting along at the science museum.

At five o'clock the sun was still high in the sky and people were getting sleepy. Everyone was getting sleepy except Little Freddy, who had slept so long in the car there was no hope of him taking a nap.

"We'll spell each other," Freddy said. "You nap first and then I'll nap. I want to take him down to the edge of the woods and leave some food for Alabama. You don't mind if I take him that far, do you?"

"Take the gun then, will you? Wear the holster and cover it up. I don't want him to see it but I want you to take it."

"I don't know about that. What's the big secret? If you have a gun you explain it to them."

"All right. I'm going up and sleep in the loft."

Freddy got the .38 revolver out of the glove compartment of the car and checked to make sure it had shells. He had never owned a gun until Adrien Searle was killed in a hotel in Berkeley after reading at Clara Books. Adrien's death had wiped out a lot of Berkeley liberal bullshit. He had bought a gun, and both he and Nora Jane had learned to use it.

Freddy put on the shoulder holster, put the gun in the holster, and then opened the trunk and got out an old photojournalist's vest to use to cover it. He zipped up the vest and walked to where Little Freddy was arranging rocks on the bottom steps of the stairway.

*   *   *

From the stairs there was a wonderful view of the woods with the sky stretching out beyond them. There were always clouds in this vista, because of its nearness to the sea. It was a landscape that changed its colors all day long. In the center of the view was a rock outcrop where the old mountain lion Freddy called Alabama loved to come and sun himself. It was there that Freddy had first seen him. For fifteen years since that time he and Nieman had left treats on the rocks when they were there. It was a ritual.

Freddy had been an overprotected child who had not had a father to teach him to be brave. He had had to figure it out for himself or with Nieman's help. They figured it out intellectually as they did most things in their lives. If there was a wild animal who had the potential to be dangerous, they studied it and were cautious in their dealings with it.

Still, Freddy liked to walk down to the outcrop and leave dog treats on the rocks. He liked thinking of the old lion's pleasure when he came upon these windfalls. Also, he liked to believe that the lion could smell his hands on the treats and would know they were gifts from a friendly member of another species. Usually he carried a heavy walking stick and a can of Mace on these excursions. Now, rather than argue with Nora Jane, he had added the gun.

"Would you like to walk with me down to where the old lion lives?" Freddy asked his son. "We can take him some dog treats and leave them on his rock and then we can sit on the balcony and watch to see if he comes to get them."

"Like dog food?" Little Freddy asked, looking up from his rock work. He had lined up ten rocks to make a rock family.

"Better than dog food. These are dog treats, very special. To animals these are like candy. See, they come in different colors, like the cereal Grandmother Annie gives you when our backs are turned."

Little Freddy studied the box of dog treats. If there was one thing he really liked to do it was get his grandmother's poodle's dog food and go behind the sofa and eat it. If his grandmother or her maid caught him they went crazy. They ran around and yelled and held their hands up in the air. Dog food was good! It was hard, like eating salty rocks, and you could keep it in your mouth a long time, like the gum the baby-sitter gave him once. Like those round chewing gums they never let him get out of machines, only once that baby-sitter had gotten him some, and he had never forgotten it.

"You remember that baby-sitter that time that give me that gum?" he asked his father.

"Well, these aren't for you to eat, son. These are for our friend, Alabama. He isn't our friend really. He's a wild creature and we have to be careful, but we can go and leave him treats. He doesn't care about us one way or the other. He hunts for a living."

"Well, okay. If you let me carry the box."

"Okay. Let's go." Freddy held out his hand.

"Wait a minute. I got to put the daddy rock on the top." Little Freddy picked up the largest rock in his collection and put it on the highest step he could reach from the ground. Then he stepped back to look at his creation.

"What are they doing?" Freddy asked.

"Them are watching *The Wizard of Oz.*"

"Who all is there?"

"Momma rock, daddy rock, sister rocks, these ones are friend rocks that came over to play, this one is the baby-sitter rock." He held up a pretty granite formation split to show pink inside. His favorite baby-sitter wore pink all the time. It was her signature color. Freddy shook his head in wonder.

"Okay," Little Freddy said. "Let's go down there then."

They started down the long sloping hill to the woods, thick stands of Douglas fir and cedar and madrone trees. They were the pride of the property and the reason Freddy and Nieman had chosen this piece of land on which to build their house. It was virgin woods, sprung up when the cataclysms that built Northern California had stopped long enough for plants to begin to grow. "Birds brought these seeds," Nieman loved to say. "Or they were carried on the hides of animals or blew in with the wind. It is dazzling to imagine how it came here."

"Uncle Nieman says birds brought the seeds that made those trees grow here," Freddy began. "We should get some of the seedlings and plant them in town. Would you like to do that with me?"

"Is the lion going to eat this whole box of treats?" Little Freddy asked. "Every one of them?"

"Well, he's a pretty big lion, for mountain lions. He's old. He probably isn't a very good hunter anymore. He's probably hungry a lot of the time and he needs a treat. I have some treats for you at the house. When we get back we'll have them."

"What treats do you have for me?" He was hoping it was gum but he knew it would not be.

"Well, some oatmeal cookies for one thing, with raisins in them. And some graham crackers for another."

Davi saw them coming. "Allah brings the man to us," he said. "Now it is revealed." And he thought suddenly that his whole life had been lived for this moment, when he, Davi, who had been sent from his mother at the age of seven to live in the hard camp and learn a warrior's ways, who had been beaten and despised and risen up from his despair and become so good at his work that he was chosen to go to the United States to do Allah's work on earth and earn his way to heaven, he, Davi, now stood moments away from that reward. Allah is good, he knew. And he rewards the faithful.

"Abu, can we take him with the child watching, or must we wait?"

Abu bowed his head. He was quiet for a long moment while he sought help in prayer. "Now," he said finally. "Allah guides us. We will follow. You, Petraea. Take him quick. I will get the child out of the way."

The old lion moved back toward his den smelling the sack of treats that was moving his way. Nieman and Freddy had been leaving them for fifteen years. Occasionally, he walked out of the woods and sunned himself on the rock outcrop visible from the house. That was the whole encounter for all those years. A bowl of dog treats on a vertical uplift near an old madrone. A lion walking out and sunning himself within smell of men.

But these smells were confused. The good smell of the treats and the familiar smell of Freddy's photojournalist vest, then another smell, of fear and musk and oiled guns. The lion knew that smell and knew its danger.

The lion moved through the high grass and out onto the glade until he was about twenty feet from Davi and Petraea. He stopped and waited.

Freddy was almost to the outcrop where he always left the treats. It was a group of three large rocks with an opening in the center. On top was a large flat rock with an indentation like a bowl in the middle.

Petraea moved a few feet. The lion moved with him.

Freddy sat Little Freddy on a flat rock and let him fill the stone bowl with the treats. Little Freddy filled the bowl half full, then took a blue treat and raised it to his mouth, watching his father as he did it.

"You know better than that," Freddy said. "Those treats are for animals. We have human treats at home for boys."

Little Freddy held the blue treat up into the air, then dropped it into the bowl and continued very slowly filling the bowl from the sack.

Petraea moved several feet, then stepped out in view of the rocks and raised the rifle. Little Freddy saw the lion before he saw Petraea. He saw both of them before Freddy did. He was looking right at Petraea when the lion leaped on the man and began to mangle him.

Freddy threw himself on top of Little Freddy and pushed the child down into the crevice between the rocks. He took out the revolver and stood up and raised it. He did not want to shoot a man or a lion or anything that lived, but he shot. He shot at the lion's flank and then the field was full of men. Two men were on top of him and talking.

"FBI," one of them said. "We are here to help you. Don't move. Where's the child?"

Behind them two other men were running into the woods. The old lion was heading down a path to the river, disappearing like a streak of sunlight.

"Did I hit Alabama?" Freddy asked. "God, I hope I didn't hit the lion."

"He ran off all right," the agent said. "I don't think you could have hurt him much."

Little Freddy was still in the crevice. It was a nice, roomy place. He had brought the sack with the remaining treats with him and was lining some of them up on a ledge in front of him. He put two on the ledge and then he started eating some. He was eating a blue one and a reddish one. They were good. He liked them almost as much as he liked his grandmother's dog food that she kept in the closet in her big house with the big pool.

Nora Jane heard the shots and came running out onto the balcony. She stopped and looked and then ran down the stairs and then down the pasture as fast as she could run.

"Let me go," Freddy said. "She'll be hurt." But an FBI man got to her first and took her arm and began to explain what had happened. "Your husband and child are all right, Mrs. Harwood," he said. "Everything is under control. Let me take you back to the house."

"I want my child," she said. "I'm going to my child."

★   ★   ★

They were in their bedroom. The drapes were drawn back. A cool blue sky was visible through the windows. It was eleven o'clock in the morning.

"Arabs and Palestinians have their side to things," Nora Jane said. "They have families. They eat and sleep and need houses and security, they need part of that goddamn sand the Jews were crazy to want in the first place. Peace is never going to happen over there until the Israelis give back some of the sand. But I live here, in Northern California, in the richest country in the world and I won't be involved in that mess. I have one political idea. To protect my children. You can help me with that or I'll go away and do it by myself."

"I'll do whatever you want me to do."

"This is it, Freddy. This is how the world works." She opened the sliding glass doors that opened onto her walled garden, which was modeled on the Japanese garden at the Metropolitan Museum of Art. She went out and sat upon a bench and looked at the designs in the windows of the wall and she thought about the carpenter who had made them for her and she thought about design and patterns and how space was bent into time and the heart of matter and the universe of stars and all the work there was to do to get ready to go to New York and the reality of evil and how it never leaves the world, never, never, never goes away. Greed, envy, cruelty, hunger, disease, and death.

And in the face of that, beauty, "the frail, the solitary lance." I will sing my heart out for that audience, Nora Jane decided. I will walk out on the stage in my blue velvet dress and for a moment beauty will win and I will be its helper.

*   *   *

By the time she got to the outcrop Little Freddy had his mouth full of dog treats. "What are you eating?" she said. "Oh, my God, what do you have in your mouth?"

"Sometimes when they eat things like that you need to get their sodium and potassium checked," the young officer began. "We had a problem with one of ours eating dirt after it rained. It turned out he was low on sodium because of some allergy medication we were giving him."

Petraea had been mauled but not badly. His left cheek was cut and there was a long tear on his upper arm and he had sprained an ankle. The medevac crew decided to helicopter him to Fort Bragg before they stitched up the wounds. "I don't want to go sewing that up until we culture some of the saliva," the young M.D. decided. "We'll clean it and wrap it and take him on in."

"His blood pressure's very low," a male nurse insisted. "I think he's in shock. How are we going to sedate him? I think we should get the truck and do it here."

"Well, it's not your call," the M.D. said. "Goddammit to hell, I'm the doctor here."

It took several hours for the National Guard and the FBI to find Davi. The Guard brought in German shepherds and they tracked him to a madrone tree. He was covered with insect bites by the time they got him down. He was armed with a Ruger and an old Ortigies calibre 7.65 but he did not shoot when the tree was surrounded. Like all terrorists he knew better than to fear incarceration in American jails. It was hard to escape from them but they were easy time. No one feared being put in an American jail.

Abu had been harder to take. In the struggle he had wounded a young guardsman from Petaluma. The young man would never throw a football again or hold a woman against his chest without pain. He would try playing soccer with a group of wealthy men in Marin but it would never be the same. Still, he would have five hundred thousand dollars in corporate bonds with which to build a great house with a recreation room in which to watch other men play sports, and that was something. Fortunately, both his children were girls. It's not as if he had a son he could have taught to be a quarterback.

They had surrounded Abu in a grove of young trees. The dogs had him. There had been no need for the young man to go in but Abu had shot a dog and the young man had gone crazy and charged. He shot Abu in the leg before Abu got off the shot that ruined his arm. After he was down one of the big dogs came over and lay down beside him and whimpered like a child. It had been the young man's job to care for the dogs and he was fond of them and they of him.

"Is this ever going to end?" Nora Jane asked. It was several days later. They were at home in Berkeley, in their own home, in their bedroom. "If it isn't we have to go somewhere and change our names. I can't live like this, Freddy. I want you to take Salman's books out of the store and put an ad in all the papers saying you won't carry them. If you don't do that I will take the children and go away. I will not be part of this. I am not a revolutionary

or a political person. I hate the books anyway. They aren't any good. The only reason anyone reads them is because of all of this."

"The death decree was lifted. This sect is a bunch of crazies. They have to have enemies to exist. I was just in the line of fire."

"They killed Holly Knight. We had dinner with her in Portland last summer at the Association meeting. Adrien Searle, then Holly Knight, that's two people that we *knew*. And Little Freddy was there when armed men came running out from all directions. I think he'll remember that. Plus, the girls know everything because it was in the papers. God knows what it will do to them to know their parents were almost killed in a Holy War."

"I'll sell the store, Nora Jane, if that's what you want. I'll call a broker and put Clara Books on the market. Say the word. If you want me to, I will."

"I don't know. Let me think about it."

"Are we going to New York still?"

"Yes. I think we are. I have a lesson with Delaney this afternoon. She's been calling every day. She thinks you should give in and take the books out of the store. It's not as if they were asking you to quit selling Shakespeare."

"It's the principle. I'll sell the store but I won't refuse to stock books because of terrorist threats."

"Then sell it. Principles are abstractions. I'm talking about live children, live lives."

"Then I'll sell it."

"Then I want you to."

★　　★　　★

The old lion could still smell the dog treats on the stone. The two pieces Little Freddy had left in the crevice were still on the ledge where he put them. The lion had bloodied his paw trying to get them a few days before so now he just climbed up on the flattest stone and rested in the smell and the warmth from the sun. He had eaten well the night before, a snake he caught by the falls and a crippled rabbit he found in the woods. Hunger was leaving him alone on this fine September day and he fell into a light sleep. A memory of spring came to him, waking up and moving out into a field deep with grass. The smell of flowers and the luxurious smell of another creature, a mother, warm breathing softness and play and a den high on a bluff, softness, smallness, the other one, the other smell.

It was some days later. Nora Jane was in her house being talked to by a man in a suit who had once been the star of a college track team. It was very hard to be in Nora Jane's presence without being distracted, but the man was trying. "You are being guarded twenty-four hours a day by the best and most highly trained men and women in the world," the man was saying.

They were in the sunken living room with the pianos. There was a tray with tea and cookies. There was a pitcher of lemonade and tall frosted glasses and a plate of lime and lemon slices. Nora Jane was wearing a yellow playdress and her hair was pulled back into a bun like a dancer's. A yellow flower was in the bun.

Tammili and Lydia were listening from the upstairs balcony, sitting very quietly on the floor, not hiding, just being quiet.

"You are being guarded as if you were the president of the

United States," the man continued. "This is the treatment we give federal judges when they are threatened. We don't think there is a threat to you. We think we have most of the group. The one named Davi is talking his head off. An Afro-American preacher got to him on a television show. We've been letting him watch television as long as he keeps on cooperating. I don't think he's playing us. We think he's spilling his guts. It's a huge wind-fall. It's what we wait for. We've got this shrink talking to him. Davi's telling him about the camps where he was raised. He's crying all the time. Everything he's told us so far checks out. The position of the camps, the number of personnel, everything. We think we have rounded up the entire group in the United States. I don't think you have anything to worry about, Mrs. Harwood. We think we can keep you safe."

"If we go to New York?"

"You'll be safe there. We'll have personnel in the hotel. We will stay on this. We have orders to stay on it."

"Please have lemonade. I made it an hour ago. It's very good, I think. Please let me pour you some."

"There's one other thing." The agent took the lemonade and sipped it. "The man in New York City who found the list is a re-tired surgeon. He knows about your concert. He asked if he could meet you when you're there, after your concert, of course. It's unprofessional of me to give you this message but he's been hounding us to get in touch with you. He's from New Orleans originally. He knew your father or something."

"My father died in the Vietnam War."

"We know about that. Well, I just wanted to give you his name if you ever want to call him."

"Okay. Give it here." She waited, here it was, the part she hated about performing. But this man had been instrumental in saving Freddy's life. And he had known her father. It might be all right to talk to someone about that at last.

"His name is Dr. Rivers. I'll write it down for you." The agent took a pad and pencil from his pocket and wrote down a name and address and handed it to her.

"I'll write to him," Nora Jane said. "Thank you for giving this to me."

"This lemonade is fine. I haven't had a lemonade in many years. It's good. It's really good."

"Let me pour you some more." Nora Jane leaned over and poured the lemonade. She was so near the agent that for a moment he thought that he might faint. It was all right for someone to be that beautiful, he decided, but it took some getting used to for a working man.

"We're going to New York," Tammili declared. "She's going to do it."

"I knew she would. She's brave, Tammili. She only worries because of us."

"Let's call Grandmother Anne and get her to take us shopping. She's the only one who's going to let us buy something we really like to wear up there."

"She's the best one to shop with."

"Let's call her now."

"Okay."

The Abortion

McCAMEY LYONS WAS SITTING on the porch watching it rain. It was raining out Fayetteville High School's last football game of the season, his last game in high school and probably the last game on a real team he would ever play. He was a tight end, a strong, fast runner and a tough, smart player but too fine-boned to play college ball. Not that McCamey would ever be able to talk his mother into letting him play college ball anyway.

His father came out on the porch, pulling his jacket on over a white cotton shirt. "Come on, Son," he said. "Let's go over to the job and see if the electricians got anything done. Come on, sitting out here pouting won't get you anywhere. Springdale might have beat you by forty points. They sure beat us every year we played. You can't do anything about Springdale."

"They wouldn't have beat us by forty points. Bobby Harting hurt his ankle. He wasn't going to get to play."

"Come on. I'll take you down to Dickson Street and buy you a hamburger when we get through. Come on, earn your keep."

McCamey got up and followed his father to the pickup. His father tossed him the keys when they were in the driveway. "You drive," he said. "I like to get chauffeured." McCamey took the keys and started down Lighton Trail and around the new park to Sequoyah and on down to where Will was building a house on top of an abandoned water tank. He had filled in the tank and used it as the foundation and was building a curved house with glass walls facing south. McCamey had worked on it the past summer, helping the masons lay the stone chimney and walks and the back wall. He was proud of the house. The sight of it cheered him up and made him forget his lost football game.

"It looks good in the rain," he said. He pulled the truck into the wooden carport and shut off the motor. "You did good, Daddy. How close do you think it is to being finished?"

"Another month. We've already had an offer, did I tell you that? So I guess you can go to college without breaking us."

"I guess I can." It was a joke. McCamey had already made a 1350 on a PSAT. He was going to be able to go anyplace he wanted to go, as long as he didn't fuck up in the next six months.

"You don't want to leave that girl, do you?" Will sat back and rolled down the window to keep himself from smoking a cigarette. He took a deep breath of the cold wet air and thought about Ted Hardcastle lying down in his house dying of lung cancer.

Hardcastle's daughter was McCamey's girlfriend and had

been since they were in kindergarten. That was that. He'd never leave her behind and she sure wasn't going to leave her daddy when he was dying and that's how the world worked. It even worked that way for seventeen-year-old kids in Fayetteville, Arkansas, in the middle of the biggest boom years in the history of the world.

"It's hard," Will said. "Well, you don't have to leave her. Go to school here. They've got as good a pre-med program here as they have at Princeton University."

"No, they don't."

"Okay, they don't. Let's go inside and see if the electricians got anything done. They can't figure out how to get the wiring underneath the front windows. I don't know why it's got to be there but Peter says it has to be." Peter was Will's partner. He was the architect and Will was the builder.

"Peter's right," McCamey said. "You don't want to have those windows up there on the front if you can't light them up."

"I don't want people on the outside to always be watching a house where I live. A house is where you have your private life that the public only gets invited to see."

They got out of the truck and started walking into the house through the covered walkway. Because the house was built into the side of a hill there were stone drains beside the walkway and around the sides of the house. They were small versions of Roman aqueducts, made of red and black granite slabs and fitted together but not mortared. The walkway was made of the same stone but the slabs were larger. When the stones settled Will planned on planting thyme in the crevices. He had seen it in an *Architectural Digest* and been wanting to try it.

"The walkway and the drains look good, Son," he said. "That's your work from the summer. If they can stand this week's rain they'll take anything. They're settling in."

"I almost broke my back getting those stones to stay on that hill. Billy Joe wasn't helping a bit. I spent two days on it before finally Peter came over and showed us how to start at the bottom and work up."

"You started at the top?"

"How was I to know? You were in Talequah that week. They had dumped the stone by the carport so we thought we should start up there."

"Well, it's a good job, Son. You ought to be proud of it."

At the end of the walkway they stopped and looked back over the hills to the south. Lightning was covering the sky, huge networks of lightning, a vast array of energy, heat, light. In between the lightning flashes, the clouds were as black as night on the horizon. It was one big storm, and this was its second day. By the time it was finished there wouldn't be a river or creek in northwest Arkansas that wasn't filled to the top of its banks. "Goddamn, we used to have some fun on the Mulberry after weather like this," Will said. "Now your mother won't go."

His cellular phone was ringing and he pulled it off his belt and looked at it. "It's her," he added. He handed a ring of keys to McCamey. "Open the door while I answer this."

McCamey opened the door and went into the beautiful circular kitchen. The house was really nice. He was going to hate to see his father sell it. It was the best one they had built in a while. He stood looking at the deep blue countertops and the pattern in the wood floor, thinking maybe he'd change his mind and go to architecture school instead of medical school.

His father came up behind him and handed him the phone. "Here, it's your mother. Suzy's dad's back in the hospital. You better get on down there. Take the truck. Your mother'll come get me in a while. Go on. She needs you."

McCamey turned and faced him, then he started moving. He was out the door and down the walkway and into the truck and backing down the drive before Will remembered that Amanda was still on the phone. "He's gone," he said. "How bad is it?"

"He's got fluid in his lungs. Should we go down there too?"

"Not yet. Come get me in thirty minutes. I'll be done by then."

He closed the phone and put it back on his belt and went into the living room to try the lights below the windows. The wiring was still uncovered but it worked. He flipped the lights on a time or two and then stood in the center of the room watching the storm and thinking about his son and his son's girl. They're too young for this, he thought. It's the year 2000. They aren't supposed to be having people die on them when they're seventeen. I got to quit this time and that's that. I'm not smoking another goddamn cigarette no matter how much I want one. Ted Hardcastle is dying from cigarettes and these kids have to watch him die.

He shook it off and turned on the lights in the windows so Amanda could see them when she came up the drive. Then he walked back into the kitchen and turned on the lights in the carport and the walkway and then he started walking all over the house turning lights on and off and working the rheostats. It didn't stand to reason that a man he'd gone to high school with should be in a hospital dying and leaving his wife and daughters just at the age when they needed him most.

"Will. Where are you?" It was Amanda, coming in the kitchen door and calling for him and he hurried back to her and took her in his arms and held her and desired her and took her into the living room and made love to her on the floor with the lightning filling the windows with glory. "I love you so much, Baby. It could be me and you. It could be us watching the other one die."

"It is us," she said. "It's McCamey and us and everyone else who knows them." She rolled over and lay quiet in his arms. "I'm not forgetting I almost lost you the night McCamey was born. I still remember every minute of thinking you were gone."

"It's the price you pay for loving. It's how it ends."

"No, it doesn't. It ends with children being born and watching them grow up and loving them, knowing they'll go out and have their own children and knowing them too if you're lucky and then letting go and letting it go on without you. It doesn't have to be a tragedy. It's what we have now that matters."

"I really like this house," Will said. "Why don't we move in it and sell ours? McCamey's leaving next year anyway. We could sell ours for as much as I'll get for this one. Peter wouldn't care."

"You always want to move into your houses but I don't want to move out of mine."

"Not like I want to move into this one. Come here and let me show you the windows in the master bedroom. They're curved more than these."

★　　　★　　　★

McCamey pulled into a parking place in front of the Washington Regional Medical Center. He turned off the motor and got out and hurried across the rainy parking lot toward the door. He had his jacket over his head but he wasn't thinking about the rain. He was thinking about his girl and her sorrow and how helpless he was to do a goddamn thing about it.

McCamey stopped at the front desk and asked the room number, then he got on an elevator and went up to the floor and got off and started down the hall. He met Doctor Fleming in the hall. Doctor Fleming had been on his father's teams at Fayetteville High. McCamey could hardly turn around in Fayetteville without running into one of his parents' friends.

"Hey, Mac," the doctor said. "Where are you going?"

"To see about Mr. Hardcastle."

The doctor stopped and took his arm. He looked him in the face, studying him to see what he should say.

"Suzy's my girlfriend," McCamey went on. "I guess you know that. I came to see about her."

"I think we have him stabilized now," the doctor began. "If we're lucky, he'll pull through this. But after this, it isn't going to be long, McCamey. He's a strong man or he wouldn't have lasted this long."

"What did you just tell them, Suzy and them?"

"What I just told you. Take care of her. That's all you can do. How are your folks?"

"They're good. Dad's just finished a house. He wants to move into it." McCamey laughed. "He wants to move into every one he builds."

"How are your college plans? We've got Alice set up to take

the Princeton Review class this winter. Why don't you take it with her?"

"I'm okay. Listen, I better get on in there and see about Suzy. It's nice to see you. Alice'll do good. She's a lot smarter than her grades show."

Doctor Fleming stood watching McCamey go into the sickroom, thinking what it would be like to have a son you could be proud of, instead of an anorexic daughter with tattoos on her arms.

Maybe it's not too late, Doctor Fleming decided. He could get married again and have more kids. I could dump Jeannette's ragged ass and marry Annie and have some kids like McCamey Lyons, class president and a good second-string running back and a young man who looked you in the eye when he talked to you and listened to what you said. If I had the balls to do it and the time. He looked at his watch. He'd been awake since five that morning and he still had three more patients to see and sometime he was going to need to eat.

He stopped at the nurses' station and called Annie on his cell phone and asked if he could spend the night. She said yes. He called his service and told them to call his wife. "Wait until ten to call her," he said. "That way she won't have a head start on getting drunk."

McCamey slowed down as he came in the door. Suzy was standing by the bed holding her daddy's hand. She turned her head and smiled at him and he went and stood against a wall and watched her. Her mother wasn't there. It was just the three of them. Him and his girl and her dying father. If the world was right we'd be out on the football field getting our asses whipped by Springdale, he was thinking. I wish we were playing them. I wish we could play them all night and all day tomorrow and until all of this is over. "He wants to talk to you," Suzy said. "Come on, he wants to see you."

She stepped back and McCamey took her place by her father's free hand. Mr. Hardcastle held up his hand and McCamey took it.

"Take care of her," he rasped out, looking right into McCamey's eyes. "Don't let anything happen to her."

"It's all I do, Mr. Ted," he answered. "It's all I think about."

Later, after Suzy's sister and her sister's husband got there he took her to McDonald's and they got cheeseburgers and fries and sat in the truck eating them.

"What do you want to do?" he asked.

"I don't know. Nothing."

"Are you going back up there tonight?"

"Sometime I'll have to get my car. They're going to put him to sleep in a while. They don't want us there at night."

"Doctor Fleming talked to me in the hall. He said he'd pull through all right."

"I guess he will."

"The rain's stopping. You want to go over to the house on Sequoyah Dad's building and look at that? It's really pretty. That rock drain I built was like a river this afternoon. I wish you could have seen it."

"Sure. I'll go look at it." She shivered and he rolled up his window and took off his jacket and put it around her shoulders. "I'm sorry your dad feels so bad. I was thinking this afternoon, over at the house, that I might not go to medical school. Maybe I'd just be an architect. Then after I saw your dad I changed my mind back."

"I'd like to blow up every cigarette company in the world. That's what I'd like to do." She folded most of her cheeseburger back into its wrapper and put it in the sack. She put her french fries in on top of it. "Let's go, then. Let's go look at it."

"Scoot over here," he said. "That's the good thing about a truck. You can have your girl next to you."

McCamey still had the keys to the house. He'd forgotten to give them back in his hurry to get to the hospital. He opened the door to the kitchen and began to turn on the lights. "Do you still have that camping stuff in the truck?" Suzy asked, still standing in the door.

"I think it is."

"Go get the bedroll, will you? Bring it in here." She was always the one who started it and he always let her, not so he could blame it on her but because no matter how long he knew her or what went on between them she always seemed so fragile to him, so precious, so small.

"Are you sure?"

"Go on. Go get it." He moved past her through the door and went out to the truck and got the bedroll and brought it in and carried it into the living room and put it down before the windows. It did no good to swear they wouldn't do it anymore. They always did it and they always would and that was that. "I guess I have a rubber," he said.

"It doesn't matter. I'm still on the pill."

"You said you were going to quit."

"Well, I didn't because I still had them and I decided to use them up." Only Suzy wasn't really on the pill because she had forgotten to take one that morning and she had forgotten to take one the day before because that was after the night her father started coughing and maybe she had forgotten the day before that too because her aunt had come and her mother had been crying and all she cared about right now anyway was forgetting about her daddy lying in a room at Washington Regional Medical Center with needles in his arms and an oxygen tube up his nose and his eyes so blue and beautiful looking up into hers like he was trying to cheer her up and the chance that they might lose him. Might lose her daddy, not have him anymore.

And that was that.

"They're fucking," Will was saying. He was putting on a pair of pajama bottoms to sleep in because Amanda didn't like the sound the heat pump made at night and her hippie friend, Katie Dunbar, had made her cut the wires off of the electric blanket and it was cold as hell in the stone house in the winter.

"No, they aren't. They might be necking heavily, but they aren't fucking because I asked him and he said they weren't."

"Well, they are and I was too at that age and so were you."

"No, I wasn't, Will. After I had Barrett I wouldn't think about that for a long time. They are not fucking, they are just doing things."

"If Ted doesn't die, she can't leave, and if he does die, McCamey won't leave her, so you can forget about Princeton University, Amanda. We have to deal with this the way it is."

"I'm not set on Princeton. I'd rather he went to Vanderbilt anyway. That's not far away. A plane ride. If she's still here he can come home and visit. She can go there. If she can't get in Vanderbilt, there are plenty of other schools near there she could go to. Let some time pass. It will all work out. He'll get a good education wherever he goes and be a fine doctor someday and have a prescription pad when I'm old and need it."

"Could I turn the heat on until it wakes you up? It's cold as hell in here, Amanda. I think you ought to think about moving to Sequoyah. I thought about you the whole time I was building that house. You could put your collection of pots on those light beams in the main room. It's got closets everywhere. The roof's new. Why do we have to live in this house the rest of our lives? The backyard's no good for swings. McCamey didn't ever have a good swing. I could build a fort with swings in the backyard at Sequoyah and if we got grandchildren they could play there."

He was moving in on her again and she was softening. He walked to the thermostat and turned it up and went over to her and began to run his cold hands up and down her thighs and ribs and pulled her into his body and lay down with her upon the bed.

"I'll think about it," she said. "I'll let you know."

Two and a half weeks later, when it was time for Suzy to get her period, it didn't happen and didn't happen and didn't happen. She looked it up on the Internet and the news was not good, especially when she started feeling nauseous in the mornings.

McCamey went with her to the doctor's office. The only doctor in town who did abortions was also Suzy's regular gynecologist. He was a brave man who had risked his life for twenty years to give women the choices he thought they deserved. His office was on a main street of town and it had been the target of protests, sit-ins, and bombings. Both Suzy's mother and McCamey's mother thought of him as a hero and loved him and supported him in any way they could.

It was a beautiful clear day in the Ozarks. One of those bright December mornings that make you forget it's winter. Amanda was teaching a translation workshop at the university three days a week and it was taking up more of her time than she had thought it would. So a morning all to herself with no papers to read was a blessing and she treated it like one. After Will went off to work and McCamey left for school she poured a cup of coffee and went out on the back porch to lie in the swing and read the newspapers. She half read the papers, then she went back inside and brought the phone out to the swing and called her mother, and then her older daughter, Barrett, in New Orleans and then she called Katie Vee Dunbar to see what she was doing.

"Take the morning off and come see me," she suggested. "Let's go for a walk and see the town."

"Not today," Katie answered. "What's going on? How's Suzy? How's her dad?"

"He's dying. It may take a month, it may take a year. In the meantime everything's on hold. Why? What did you hear?"

"I didn't hear anything. I saw something. I've been meaning to tell you but I didn't know how."

"Say it."

"I saw McCamey and Suzy going into Doctor Alford's office. I was on my way to an art supply place out on the highway. It was two days ago after school and McCamey and Suzy were going in the office. What do you think that's about?"

"It could only be about one thing."

"Yes."

"Oh, God, Will says they're fucking."

"I wouldn't have told you if you hadn't called but I might have. If they're in trouble you need to help them. That girl has enough trouble without that."

"Thank you, Katie. Thank you very much. You're a real friend."

"I try to be."

The day was ruined. Amanda went into the house and took a shower and dressed and straightened up the house and went outside and got in her car and drove over to the house on Sequoyah Street. Will's car was there so she parked and went in.

"It's all yours if you want it," he said when he came to meet her at the back door. "Let's walk around and go in the front way."

"It's not about the house," she answered. "Come out here. I have to tell you something."

"So what do we do?" he asked when she was through. "They couldn't have had an abortion this week or we'd know. Suzy's been over at the house every night."

"Maybe they didn't have an abortion. Maybe they just went to find out. There's no other reason a young man and a young woman would be going in Doctor Alford's office together. Unless they caught a disease. Do you think they caught a disease?"

"We have to find out. We have to ask him."

"Who's going to? You or me or both?"

"What do you want to do?"

"Let me talk to him first. I'll see him this afternoon when he gets home from school. There's no practice now. He'll be home by four. I'll just tell him what Katie said and see what he says."

"Be careful, Amanda. I don't know. I think I should be there." He stepped back. He waited. She didn't answer. "Let's walk a few blocks. Let's really think this through. Let's know what we're doing." He took her hand and they walked down the driveway to Mountain View and began to walk along the old curved road, past the eye surgeon's mansion and several wooden houses built into the mountain and in various degrees of almost falling into the road. The leaves were gone from the trees and you could see into yards, piles of garden hoses and wheelbarrows and the bright green containers for the recycling program which for some reason no one tried to hide as they did their trash cans, as if only organic trash needed hiding but cardboard and plastic bottles and old newspapers could be known.

"Say it," Amanda began. "Say what you're thinking."

"Her father's dying. What if she's pregnant? That would be that. She'll have the baby."

"And ruin McCamey's life?"

"Not if we don't want it to. Maybe they love each other. They do. Some of the best marriages I know started in high school. She's a sweetheart. I like her. If that's what they want we have to help."

"Go on."

"I know you're spooked about it because of what happened to you when you were young. But you wouldn't want Barrett not to be in the world. Keep thinking that. If you didn't have Barrett you wouldn't have Charles or Philip or Aimee. So don't think this is a full-blown tragedy. We aren't talking about a tragedy. We're talking about two young seventeen-year-old kids we love. All we are supposed to do is help them."

"Why were they at Doctor Alford's?"

"He's an obstetrician. Maybe they were going to get her some birth control pills. We don't know. When he comes home this afternoon we'll ask."

McCamey was waiting when Suzy came out of her World History class and he held her arm and walked with her to the cafeteria. They got food and took it to a table in a corner and began to eat without talking. "We have to tell your mother," he said. "I don't like this, Suzy. We have to be sure you're doing everything you have to do, taking all the vitamins and all of that."

"No. We can't tell any of them. We can't. I don't want Daddy to know. She'd tell him. She'd have to. I haven't said I'll have it, McCamey. I haven't said that. What would we do? Where would we live? We have to go to college. I don't think I want to have it."

"I want to have it. I'll take care of you as long as you live and of our baby. I can go to college and have a baby. I can go to high school and have a baby. I'll do everything you have to do. Don't talk about not having it. I can't stand to hear that."

She picked at the Jell-O salad on her tray. She ate a cracker. She sipped her tea. Nothing occurred to her. She was stopped.

"Listen to me," McCamey said. He leaned nearer to her. "This is all right. We aren't kids, Suzy. We can do this. Your father might be glad. He knows I'll take care of you. He knows me. He knows I would never let anything happen to you."

"It already has. It's happening now." She picked up the cracker and ate a corner of it. She drank more tea. She was feeling terrible. She'd been feeling terrible all day. "I know I look like hell. I look like I'm sick. I might go home but then they'd make me see the nurse. She might know. Do you think she would know?"

"Yes. I think we should tell people. We don't have to keep it a secret. I love you. I'm going to tell my folks this afternoon."

"Don't do that, McCamey. I'll never forgive you if you tell them."

Amanda and Will were waiting for him when McCamey drove up to the house and stopped. They were on the bridge that went from the front door to the parking area, just standing there and waiting. Amanda was wearing a jacket and Will was wearing a heavy shirt so they'd been out there awhile. As soon as McCamey saw them he knew and he was glad they knew.

He got out of his car and walked toward them. "What do you know?" he said. "What's going on?"

"Katie Dunbar saw you and Suzy going in Doctor Alford's office on Linwood Avenue. So we think maybe you need to talk to us."

"She's pregnant," McCamey said. "I was going to tell you anyway but she told me not to. I was going to anyway." He stood before his parents in all the glorious good health and beauty of seventeen years old. Their only child and not their hope for the future, their here and now, their darling, their joy, their pride, their son.

"What do you want us to do?" Will said. "How can we help you?"

"Tell her not to get an abortion. She doesn't want her dad to know. She can't stand for him to know." He didn't bow his head. He kept on looking right at them. They had always done everything he needed done. He believed they could do it now.

"Let's go inside," Amanda said. "It's cold out here. Let's build a fire. We'll figure it out." She moved to her son and touched his arm. She gloried in the touch of him. And something else, a dawning thought of a baby, a grandchild. It was ethereal, like the feeling she had when she became pregnant with McCamey, as if it were a promise too fine to be imagined, a field of promise, too fabulous a possibility. Amanda had had a daughter when she was fifteen and been forced to give her away. She had not become pregnant again until she was forty years old and had McCamey. The same year she had him she found her daughter and began to heal that wound but it was not the same. It was always the memory of loss and sorrow. So the thought of a new child was not the same as it is for ordinary women. It was a miracle, a field of light.

"This isn't going to keep me from going to college," Will said. "Or her either. Plenty of people do both things. And she feels bad, Mother. She's feeling really bad and she won't tell her folks and I think something might go wrong if she doesn't know how to take care of herself."

"Come on in. Tell me what Doctor Alford said."

They went into the house and Will built up the fire in the living room and they sat around it and McCamey told them what he knew.

"He says it's just a normal pregnancy and she's six weeks pregnant and we figured that up and it would come in May or June. About the time we graduate so she can finish high school. Then we'd have all summer to get used to it and then we'll go to college. We can just go here. I bet we'll both get big scholarships and then if we do well we can transfer to Duke or Princeton or Vanderbilt later. All we have to do now is do what happens now. She's going to have a baby, Mother. That's it. You had a baby when you were younger than she is and you're all right, aren't you?"

"Watch it, Son," Will said. "No one here's mad at you. All we want to do is help you. Don't say things about your mother."

"It's okay," Amanda said. "It's all right. She hasn't told her parents?"

"She says she isn't going to. I want you to talk to her, Mother. I want you to tell her we can take care of her."

"Of course I will. Well, do you want to call her and ask her to come have dinner? Or what do you want to do?"

"She won't come over here. I'll ask her to go out somewhere and you can come there."

"All right. How about the Thirty-Six?"

"Not Dad. Just you."

"Of course. Whatever you want."

So McCamey called her and she said she'd go to dinner with him at seven, and at six thirty Amanda put on her best wool suit and high-heeled shoes and drove down to Dickson Street and parked the car and went into the restaurant and found them at a back table. The minute Suzy saw her she got mad. "I told him not to tell you all and he did, didn't he?"

"May I sit down?"

"Yes."

"I came here to tell you that we love you, Suzy, and we will do anything we can for you as long as you live. We will take care of you. We will take care of the baby. We will send you and McCamey to college. We aren't wealthy people but we have enough money to always take care of you. That's all. That's all I came to say."

Suzy didn't answer. She sat across the table as still and cold as a stone and Amanda started to speak again but looked at McCamey and he shook his head.

A waiter came to the table and Amanda ordered a cup of coffee and then the waiter brought bread and Amanda began again. "I'm sorry McCamey told us if you didn't want him to," she began. "But we love you and he knows that. I'm not going to stay here. I only came to tell you you can count on us for anything. Any help you want of any kind we will give you."

"She's going to have an abortion," McCamey said. "She's going to do that."

"Will you help me with that?" Suzy asked. It was the first thing she had said. "But I don't need any help. I shouldn't have said that. I like you a lot, Amanda. I just don't want to talk about this right now to you."

Amanda got up and took her jacket off the back of the chair. McCamey stood beside her and held it while she put it on. "Call me," she said to Suzy. "Call me if I can do anything."

McCamey walked her to the front of the restaurant. Several people spoke to her and she nodded to them, then she and McCamey went out the front door. "Don't worry about me," she said. "Go back in there."

"I don't know what to do," McCamey said.

"Beg her," Amanda said. "Or give up. When you finish eating take her home and come home yourself. We'll be waiting for you." She kissed her son and patted him on the shoulder and walked off down the street without looking back. He was a man. There was nothing she could do now but pray and she had long ago forgotten how to do that.

That was Thursday night. The next day was Friday. A cold, clear day in the Ozark Mountains. Blue skies, white clouds, black barren trees, Christmas music playing on every radio station, in every grocery store, at the Northwest Arkansas Mall.

Suzy left the house at seven forty-five. She was driving her father's automobile, a 1997 five series BMW. It was green. She had an appointment at eight. The doctor's office was one block from the hospital, and she thought perhaps she might have time to stick her head in her father's room and say hello, then decided against it. Doctor Alford had told her to bring someone to drive her home. She told him McCamey was going to come to the office later and he believed her. He had known her all her life. He knew her father. He knew about her father's illness. He knew her mother. She had become eighteen years old on the tenth of October and she had a right to walk into his office and have an abortion without telling anyone and he conceded her that right.

So at ten to eight she parked in a parking space below the office and got out and went inside and went to the nurse's desk and the nurse told her to go upstairs. In the upstairs hall a second nurse took her blood pressure and temperature and weighed her and put her in a room at the far end of the hall. It was a nice room with paintings on the walls and a stack of good magazines on the table.

A third nurse came in and prepared her for surgery and offered to give her a pill to make her woozy but she refused it. "He said it wouldn't hurt much. I don't have to take that unless I want it. I want to be awake."

"All right. I'll tell him. He'll be right in."

She lay on the table with her feet in the stirrups and thought about nothing. She concentrated on nothing. I will have a future, she decided. Maybe my father isn't going to die. I will get this over with and that is that.

Doctor Alford came into the room and took her hand and asked how she was.

"I'm fine. I just want to get it over with. I didn't take the pill. I want to be completely awake."

"All right. This won't take long, Suzy. It's very simple, really. Catherine's going to hold your hand. Tell her if you are uncomfortable. Tell me. My hands might be cold. I'm sorry."

Then she felt the cold steel, very smooth, not painful, and then a prick when he went in the cervix and then suction, not painful, nothing. It was nothing. It was what she wanted. She, Susan Montgomery Hardcastle, straight A student, homecoming queen, girl whose father lay dying one block away and who knew what to do to save herself and if McCamey didn't speak to her again he could do anything he wanted to but she was not going to be a teenage mother and take a baby off to college if she ever got to go to college anyway because when her father died they might be poor and, "God, that hurts. What hurts?"

"I'm taking the speculum out. There. It's done. It's over. Just lie there. Are you cold?"

"A little."

"Put a blanket on her, Catherine."

He stood with his big sweet hand on her thigh. He was looking at her. "You're a brave girl. I'm going to put a pad on you. Catherine will get you a belt. I want you to wear them for a few days. Don't wear Tampax. And I want you to take some antibiotics. I'll give you enough samples. It's a once-a-day dose for seven days. When Catherine gets you dressed, I want to talk to you in my office." He kept standing there, touching her with his hand. He moved it from her thigh and took her hand from the nurse. "You don't have to tell your parents or anyone, Suzy, but you have to check in with me, tomorrow and then every few days until you have finished the pills."

"Thank you so much," she said. "You are a hero. My mother always says that."

"I'm just a doctor," he answered. "I do what I can."

After a while the nurse gave her a glass of orange juice and she drank it and asked for more and they gave her that and she drank it too. Then she sat up and slowly got off the table and got dressed. There were two nurses in the room. One of them knew her mother. The other one knew both her parents. They waited until she was standing and asked if they should leave and she said she didn't care so they waited until she was dressed.

"I have the money to pay the bill," she said. "Where do I go to give them the money?"

"Don't worry about that now," Catherine said. "He said to tell you not to worry about that today."

"I want to do it today. I'm all right."

"Let me go see if someone's downstairs to pick you up," Catherine said.

"There won't be. No one's coming. I need you to call me a taxicab." She looked the nurses straight in the eye. "No one knows I'm here. I came alone and I'm going home alone. It's all right. This is how I want it to be. I'm eighteen. I don't have to have someone."

"All right," Catherine said. "He wants to see you a minute in his office if you're ready."

They walked into Doctor Alford's office and he was waiting for her at his desk. He gave her some instructions and she promised to call him the following day. He came around the desk and watched her go down the stairs with the nurse. He put his hands in his pockets and thought about her father dying and about his new grandchild and about the twins he had delivered at four that morning and the twins he lost the first week he practiced medicine, down in a small town in the Delta where there was no adequate neonatal equipment. They would have died anyway, he told himself as he always did when he thought of them. I did everything I could.

Suzy and the nurse walked downstairs and Suzy got six one-hundred-dollar bills out of her purse and gave it to the nurse behind the desk. "He said this is how much it would cost. I have more if you need it."

The nurse took the cash, wondering where to put it. She hadn't been paid in cash in months. It wasn't exactly six hundred dollars anyway, there were taxes and a surgical fee, but Doctor Alford had said to take care of her, not to even charge her if it was a problem of any kind so she took the cash and made a receipt and gave it to Suzy.

Catherine had been on the phone calling a taxi. She came back and stood by Suzy and told her one was on the way.

"I want to go outside and wait for them," Suzy said.

"I'll go with you," Catherine said.

"You don't need to do that."

"I want to. The doctor wants me to."

They stood outside the front door of the pleasant, pretty building that had once been an insurance company. There were pots of yellow chrysanthemums along the borders of the flower beds. Everything was very neat, well-ordered, cared for.

"I'm okay," Suzy said. "I'm going home and go to bed. I took the antibiotic, didn't I?"

"Yes. You don't need another one until tomorrow. You're sure you're all right?"

"I'll never give this another thought. You can believe me when I say that." Suzy turned and looked the nurse in the eye. And as she said it she knew it was almost true. "I don't regret things," she added. "I knew what I was doing."

The shiny new white taxi-van pulled up beside the sidewalk. It was the first real taxi ever to be in Fayetteville, Arkansas. There were three of them now. Three shiny new white taxi-vans.

Suzy walked down the sidewalk and got into the van and told the driver to take her to the place where her car was parked. He had to go around the block to get to it. When she got there she gave him a five-dollar bill and got out and got into her father's car and drove to her house and parked in the driveway and went inside. Her mother was playing tennis. If her mother had been there she would have told her why she was home. When her mother came home she would tell her.

For now, she went into her bedroom and unplugged her phone without getting the ten messages the lighted dial said she had waiting. Then she took off her clothes and put on a baby blue velour robe and tied it around her waist and got into her bed and used her remote control to turn on her CD player and curled up in a ball listening to Sarah Brightman sing "Scarborough Fair" from the album *La Luna*. Three times she listened to it and three times she punched the button on the remote control to make it play again. Then she fell asleep, safe and warm in the robe her grandmother Anne gave her for her birthday and the down comforter her mother ordered her from Land's End.

Second-period class began at nine forty. It was the first class of the day that McCamey and Suzy shared together. It was Advanced Placement Chemistry and Suzy had the highest grade in the class and never missed it no matter what. When McCamey saw that she wasn't there he asked to be excused and went out in the hall and called her house but no one answered. When the class was over he called again and still there was no answer. At eleven thirty he gave up calling her house and called Doctor Alford's office. "I was supposed to pick up Susan Hardcastle," he said. "Is she still there?"

"She left a while ago," the nurse said. "She took a cab."

McCamey went to the school attendance office and told the woman in charge he was leaving for an emergency. Before she could answer he was gone. He drove by Suzy's house and saw her car and sat for a few minutes across the street fighting the urge to go and confront her.

Then he went home and went into the storage shed and found a tent and a Coleman lantern and a backpack and went in the kitchen and got a loaf of bread and some cheese and a couple of bottles of Gatorade. He went to his room and threw some clothes into an athletic bag and walked out of the house and started driving toward the Buffalo River. I don't need this shit, he told himself. I know the way to the woods.

He drove up the winding country roads toward the east and

north, the country getting wilder and less inhabited, the old hills called Ozarks getting higher, the day colder and the air clearer.

In the small town of Kingston he stopped and bought gasoline. "Awful cold to be going to the river," the proprietor of the store told him. "All the canoe rentals are closed now."

"I'm going camping," McCamey answered. "I don't need a canoe."

"You running away? Is that it?"

"I'm running away from women, if you want to know. I'm just going to get some quiet."

"They're all crazy," the man agreed, handing him his change. "Sometime you think you've found a sane one but it's never true. They like to be crazy. It's their favorite thing."

McCamey took his change and stopped a minute and then bought a package of potato chips. "Good," the proprietor said. "Keep eating. Don't let them get you off your feed."

The sun had started down the sky behind a wide cover of clouds. It was a really pretty sky in four directions and McCamey opened the potato chips and ate them standing by the car. Then he opened the car and took out the phone and called his father's answering machine and left a message. "I guess she did it. I'm going up and camp near Lost Valley. I'm okay."

He curved on down to Ponca and found a canoe rental place behind a soft-serve ice cream stand and talked the owner into renting him a canoe and a life vest. He paid him forty dollars cash and stowed the canoe in the back of his Bronco and drove to the bridge with the back open and the cold air freezing his face. The colder he got the better he felt. He had somewhere to go and he knew how to get there. That's as good as it gets in the world whether you're sad or not he decided. He would not think about Suzy. Whatever she had done was done. And he was never going to fuck her again as long as he lived or maybe any other girl or woman or whatever they called themselves.

They gave babies away and killed them or whatever they wanted to do. They loved you one day and killed your children the next day. And lied. They always lied. They had to lie. It was in them like lust was in a man, hardwired into every cell.

At the little bridge that was the put-in place for the Buffalo he lifted the canoe down from the Bronco and got his gear and stowed it in the boat and then he changed clothes and put on his foul weather gear and locked the Bronco and got into the canoe and pushed off and let the river take him. The water was low compared to what it was in the spring, but it would do. It would take a man downstream.

It was four in the afternoon when Will got the message from his answering machine. Amanda had a class that lasted from three to six thirty so he didn't wait for her. He pulled his canoe down from its rack and put it in the back of his truck and started driving. He was twenty miles from town when he remembered to call and leave her a message. He called his house and then he called Katie Dunbar and told her what was going on. "Go find her," he said, "when she gets back and tell her McCamey's okay and I'm going up there. There're only one or two places he could be. I'll find him and I'll call her if I can."

"Suzy got an abortion?"

"That's how it looks. I've got to go, Katie. Take care of Amanda and tell her to call Peter."

Will drove the speed limit to Huntsville because it was after school but when he got on 23 going to 74 he floorboarded it and drove the truck. He kept on driving, stopping once to piss by the side of the road and wishing he'd brought a heavier coat and some gloves.

At Ponca he went straight to the soft-serve place and talked to the kid in charge. "He's about two hours ahead of you," the kid said. "You want something to eat before you leave? You better get some food."

"What do you have that's ready?"

"Hot dogs."

"Give me two, please, with mustard and relish. Wrap them up. I'll take them." The young man hurried and got them ready. "You don't have a pair of gloves you want to sell do you?" Will asked. "Name your price if you do."

"I got this old pair of fishing gloves." The boy produced a worn pair of thick cotton gloves. "I'll sell you them for five dollars."

Will gave him a ten and thanked him for the food and got back in the truck and started driving. How many times in his life had he followed this road to this river, alone and with his childhood friends and with Amanda. Hell, he thought, this is proba-

bly where we conceived McCamey. That time we forgot the rub-
bers, not that we ever used them. He put on the gloves as
he was driving. They were lucky gloves.

McCamey pulled the canoe up onto the sandy beach below the
cave and tied it down good and set about making a fire. He had
forgotten to bring good matches and was going to have to make
do with a pack of folding paper matches he'd found in the glove
compartment that were stuck together and old. He searched
carefully for tinder and kindling and laid the fire carefully in an
old fire site above the beach. When he had it laid he set up the
tent and brought his gear in and zipped it up and then he sat on
a limestone outcropping and watched the sun going down on the
worst day of his life. This is the first day of knowing what's really
going on, he decided. I've just been a punk kid and now that's
over. No wonder I couldn't get a woman to bear my child. What
did I have to offer her? Sending my mother to tell her my parents
would take care of her. And Ted is dying and we're all going to
die sooner or later and she killed my son this morning. Just went
in and had him vacuumed out. I could have taken care of her.
And of him. I am an eighth Cherokee Indian. I could make a safe
place out of nothing if I had to.

The sun had reached the point where all the light above it
was a thousand shades of red and violet and colors too beautiful
to name. The clouds gathered above the sinking sun to catch
every bit of light and turn it into beauty.

McCamey put his head down on his knees and began to cry.
He hadn't cried in so long he had forgotten how. The last time he

had cried was when Basic Builders lost nine to thirteen in the last inning to Flying Possum and he made the last out. That must have been nine years ago. I was going to give him my baseball glove and save my team jackets for him and all my Transformers. I was going to be the best father any boy ever had and a great doctor and make plenty of money for both of them. But she couldn't wait. She had to do this thing. He kept on crying until he was cried out and then he got up and lit a piece of paper he had in his billfold and used it to light the fire.

The last light was almost gone from the sky but Will kept on coming. He knew this river like he knew his name. Light or dark it didn't matter and he had two flashlights and a Mag-Lite. He had tied a towel around his head over his baseball cap and with that and the fishing gloves he looked like some homeless person in New York City, sitting in the long canoe in his old hunting coat and wearing a pair of boots he had had for twenty years.

He saw the light from the fire reflected in the trees before he saw the camp and paddled harder and turned the bend and started calling to his son. "It's me, Mac. It's Dad. Come take me in."

When he got to the beach McCamey walked out into the shallow water and pulled the canoe up on the beach. "You didn't need to come," he said. "I was doing all right."

"I brought some fishing gear," Will said. "I thought you might have forgotten to bring some." He got out of the canoe and took his tall son into his arms and held him there. There is just so much you can do in the world, he knew. In this beautiful, unjust, and only world there is.

*   *   *

In Fayetteville Suzy's mother had gotten Amanda on the phone. "I'm going to kill him for doing this to her. I'm going to tell the principal for one thing. And we're going to sue Randy Alford. She is barely eighteen years old. He should have called us. He should have told us. She was by herself. Not a soul was with her."

"I know McCamey would have been there if he'd known. He was begging her not to do it, Stella. He had me talk to her and ask her not to. We told her we would do anything to take care of —"

"You knew this and you didn't tell me! That's contributing to the delinquency of a minor. Where were they doing all this screwing, Amanda? At your house? Is that where?"

"Stella, I don't think I deserve all this. McCamey is going crazy over this. He's hurt too."

"TELL HER TO GO FUCK HERSELF," Katie Vee was saying loudly enough for Stella to hear. "Give me that phone. Let me talk to her." She wrestled the phone out of Amanda's hands and moved across the room. "Stella, you're acting like you're crazy. Amanda and Will had nothing to do with this. Two kids got pregnant. Now it's over. Calm down or we're hanging up. And stop threatening to sue people. Your husband's dying. Don't you think maybe this is more about that than about Suzy?"

Amanda took the phone back. "What can we do to help you, Stella? Is there anything we can do for any of you?"

"I'm sorry. My child is in bed crying. What am I supposed to do? I need to be at the hospital. I'm only one person. I can't do everything."

"Ask Suzy if we can come there while you go see about Ted."

"Wait a minute." Stella left the phone. "She said no. She says she's okay. I've got to go. I'll talk to you tomorrow."

Amanda hung up the phone and turned to Katie Vee. "Where do we go from here?" she asked.

"We go out on the porch and look at stars and count our blessings, Amanda. And then we sleep and get ready for what happens next." She pulled two parkas out of the coat closet and handed one to Amanda. "Come on. Let's get out of the house."

"We fought for this," Amanda said. "You and I. We fought for her right to abort my grandchild."

"And we did right," Katie answered. "And we would do it again. Nothing human is easy, Amanda. It's all a balance, good and evil, right and wrong, just and unjust, just like the Bible says. Let's go outside and talk. Let's talk until we're through."

Remorse

BUDDY ADAIR WAS CLOSING HIS SALON for the night. He locked the back door and checked to see that the water was drained from the hot tubs and the tanning beds were unplugged. He went by each station to make sure curling irons were turned off and tops screwed on bottles and so forth. Usually the receptionist did this but she wanted to leave early to go to her nephew's high school football game and of course Buddy let her go. He did not think he was on the earth to run a slave ship.

If he had looked in any of the seven mirrors he passed he would have seen a pleasing sight. He was a thirty-six-year-old man with a tall, athletic body, short brown hair, brown eyes, and a beautiful, actually an unforgettable, face. It was a face that welcomed the world, a good face, not only beautiful but a face that seemed more or less permanently happy.

And why wouldn't Buddy have been happy? He had grown up in a small town that was about as close to paradise as human towns get. Plenty to eat, no racial troubles, a university to lend variety and élan to the population, beautiful trees, a lake, nearby rivers, small friendly mountains to climb. The town was called Fayetteville and it was situated in the extreme northwest corner of the state of Arkansas, just where the Ozark Mountains begin.

It was a town that had once been poor and now was rich. In Buddy's thirty-six years it had gone from being a place so poor that everyone had gotten in the habit of being nice to everyone else to a place where many people were rich but had not yet gotten to the point where they stopped being nice. "Maybe the right people got rich," Buddy's mother always said. "The Tysons and the Waltons are nice people and they have brought nice people here. I should know. I've been doing their hair since before you were born. I know the good hearts of those people."

Buddy's mother was retired now but Buddy still dragged her out for big weddings. Also, she spent one day a week doing hair at Melvaney Gardens for some of her old customers who didn't like for strangers to touch their heads.

Buddy's mother had always known he was gay. She had a gay brother and a gay first cousin. She knew it the day he picked up a comb and started making a ponytail on Sally Sue Dalton's Barbie doll.

It was a good time to be gay. Buddy was born in 1963, when anything went in the United States. It took a little longer for that feeling to get to Fayetteville, but not too long. There was the Art Department and the Creative Writing Department and the

Political Science Department and History and Philosophy and Foreign Languages to draw upon. Plus, the Episcopal minister was gay even though he didn't let it show. Plus, one of the bankers in town had a boyfriend. A couple of physicians, the best-loved veterinarian, three florists, the main chef at the Old Post Office Restaurant, and a couple of professors at the law school pretty much finished up the score of gay men Buddy's mother knew or at least was acquainted with.

Buddy's father wasn't too happy to realize his son was gay but he loved the little boy and took pleasure in his physical beauty and his joy in the world. He was a deeply religious man and when he fell on his knees on the prayer bench and prayed to have love in his heart he meant it. He played bluegrass music with a group he had known since high school. They played together nearly every Friday night. If anything worried Buddy's father, he usually took it out on his guitar.

So Buddy was okay. He had loving parents and a beautiful face and he lived in a place that was safe and rich. He had left Fayetteville several times but had always returned.

He stopped by the cash register and looked at the receipts. One was a Visa charge to Sally Sue for the hairdo he had done the day before. He had told the receptionist to leave it out. He punched in the numbers and canceled the charge. He didn't like charging Sally Sue for things. She was his best friend. "I learned on this hair," he would say, and tousle the curls he made for her. "Now don't go outside and comb this out. Let the curls sit for an hour before you start messing with them."

*   *   *

He turned out the rest of the lights, threw his jacket over his shoulder, and went out into the night. There was a new moon with Venus near its horns. It was set against a blue-black sky with a line of white clouds drifting across the moon at exactly the place in the sky that a painter would have put them if the painter was a genius. Oh, my, Buddy thought, and stood in the empty parking lot watching the clouds move nearer and nearer to the star. It reminded Buddy of Hoagy Carmichael's "Stardust," sung by Willie Nelson, and that reminded him of the year he was seventeen and was in love with their veterinarian and would drive around in his old Pontiac singing along with Willie and waiting until it was late enough to drive by the vet's house and imagine him in bed.

Fortunately the vet was an honorable man and had told Buddy's mother to use another vet until Buddy's passion cooled.

"Got to hear that song," Buddy said to the skies. "I can have a CD if I want one. It won't take a minute to go by Hastings on the way home. It's Friday night, for God's sake." He got into his Outback and drove down Spruce Street to College Avenue and down to Fiesta Square and parked and went in the record store and went straight to the Country and Western section and picked *Stardust* out of the N bin and started to the checkout counter. It was nine forty-five. He was trying to get home to see the ten o'clock news but there was a video he'd been wanting. Al Pacino in *Looking for Richard*. He loved *Looking for Richard*. He was thinking of using part of it for a benefit performance he was giving in December.

He went back to the Drama section, plucked the video from

the wall, and carrying his two treasures went back to the checkout counter. "I was not thinking about Sally Sue," he kept telling people later. "I had put her out of my mind. I had not the slightest premonition. I was mad at her for going off to Little Rock alone but I was relieved I didn't have to go with her. I was buying a CD. I wasn't thinking about a thing but Willie Nelson and 'Stardust.'"

He paid for his purchases, went to the Outback, opened the CD and stuck it in the player, and drove off toward his home listening to Willie and thinking about how gorgeous it is to be in love. He thought for a minute he might go out to a bar and see if it could happen again, then thought better of it.

He listened to "Stardust" all the way through to the end of the song. He was almost to his driveway. He reached down and hit a button to listen to the track one more time before he took it inside to his CD player there. But he hit the wrong button and changed the format to the radio. "A one-person accident on the Pig Trail has claimed the life of a local woman," the announcer was saying. "Highway patrol officers say the car left the road and slammed into a tree near the bridge on the Mulberry River. . . ."

"No," Buddy said. He pulled to a stop in his driveway and sat staring into the steering wheel. The headlights made strange visions on the cedar bushes along his fencerow, on the flower beds and the windows on the side of his house. He pulled the key out of the ignition and ran to his door and into the house and toward his answering machine. The light was blinking. Seven messages. There were seven messages. He pushed the button. It was his mother's voice. "Buddy, something's happened. Call as soon as you get home."

"Buddy, where are you? I've been calling the shop. Call me."

"Buddy. This is Fred Dalton. I don't know if you heard. Call me. 555-4377."

He sat down on the bed and put his head in his hands. He got up and turned on the overhead lights. He picked up the phone and called his mother's house.

"What happened?" he said when she answered the phone, but he already knew.

After a long time, after what seemed like weeks but was only days he got out the hardbound journal he had bought at Barnes and Noble and began to add notes and paragraphs to the section called *Sally Sue*. He worked all night. When he was finished, the section was filled with paste-ups, liner notes, and footnotes. The sun was coming up when he was finished. He laid the journal down on his desk and put his head upon it and began to cry. Here is an approximation of those pages from his journal.

So she's dead. The girl I could have loved if I loved women. Dead by distress and I might have stopped it. If I had told her the truth. If I had said, He's a creep, Sally Sue. He's not fit to clean your boots. To hell with Thomas Cane. Let's go and have some fun. Well, I said all I could say. I said everything she'd let me say and I said volumes with my eyes when she'd come into the shop to get her hair dyed and start talking about going to church with him or out on the highway to pick up trash with his Bible class.

I wish I'd dyed it blue the night his parents came to meet her parents. Green or blue. I wish I'd done everything you always think you should have done when somebody dies. I wish she could have read my journal. I should have given it to her.

I knew he would never marry her. Or, if he did, I knew it would go bad. He was a virgin when he met her, a Promise Keeper from some country church out in the valley where his folks are from. I know those men. I knew them when I was pretending to be straight, and I cut their hair now that I'm out.

Tonight his parents are coming to meet her parents. She is determined to talk this guy into marrying her and I'm supposed to stand by and watch. I'm supposed to do her hair and keep my mouth shut.

Fallout, that's all I see around us. I have known Sally Sue since before either of us could walk. We played on the floor together while our mothers shelled peas and gossiped. We learned to swim in the same pool, Miss Adelaide's Swim for Tots. We took dance together, a move my mother now regrets. I was runner-up for Mr. Arkansas last year. I know this is about Sally Sue but you should know who's talking.

Our mothers are distant cousins. My father is a barber but Sally Sue's father wasn't content to stay in the lower middle class. He went to school at nights and piled up degree after degree. Then he got a job teaching plant biology at the university. Then he got in with a team that developed a new strain of feed corn and since then he's been set.

Sally Sue is the youngest of four daughters. I think that's why she is so desperate to marry anyone, even that creep, Thomas, if all goes well tonight.

I try to imagine his creepy Christian parents coming to meet her parents. I picture them around the dinner table. His creepy folks laying on their thick country religion like Cool Whip and Mr. Dalton pretending to be nice. I love Mr. Dalton. He is one of the first people I turned to when I got back from San Francisco and decided to come out. He is a scientist, with a broad, objective view of time and space and what passes for reality. Now Mrs. Dalton and Sally Sue have ordered him to sit at the table acting like he thinks it's okay for the Canes to throw Jesus into the dinner conversation every chance they get, which is what Sally Sue said they did the horrible weekend she spent at their house. The other three girls are already married to Born Agains. Now it's Sally Sue's turn to be sacrificed to Mrs. Dalton's dream of security.

She wants those girls married. I don't know if you have noticed, but people who aren't into religion aren't necessarily into marriage lately. I mean, they will get married, but not until they have sampled plenty of wares and are at least thirty-five or -six and getting bored with their Merrill Lynch portfolios and their pets.

In other words, the ones who think it's all right to get laid don't think they have to marry every girl who wants to be a bride.

Bride's Magazine, that's what Sally Sue was reading the last time I was over at her house. This from a girl who went to France with me the summer we were eighteen. The girl who got on the ferry to Albania and didn't complain about the smell. The girl who came to visit me in Spain. Never mind. My heart is broken. It's the American story here in the heart of the heartland.

The reason I know I'll leave even though my shop is making money and I'm so successful I can't stand it.

She is completely changed from the girl who was running track with me every afternoon last summer. The girl with the million-dollar legs. She has gained fifteen pounds since she met this creep. All she does is cook for him and watch him watch football games.

Here's the true deal. Sally Sue's father is the biggest cocksman in this town. He rides bicycles for exercise and he likes to just ride over to a woman's house, hide the bike in the backyard and get a piece before he hits the road again. There isn't a week that goes by that some woman in my chair doesn't throw in his name. I love the man but the truth's the truth as every psychiatrist knows and our parents shape our fates.

Like most men of that type he married the nicest girl he could find, one who would never be unfaithful and who is dumb enough to believe his lies. Only deep down she doesn't believe them so she goes to work to marry her daughters to the most dependable men she can find, which in the Midwest means religion. Only the Baptist Church and its satellites can hold back free love now, and Mrs. Dalton has made a specialty of finding those men for her girls.

Sally Sue had escaped her mother's plots by moving to Kansas City, but as soon as she was home her mother went to work. She found Thomas in a line at the post office and started reeling him in. Only Thomas was hard to catch.

Hard to trap, hard to marry. The harder he got to get, the

more Sally Sue liked him. I've seen that before, the slip net, the inescapable trap.

Here's how it went. Her mother struck up a conversation with him, found out he was a Born Again, and invited him to dinner.

Sally Sue had only been home three weeks. She had been working for a museum in Kansas City and had come home to get an extra degree so she could become a curator. I don't know if you know it but our little university has a top-notch Art Department. I don't know what she thought another degree would do for her that sticking to her job and waiting for a break wouldn't do, but I didn't argue. I was glad to have her in town. I'd only been back two years myself and I was getting lonely. As I said, Sally Sue and I sucked from the same pacifier. We built a tree house. We are bonded.

She had her heart broken twice in Kansas City. That's a factor. "You always start wanting to marry them," I told her. "You lose the mystery. Don't be so available. Don't be so goddamn needy."

"But I do want to marry them. How can I hide it?" She was sitting in my chair with primer on her roots. It was a perfect place to make a point if I wanted to make one. I plunged in.

"It isn't you who wants to get married. It's your mother. She's the one who put that idea in your head. She's the one who introduced you to Thomas. She invited him to dinner. She set you up."

"She met him and thought he was nice. She wasn't setting me up."

"She set you up. He's the dream son-in-law. If they are Born

Again, she likes them. How many times have you told me that about your sisters' husbands? Only Christians need apply. Remember what you told me when Sharon married into that church where they speak in tongues? Look at the patterns, Sally Sue. Stay on top of this."

"None of that has anything to do with Thomas. And my mother is not putting this idea in my head. Twenty-five million years of evolution tell me to get married and reproduce myself. It's normal, Buddy. I don't mean to hurt your feelings but the normal thing to do is to get married. Only Thomas won't ask me."

I peeped underneath the foil to see how her streaks were taking. This is when I should have dyed it green.

"It's me," Sally Sue said, sinking down into the chair. "He won't ask me because I gained weight. They always leave me. Something's wrong. I'm not pretty enough. They go on to other women."

"Shut up that trash or I'll dye you blue," I screamed. "You are a gorgeous, brilliant prize and anyone who doesn't know it should be castrated. Now get up and let's wash that off and see what we got." I pulled her up from the chair and led her to a basin.

I shampooed her and gave her a really hot new cut and curled her hair all over her head and made her go with me to Uncle Gaylord's to eat dinner. "Stop loving that boring man," I told her every time she mentioned him. "Get your degree and we'll blow this popsicle stand. We'll go to California, San Francisco or L.A. You choose."

"If I only could," she said. But that night, because I had made her look like an angel, she laughed when she said it. For a moment she believed she could find a life she really wanted to live.

Am I to blame for this? Should I have made her look that good the night she met him? She's no natural beauty. It was me who put those popcorn curls around her face and told her to wear the cerise silk and heels.

A misalliance, that's what it will be. I keep thinking Princess Di. Marriages should be made in the heaven of desire, not the Procrustean bed of the family's needs. None of this matters now. He's playing hard to marry and she's hooked. All I can hope for is a long engagement during which she can see how dull he is. If he asks her I will not pretend to be glad. I will keep on telling the truth until the moment they say the vows. Only I haven't really been telling the truth. There are plenty of things I could say that I haven't said. What is keeping me from doing it? This is Sally Sue's life, her future, her fate. Is it in my hands? WHO DO I HAVE TO FUCK TO STOP THIS TRAIN?

Delve deeper. Why is Mrs. Dalton able to make her daughters marry men she chooses for them? Is it because there are so many of them and they are still fighting for her attention and approval as they had to when they were young? How did she take three, now four, reasonably attractive, intelligent, well-educated young women and convince them they have to marry anyone who keeps a job and is faithful? I can't figure it out. They aren't beauties but they're good-looking girls. They could do better than what they've done. She was picking up trash on the highway with HIS BIBLE CLASS. This from the girl who went with me to march on Little Rock over abortion rights.

*　　　*　　　*

Mea culpa. I am the one who dyed her hair golden blond the day she met him. I dyed her hair the color of buttercups, the color of eighteen-carat gold, the color of hickory trees in autumn and then *I curled it all over her head.* I made her a halo.

This was before she gained fifteen pounds from making sandwiches while he watched football games. This was when we were running four miles every afternoon on the university track. Then doing ab exercises on my Turkish rug.

Also, I own the shop that provided the facial, the pedicure, the manicure, and the new Windsor Red nail polish and matching lip liner and lipstick. I'm the one who showed her how to widen her upper lip with the darker pencil, then fill it in with color. It was her birthday present last year, The Works at my shop.

So she used it to seduce this jerk, this Promise Keeper to Jesus. She became so beautiful that he fell from grace and let her teach him how to get off on something more interesting than self-abuse.

The third time she went out with him she got him in the sack. Also my fault. She had him to her place for dinner. I supplied the beef Stroganoff, the imported noodles, the salad dressing, and the wine. I thought it was a joke to help Sally Sue seduce this Promise Keeper, but the joke was on us. How was I to know she would mistake a few orgasms for love?

There is a passage from Faulkner that keeps occurring to me.

"Maybe she was bored," I says, and he says:
"Bored. Yes, bored." And that was when he began to

cry. "She loved, had the capacity to love, to give and to take it. Only she tried twice and failed twice not jest to find somebody strong enough to deserve it but even brave enough to accept it. Yes," he says, sitting there bolt upright with jest the tears running down his face, at peace now, with nothing nowhere in the world any more to anguish or grieve him. "Of course she was bored."

During the months when she dated him my worst nightmare was the wedding. It would be in one of those hideous new Baptist churches that have sprouted like malls in the pastures between Fayetteville and Springdale. Piles of brick with crosses the size of trees and interiors that smell like carpet factories. Plenty of our friends have been married in those churches. Sally Sue and I have giggled through many long ceremonies, some of which were the weddings of her sisters.

But that is not what happened. Sometime around the first of July Thomas's attention began to waver. He was not over at Sally Sue's apartment every night watching baseball games and eating popcorn and pizza. He was not showing up.

It was because Sally Sue's mother had made her ask him if they were going to get married. I guess so, he had answered, but I don't know when. When do you think? she countered. Next year or the year after that, he said.

The afternoon after this conversation she was in my chair getting a touch-up. "I guess he just likes things the way they are," she said.

"Who wouldn't," I answered. "You cook and he watches television. You pay for your apartment and he lives in a room at his cousin's house."

"He's been acting funny about sex," she said.

"In what way?"

"Not wanting to do it."

"Fifteen pounds," I answered. "Let's go to the track this afternoon. Let's start running."

"I can't. I have to drive to Memphis with him to his family reunion."

Only she didn't get to go to Memphis. Thomas came over to her house when he got off from work and told her he wanted to break off the relationship. He said he had decided to go back to being chaste. He said he couldn't marry her after they had already sinned. After she had made him break his promise. He said he couldn't take her to his family reunion as that would lead her on. He said he wasn't really sorry because it was her fault that they had sinned. He said that he would pray for her but she told him not to bother. Then she called me.

It was a Friday afternoon and we keep the shop open late. I would have gone to her the minute we locked the door but she wouldn't wait for me. When she got through talking to me she started calling everyone in her Rolodex. She found an old sorority sister down in Little Rock who was having a party and she called me back and told me she was going there.

"I can't stay in this town," she said. "I'm going to visit Gaye. This is it. The final proof that life is not going to give me anything I want no matter how hard I work to get it."

"You're getting your master's degree in August," I answered. "You have three thousand dollars in the bank. You have me."

I have to admit I was relieved. I had Augustine Wills in my chair and I remember exactly what I said to her. "That's the best news I've had all year," I said, as I twisted Augustine's hair up into a French braid for the Kiwanis Club dinner. "My best friend just got saved from a disastrous marriage. She thinks she has a broken heart. What she got is a reprieve."

That was about five fifteen. At six Sally Sue called me back. "I'm leaving," she said. "I'm going to Little Rock."

"Wait until tomorrow afternoon and I'll go with you," I offered. "Don't go running off alone with this. Come on over to the shop and we'll go to the new Thai place as soon as I lock up. Don't go to Little Rock alone."

"I'll be there by ten. I used to know how to have fun. I'm going to see if I remember how. He said he'd pray for me. My God!"

"Well, at least you're mad. Stay mad. You don't want to come by and get curled some more before you leave?"

"No, I'm leaving. I'll call you Sunday when I get back."

She got into her little Miata and struck out for Little Rock. I didn't have a single premonition. Every thought I had was good. Good, she had broken up with the jerk. Good, I would have her back for a playmate. Good, she would collect her degree and go off and work for a fine museum and be my friend forever. Good, I would never have to talk to Thomas again and pretend I didn't know he hates me for being gay.

*   *   *

Sally Sue had two drinks before she left home. We think two. Then she put a bottle of wine on the seat beside her and started driving. She didn't go up highway 71, the most dangerous road in the United States where sixteen people died in the last three years. She knew she was drinking so she took the Pig Trail, the old, curving country road down through the national forest. It's the road the students use. It's a sweet, crazy little road we love.

She hit the tree going eighty, one of the old oak trees on the curve right before you cross the Mulberry River. A mile from the country store where we always stopped for snacks when we'd drive to Little Rock. Cookies or potato chips or soft drinks or just to stand and watch the river if the water was high.

You know what haunts me? Thinking she was crying when she died. What did she do to deserve this fate? Maybe her momma is right and there's some terrible, punishing God in charge and we should all marry Born Agains and get fat and watch television until we die.

I have figured out I was on my dinner break when she died. Sitting at my little walnut table in my back office with the Lean Cuisine I microwaved on a Limoges plate. I was eating it with a silver fork. I always eat with silver. It's my thing.

You know what haunts me even more? The thought of that winding country road, that vein of blacktop winding through the trees and her moving on it to her destiny and me eating rice and listening to Santana and never even knowing anything was wrong. What else don't we know?

That it can end any moment. That these sunrises and sunsets and glorious colors of the earth and sky and all the good fun of eating and smiling and laughing and planning weddings and having it rain and putting on our running shoes in the early morning can come to an end. A poet wrote a book called *The Names of the Lost*. I am going to have to start one. I'm only thirty-six years old and already I am losing people. Already the list of people I can call when I am blue is getting smaller.

Sally Sue was half her scared mother, full of anxieties and longings, and half her sexy, ambitious father. She was part her fat, satisfied sisters and part me, all the jokes we had and the things we learned and the nights at the Cabira of our youth. Then she was a body in a wrecked car stuck in a tree.

I have to go to work now. Because of me women all over town will be more beautiful, or think they are, which is the same thing. Am I sending them out to meet Thomas Cane, to squander my work on men who aren't worthy to smell their hair spray, much less mess up their backcombing? Or am I making one afternoon worth having and remembering? I saw one of my women stopped at a stoplight the other afternoon. It was only an hour since I had done her hair. She pulled the rearview mirror down and smiled at her sixty-year-old reflection and I said to myself, It's okay. This is work worth doing. This is what I am.

If I have to think about Sally Sue, from now on I'm going to replace bad thoughts with good ones from the past. I'm going to remember the afternoon we took my mother's car and drove it around Wilson Park and didn't get caught. We were twelve. We were sitting on the porch reading books when Mother got home from work. That will be the memory I save. Sally Sue had on an orange-red sundress I had helped her make on her grandmother's sewing machine and little white Capezio sandals I helped her pick out. The little fat places on the tops of her arms were sticking out around the straps of the dress and she was so sweet I wanted to kiss her on the neck. Tell me I don't love women. I have given my life to them.

I will not cry. I will not cry. I will not cry.

Alone

MY BEST FRIEND IS SABRA LARKIN. She has been at my side through kindergarten, first, second, third, fourth, fifth, sixth, and seventh grades. Other girls worry about whether they'll be popular or get elected cheerleader but not me. Sabra Larkin is my best friend and where Sabra goes the herd follows. Sabra lives next door to me. Or at least she did until tomorrow when she goes to Canada to live.

She is going to Canada because we found her mother's love letters to her boyfriend and mailed them to her father and that was that. As you sow so shall you reap. I helped her copy them on the copy machine at Collier's Drug Store and I helped walk across the street to the post office and weigh the envelope and buy stamps and put them in the mail. So it's my own fault that the main person I like is moving to Toronto, Canada, and leaving me alone.

She leaves tomorrow afternoon. Two days later I go to Woodland Junior High alone. Get out of the car alone. Go in the school alone and pray that Janise or Sarah or Ally are going to let me hang out with them. All my life it's been Sabra and I saying who can hang out with us or eat lunch with us and now it's me.

Let me tell you about Woodland Junior High School. That place is so mean people have committed suicide from going there. Fact, not fiction. There are cliques and cliques within cliques and if you're not in one you're alone. Only Sabra and I managed not to be part of that. We took dance three afternoons a week and on the other two we lifted weights at the health club or ran on the university track. We strove to like everyone at the school and were democratic about letting people walk and talk with us. We were elected cheerleader, together, and now I am going to cheer alone.

We had to mail those letters to her father. If we hadn't, Sabra would have ended up living in a house with a man who was looking at her legs every chance he got and getting drunk and sleeping on her sofa. We had to stop that. It never occurred to us that her father would get a court order and take her to Canada to live. The letters were written to the lover before her father got the divorce that took him to Canada to begin with. The letters are bad, really bad. Maybe Sabra had to leave. Maybe it will be the best for her. I should want what's best for Sabra, as my mother has been telling me every day. Still, when she is gone I will be alone.

Mother got me a psychiatrist to talk to as soon as all this became public knowledge and the lawsuits started. My mother is a very kind and useful person. She teaches Political Science at the university and is a good friend of Hillary and Bill Clinton. She and my dad have spent six nights in the White House in the last seven years, and they didn't have to pay to sleep there. Well, I don't want to brag about that and I won't. I have enough to worry about.

The psychiatrist is this chubby good-natured sort who tries to be buddy-buddy with me and establish a transference so I'll have him when Sabra leaves but it isn't working as well as he and Mother hoped it would. I like him, don't get me wrong, but we are not rich people and I can't help wondering how much it's costing. Plus, I don't like the idea of buying friendship. I guess that's just resisting therapy. My parents are tenured professors at the university and our insurance is paying for it.

I am an only child and they feel guilty about that. As long as Sabra lived next door they could go about their merry lives thinking I was okay but now they have to face their decision to cut my father's sperm supply when they were thirty-seven.

There was talk of Sabra and me going together to Interlochen, Michigan, to go to art and drama school for a year and that may be in the works for 2001, but it is August 2000 and I am facing Woodland Junior High alone.

The psychiatrist said I shouldn't feel guilty about helping Sabra copy and mail the letters. "She sounds like a very willful girl," he said. "She would have done it whether you helped or not."

"This guy, Dave, was getting drunk about three nights a week and sleeping on the couch, or with her mother. How would you like to be a fourteen-year-old girl and wake up with a drunk in your house? Think it over."

"I think you did the right thing. It's a shame that she is leaving town but it may be the best thing for her. What did the letters say, Ginny? Do you feel like telling me what was in them?"

"No. It's too gross. I wish I'd never seen them. It's about what she wants him to do when her husband is away. Most of them were written before she got the divorce and Sabra's dad went to Canada."

"So is Dave living there full-time? I still don't understand how you got her letters if she mailed them to him."

"She kept copies. They were on a table in this room she calls her office. Sabra wasn't even looking for them. She just found them sitting there in a box."

"Okay. I see. So did her father get full custody? Will she come back in the summer?"

"She can come visit if her mother proves Dave isn't there. Her dad says she can come and visit us. But I'm still going to Woodland Junior High alone. People have moved across town to get their kids out of Woodland. It's a killer place."

"I know. I've heard the stories. Well, you made it all right last year. You got elected cheerleader. You're in the in crowd, aren't you?"

"You never know. It can change overnight. One pimple in the wrong place, gaining a little weight, anything can happen. I feel like a Siamese twin who is getting separated to save both their lives. Think about that baby in England who's getting cut off from the one who's dying. What's she going to think when she wakes up and half of her is gone?"

"There are phones, there is e-mail, there are fax machines, there are old-fashioned letters. Keep in touch with Sabra. Don't let her go. Things may change. She may come back here. You have to be strong for her."

"I'll try."

"Meantime, I want you to keep a journal for me. I want you to write down what happens at school and how you felt about it and when you were strong and when you were weak and what you want from junior high and how you are going about getting it. Will you do that for me, Ginny?"

"I will try."

Okay. Here are some of the things I wrote as August turned into September and the leaves began to change and autumn spread its bright mantle on Fayetteville, Arkansas. This place used to be an inland sea. It did. Right here where I'm sitting. You can find seashell fossils in the Ozark Mountains. I found seven one afternoon on the Highlands Trail. Think about that if you want to get things in perspective.

Journal Entry, August 28, 2000. Written by Ginny Colter, age 14

The morning of the last day Sabra will ever be by my side dawned warm, bright, and clear. I woke at dawn and went downstairs and let my cats outside and then I got a glass of tomato juice and went out on the back porch to look at Sabra's swimming pool and wait for her to wake up. I remember when her dad had the men come and build the pool for us. It was for both of us. He treated me like his own child and my parents treated

Sabra like she was their own. It was only her mother who was a problem. She was a problem from day one. Before she got Dave and started ruining Sabra's home with her love affair she drank by herself and said things to us she shouldn't say. She was always telling us about when she was a fashion model and lived in New York City and knew famous people, as if being married to Sabra's father, who is an English teacher, was a comedown for her. "I got preggie with you, Sweetie Pie," she was always saying to Sabra. "And that was all she wrote."

"You will keep those little boxes of yours buttoned up," she'd say to us. "Then you can't get trapped like Mommie did and have to live in the Midwest and look at fat people all day. Well, I have my writing. There is always that." Her mother likes to pretend she's a writer and has this room where she has a typewriter and a lot of books and papers. She reads all the Oprah Winfrey Book Club winners and romance novels and any kind of crap because she says the life of English departments is bullshit and she wants to write for money.

So finally she got Dave. She met him in this writing class she took over at the university. He's just this drifter, loser kind of guy from somewhere up north and makes fun of everything in Fayetteville. He pretends to be a writer too but he hasn't ever published anything. He mainly drinks and looks at Sabra's legs.

Sabra usually sleeps late if she doesn't have to go to school but I had only been out on the back porch about ten minutes when she came out on her patio and waved at me. The minute I saw her I started crying and ran across the yard and climbed the stile my Dad built on the fence and went to her and held her in my arms. "Where's your mother?" I asked. I am persona non grata in their house now as you can imagine. In the first place her mom knows I helped mail the letters and in the second place my mother testified in the custody suit.

"Let's go to your house," Sabra suggested. "She's waking up." So we climbed back over the fence and went in my kitchen and started making cinnamon toast and coffee.

"Here's what I want you to do about tomorrow," Sabra began. "I've been thinking about it. I woke up in the middle of the night worrying about you at Woodland by yourself. The first thing you have to do is get Jobe Knight and start hanging out with him. He's the smartest boy in school. You are going to have to align yourself with the smart kids now. Do the cheerleader thing but don't let it take over your life. I want you to try out for the school plays and I want you to sign up for the yearbook staff. Jobe likes us. He has always been our friend. He's the best ally you can have now. I think we ought to find him today and get him in on this."

"Okay," I said. It was the first glimmer of light I had seen since I found out she was leaving. Jobe Knight is the son of a lawyer who also knows the Clintons, so we have that in common. Also, we have been in the same grade with him since kindergarten. He is extremely tall for his age and slightly chubby and extremely brilliant and gifted and talented. I guess he has the highest grade-point average of anyone in Fayetteville, Arkansas.

"You are in Advanced Placement classes but until now you have not been putting out in them. You know this, Ginny. Well, that has to change. You must put your faith in intelligence now. We are going to be apart. We are going to be alone."

I just started crying. It was all that I could do.

*   *   *

Momma comes down the stairs and into the kitchen and hugs us and tells Sabra we will be waiting for her to call us every day and she can call collect if she needs to from anywhere. "I am going to get Ginny a cell phone so she'll be available for you. It's going to be all right, Sabra. You will be happy there with your father." Then Mother starts crying too. "We want you with us at Thanksgiving. I have told your father that. Maybe we'll all go to our house on the coast if you don't want to see your mother and Dave."

Journal Entry, August 30, 2000

I couldn't talk or write about her leaving but now I shall. The first thing that happened was we had a cheerleading meeting to get things organized and I got voted eighth-grade captain. I think everyone voted for me to make up for my losing Sabra but Mother says no, people are nice if you give them a chance to be and maybe it was because I'm good at organizing things. Plus, I'm on the yearbook staff and will be choosing the photographs that go in. That's a lot of power at Woodland although I didn't sign up to get power. Now that I have it I am going to use it, but not in a mean way. Anyone who is nice to me will get plenty of photographs and if they aren't nice to me, they won't. It's a cruel world.

The second thing that happened was Sabra called the first night she got to Toronto and said her stepmother was a bitch and she had gone from the frying pan into the fire. "She fixed me this room the size of a closet with all this plaid chintz everywhere. I will go mad trying to sleep in there. And she wants to put me in the Catholic school because she went there. And talk about drinking. She drank half a bottle of wine while she was fixing supper. It was red wine and her teeth were turning pink and after supper she and Dad watched some political bullshit on television. I don't know what to do, Ginny. I feel like I'm going to die." Then she started crying and I went and got Momma and we both talked to her for about an hour and finally she said she was going to bed.

So the next day is Monday and I have to go to school except I'm so upset I can hardly eat breakfast so Mother calls the psychiatrist, his name is Johnny, and he says he'll come to school at noon and talk to me, but I say no, that would embarrass me to death and I can't see him after school because I have cheerleader practice and tryouts for cross-country running.

Mother drives me to school and sticks high protein bars in every pocket of my backpack and generally starts losing it herself. "Don't worry about me," I keep saying. "I'll see Johnny tomorrow. I'm not going to do anything, Mother. If you want to help me, call Sabra and see when she has to start the Catholic school."

"Here," she says, and gives me her new cellular phone. "When you get a study period you call her. It's all right. I'll use my old one. It will be all right, talk to her as much as you want."

Mother manages our rental property. She lives by her phone, so you can see what a generous and helpful person she is. I gave her a kiss and walked up the walk to the school. I'm ashamed to say I kind of let my shoulders hunch so she'd know how sad I was.

I've got to say this for Woodland Junior High. When the chips are down there are some really nice people there. Everyone saw me walking into school looking like I'd lost my best friend and by the time I got in the front hall I was surrounded. My English teacher, Mrs. George, and three people in my Advanced Placement chemistry class and Jobe Knight and his best friend, Marshall McCormick, were all around me. "She's having a terrible time," I told them. "She cried on the phone for an hour. Her stepmother drinks wine and is sending her to a Catholic school. I don't know if Sabra's going to make it."

"We'll e-mail her," Jobe said. "Every one of us will e-mail her every day. We'll tell her everything that happens. We'll smother her in e-mail."

"How much does her stepmother drink?" Mrs. George asked. "That would stand to reason, of course. People run to type. I guess her father marries women who drink."

We started an e-mail campaign to keep Sabra from being lonely. Jobe gave out times to different people so it wouldn't all go out on the same day and he made a place on his site for her to send replies that everyone could access.

"You are saving my life," her first reply came. "I will draw strength from my roots like a maple tree. I will find a way to be there for ninth grade. I will get an apartment and live alone if I have to. I have to go to the school to be evaluated this morning. If I hate the place I'll just fail the test."

★   ★   ★

That was Tuesday. On Thursday we got a second reply. I had tried to call her Wednesday night but no one answered so I left a message and then Mother made me go to bed.

Here was Thursday's message. "The school they took me to, St. Martin's-in-the-Fields, is not as bad as I thought it would be. They have uniforms but they are really pretty. There are two different kinds and they are really well made and have to be custom-made for each girl. The girls are really cute. They have this beautiful accent and they want to know everything about the United States and Fayetteville and Woodland Junior High. I took a bunch of your e-mails to school today and showed them to people and they all laughed and said they were funny and wanted to know about the pom-pom squad and cheerleading and the rules for our football.

"I got invited to three different parties. One is Saturday night and it's a dance at the mayor's residence. Carlene, my new mom, is taking me out tonight to buy a formal dress for it. Wish me luck. Maybe I'll be all right up here. Will you come and visit me?"

That was fine for Sabra, but how about me? I climbed on the bus Friday afternoon wondering what I would do all weekend. Unfortunately football season doesn't start until next week so there were no extra cheerleading practices and cross-country doesn't start until Monday.

Jobe climbed on the bus and came and sat beside me. "Nineteen months to go until I get a driver's license," he said. "I don't know if I can wait."

"You have to wait. Deal with it."

"What are you going to do this afternoon?"

"Nothing. What is there to do in Fayetteville?"

"We could walk down to Dickson Street and see what's happening."

"I'm not allowed on Dickson Street by myself. Mother thinks there are too many tattooed people down there."

"You wouldn't be by yourself if you were with me. We could go to the used book store and see what they have."

I pulled Mother's cell phone out of my backpack and called her and asked if I could go with Jobe to the bookstore. Of course she said yes. She hadn't seen Sabra's e-mails. She didn't know that crisis was winding down and I sure wasn't going to tell her about it. I was getting a lot of mileage out of losing my best friend and I thought I better milk it for everything there was. I live in the United States of America in a small college town that has a crime rate of about zero. I have a constant food supply and parents who love me. I go to a junior high school that has produced fifteen National Merit Scholars in three years. I mean, people at Fayetteville High that went to Woodland for junior high.

I don't get to have many crises. I have to make the most of what I get.

"I'll go with you but I don't want to walk," I told Jobe. "I want to ride my bike. If you don't have one you can ride my dad's. He hurt his back coaching soccer. He can't ride it anymore and he doesn't mind if I lend it to people."

"I ride bikes," Jobe said. "Let's go get them. Let's go."

★　　　★　　　★

We went to my house and ate some leftover pizza and drank Gatorade and then we went out to the garage and found the bike pump and pumped up the tires and got on the bikes and started riding down the long hill from Sequoyah to Dickson Street. If your brakes failed on that hill, you'd buy it. When I'm flying down it on a bike, I usually plan what I'll do if the brakes give out but today all I thought about was the million times Sabra and I have ridden down that hill starting when we were on three-wheelers and our fathers were running behind us holding on to the seats. I started crying when we turned down Dogwood and I cried all the way to Lafayette. We stopped by the brick wall in front of the Whiteheads' house and Jobe got off his bike and tried to comfort me. "She's going to forget all about us," I cried. "She is so beautiful and funny, she will have a life wherever she goes. They will probably find her and put her in the movies. She'll look great in a uniform. She said I had to put my faith in you now, Jobe. That was her last instruction to me."

"Sabra's a phenomenon," he agreed. "My dad says her mother used to be that beautiful when she first came to town. He said people would stop and stare at her. He said beauty like that can be a curse."

"Curse me," I said and started laughing through my tears. "Throw me in the briar patch."

"Listen, Ginny, Sabra's gone but we're right here. I want to see if the used book store got in any more James Bond books. I have every one now but *Diamonds Are Forever* and *Doctor No*. Marshall's collecting them too, so if I find one he doesn't have I'm going to give it to him for his birthday."

"Okay. Wait a minute. Let me put on some lipstick." He held my bike while I got out my lipstick and put it on using the rearview mirror of the Whiteheads' Lincoln, which was parked in the driveway. Then we got back on the bikes and rode the sidewalks down to College Avenue and walked the bikes across and got back on and rode the broken sidewalks down to Ila and cut across to Dickson. This town needs some infrastructure because it's built on shale and besides the tree roots break open the sidewalks while we're sleeping. My grandfather is an engineer. He tells me things like that all the time.

We played around in the used book store for about an hour. I got on the tall ladder in the poetry section and read a lot of poetry. I started crying once while I was reading this poem about a poet whose friend died and he wouldn't go to the funeral. He just went out in the woods and sat on a hill by himself and had a private ceremony in his mind. It was called an epithalamium and I thought I should have one for losing Sabra. I got down off the ladder and went to find a dictionary to look up the word but as soon as I went around the stacks of the poetry section I saw Dave standing by the front door talking to a student and then they went out the door and started across the street to the coffee shop. He was holding on to her arm like she was his girlfriend. I went to the fiction section and found Jobe sitting on a stool reading *On Her Majesty's Secret Service*. He had found two hardback copies of Ian Fleming's books. They were old book club editions and were only three dollars each. We went to the front and paid for them and then went outside and counted our money. I had a five-dollar bill and some change and he had two dollars left so we went over to the coffee shop to spy on Dave. I didn't really think he was going to recognize me because he is mostly at the Larkins' house at night and besides, I'm not that recognizable. I keep a low profile. It's my coping mechanism.

Anyway, we love the banana nut bread in the coffee shop and we went on in and ordered coffee and two pieces of the bread and took our stuff and went to the back room where all the writers hang out. It's really dark in there and we took a table at the back. Dave and the girl were sitting up front near the bookshelves and he was leaned across the table holding her hand and talking to her like he was telling her something important.

"I wish I had a camera," I said.

"I have one," Jobe answered. He pulled a very small, very beautiful little camera out of his pocket and aimed it in Dave's direction and took a picture. Then he stood up and pretended he was photographing this ugly painting that was on the wall. It was part of a show of local art.

"You have every piece of equipment ever made," I said. "You are the most spoiled boy I ever knew."

"I make the grades. If you make really high grades they get you what you need. You're doing better this year, Ginny. I'm really impressed with the way you're paying attention in chemistry."

"Sabra told me to. She said I had to stop goofing off and really try so I'm trying. What else do you have in that backpack? Do you have a dictionary? There's this word I read in a poem I need to look up."

"I have something better than that." He pulled this very small computer out of his backpack and opened it and turned the light up on the screen and found the dictionary. "What's the word?"

"Epithalamium. I'm going to write one for Sabra leaving."

He typed it in and then he started laughing. "Not unless she's getting married," he said. "It's something you write for the bridal night."

"Let me see." I read the screen. "Well, then I spelled it wrong. It's supposed to be a poem for someone who's died. It was this poem about this poet whose friend died and instead of going to the regular funeral he went out to this hill and sat on it and wrote this epithalamium."

"I guess he was saying death is like getting married. The death of one form of being and the beginning of another. Like people who think they're going to heaven when they die."

"You know what I hate? I hate running around with someone who knows everything. It's wearing, Jobe. It really is."

"Don't get mad. The way you learn things is to make mistakes. There are three things you have to know to be happy, so my father says. Machines break, it's an imperfect world, and you learn from your mistakes. Finish your cake. I only have two more pictures on this roll of film. If we go to the park I can photograph the pollution in Rock Creek and then we can leave the film to be developed. We may need that photograph of Dave."

Two days later he got the photographs back and we put the one of Dave holding hands with the girl on the copy machine and made a big copy of it and put it in an envelope and stuck it in Judy Larkin's mailbox. I don't know why we did that. It wasn't all that carefully thought out. We just thought every little bit helps where Sabra's welfare is concerned.

Friday, October 13, 2000

There are four black crows living on my trampoline. Ravens, my father calls them and starts quoting Edgar Allan Poe. He thinks it's funny but my mother thinks it's mystical. Four crows sit on the roof when the Dalai Lama is born in Tibet. Fact. Anyway they're sitting there and waiting for the squirrels to crack open the hickory nuts which are falling from our hickory trees. When Sabra and I were little girls we used to collect the hickory nuts into big piles for the squirrels to help them get ready for the winter. We would put a big pile under every tree so they could get to them more easily. Also, this time of year we would be setting up a tent in my backyard and begging to get to sleep there. Then we'd be in the tent with cookies and flashlights talking about what would happen to us when we grew up.

We didn't know it would end up with Sabra's mother getting a boyfriend and acting like Sabra didn't exist and Sabra ending up in a Catholic girls' school in Toronto, Canada. I can't help being sad about it. This is not what was supposed to happen to us. I hate her mother. But not as much as her mother hates us. She has called the Animal Control Office about ten times to complain about our poor old Australian sheepdog being allowed to go out front at night for a few minutes and run around. The animal people think she's nuts, but they have to call us.

Andre, that's our dog, hates Judy Larkin. He knows she is dangerous and mean and he goes into this fierce protective mode and bares his teeth the minute he sees her. We are scared to death she will taunt him to bite her so she can have him killed. She hates us so much and probably even more so since Jobe and I left that picture in her mailbox, that we are going to have to sell our house. I know she knows who did it. She must.

"We have to sell this house," my mother keeps telling my father. "I cannot live next door to that. We can get something on the park so we can walk to school. I've always wanted to live near enough to walk to the university."

"But I love this house. I was born in this house. Why should we move?"

"I testified for James in the custody suit. That's that. It was my duty and I did it and I think we should move. It's depressing, if not dangerous, to have her over there."

"Then look for a house," he said finally and Mother is looking for one now.

"We obeyed our consciences, Ginny," she tells me. "That isn't always easy and it isn't always free."

"Is she coming for Thanksgiving?" I asked. "Did Mr. Larkin say he was going to let her?"

"We are going to meet her in Memphis and take her to the coast with us. He doesn't want her here because she doesn't want to see her mother."

"Then let's get cracking on that house. If we weren't so near he might let her come here."

That afternoon we began our house search. It's spooky to go poking around in houses that are for sale. Especially with fall weather and the trees starting to turn and everything so poignant and full of metaphor. Beginnings and endings. The end of my life in the house where my father was born and the beginning of moving to the park and new things happening. Jobe lives on Maple Street not far from the park. He got interested in us looking for a house and started roaming around every afternoon checking things out. He found the brick house across the street from Dr. Ladner the second day it was on the market. He called Mother and told her about it. It is a Tudor house with a slate roof and a pool.

Three days later we bought it. The day we made our offer there were two more offers for more than we paid for it. It cost $250,000 if you want to know but we are going to sell ours for more than that because it's on Sequoyah and has a view. We'll come out all right. Still, as soon as they signed the contract I went outside and looked at our trees and started getting sentimental. The new house is nicer than our old one but the lot is only half as big.

"Stay strong," Mother told me. "We did what was right and now we are finishing our work." As if she isn't thrilled to finally get a new house and get to walk to the university every day. Plus, now she gets to spend some of Granddaddy's money for something besides my college fund and the United Way and other charities.

We are moving on November the tenth. A new professor in the business school bought our house the minute he saw it and now his children will be in my playhouse and on my trampoline and have Mrs. Larkin next door screaming at them if they even look over her fence.

October 20, 2000

Jobe had his birthday yesterday. He celebrated by riding his bike around all day reciting "Poem in October," by Dylan Thomas. I was with him, and kept his present in my jacket pocket until two in the afternoon, the time that's listed on his birth certificate as the time of birth. Except for the rotation of the planets changing our clocks, that is exactly the time he was born as they did a C-section on his mother and that's when they pulled him out. I am getting really dependent on Jobe. My psychiatrist says it's healthy because we both are so gifted and talented we have to have friends who are as smart as we are. He also says now that she's gone I may find I don't have as much in common with Sabra as I once had.

Because we will be in the new house, her father has agreed to let her stay in Fayetteville for Thanksgiving instead of all of us having to caravan to Gulf Shores, Alabama, which is no fun this late in the year. The little house we go to is cold in the winter and you can't go swimming, so what's the point?

"It was my thirtieth year to heaven, woke to my hearing from harbour and neighbor wood and the mussel pooled and heron priested shore the morning beckon with call of seagull and rook and the knock of sailing boats on the net webbed wall myself to set foot that second in the still sleeping town and set forth. . . ." Jobe was quoting the Dylan Thomas as we rode down the long hill to the university and up onto the paths in front of Old Main. We came to a stop on the old stone where students kiss and leaned our bikes against it and he said to me, "Do you think we should kiss each other, or not? We wouldn't have to take it seriously, of course."

"I don't know," I answered. "I want a boyfriend, of course, and I want you to go to homecoming with me. I was meaning to ask you about that but what if I kiss you and then we get into something and start being jealous if we talk to other people and all of that."

"You've got a point. You know, boys have penises and they are, well, I won't bore you with that. Let's go." He got back on his bike and went at breakneck speed down one of the paths. He is way too tall to ride a bike that fast. I followed him.

We went all the way to Arsaga's coffee shop on Hill Street before he talked to me again. "Sorry about that," he said, when we had parked our bikes. "I shouldn't have brought that up."

"I know about it anyway. My father told me about it two years ago. He explained it in detail. It's the way we are designed. We are here to reproduce ourselves. All else is art. Well, do you want to take me to homecoming? You have to wear a suit."

"I'd like to. I will."

So that is settled and at last I have a real date to homecoming and not just some thing like last year when Sabra and I and two other girls and four boys all went together in a group.

About the penis thing. I understand that boys have a problem at our age with all of that and desire to copulate with all girls they meet and think about it many hours a day even if they try to put their minds on something else. The thing about Jobe is he has such a brilliant mind he is good at staying on top of any problem by his constant interest in the world and all its manifestations.

★   ★   ★

I don't know how I feel about it. I like little kids a lot and I can see how someday I might want to have one if you could have them in a bottle like in *Brave New World*. To tell the truth, I am hoping they will have that technology in place by the time I want to reproduce. I'd rather clone myself anyway. If I had a kid exactly like myself, I would know exactly what to do to make her happy. It's something to think about.

November 30, 2000

We moved into the house and most of our furniture fit but Mother is going crazy and ordering some really fine contemporary chairs and a table. She is spending about five thousand dollars fixing this house and buying things for it but we still are ahead after we sold our old one.

We still had unpacked boxes in half the rooms when Sabra came for Thanksgiving. Mother and I went to get her at the airport and she looked just like herself except taller and maybe even more beautiful than when she left. She had on this dark brown wool cashmere coat her stepmother lent her for the trip and a fake mink hat and she brought me one just like it for a present. As soon as we got in the car to drive into town she told us she was going to see her mother.

"She's kicked Dave out and she's going to Alcoholics Anonymous. Dad says he'll believe it when he sees it."

"But you're going to stay with us, aren't you?" I asked.

"Most of the time I am, but I'll have to stay there one night and have Thanksgiving dinner with her. I mean, face it, she's my mother. She's not mad at you anymore, either, Ginny. She said to tell you she wants to see you."

"Why didn't you tell me this?"

"I wasn't sure what I would do. I have a psychiatrist now. He is helping me figure it out. And I got to go to New York City and see two plays and the New York City Ballet. I brought you all the programs."

"I've got one too. A psychiatrist. His name is Johnny Battle. We go for walks and talk about things. And I went to homecoming with Jobe but you already know that."

"Well, my psychiatrist is a Freudian. He's very strict. You have to call him Doctor Jacobs and you have to lie on the couch and not look at him."

"I guess that's the difference between Fayetteville and Toronto," Mother put in. "Are you girls hungry? I bought you some really wonderful low-fat salmon salad at the new deli."

"I think maybe you better let me off at my mom's first," Sabra said. "I mean, she knows when I was getting here. I don't want her getting sad when she's trying to quit drinking. I better go by there first. She'll bring me over to your house later."

"Does your father know you're going to see her?"

"Yes. He doesn't care as long as Dave isn't there."

So we drove back up to our old street and stopped in front of Sabra's house and Mother decided we had better go in with her so we did. It seemed really weird to be going up that sidewalk after I thought I'd never set foot on it again. Our old house looks like shit if you'll pardon the expression. The trash cans are in the front yard and three tricycles and they are painting the whole house this terrible color of beige with a yellow door. I tried not to look at it. My father was born in that house.

Then Judy was at the front door, wearing some gray wool slacks and a short-sleeved turtleneck and she grabbed her daughter and hugged her and Mother and I just stood there and said polite things and told Sabra to come over as soon as she could and then Judy said, "Leave her luggage here," so I went back to the car and got her suitcase and her cosmetic kit and took them in the living room and put them down. Judy came up behind me and took my arm.

"I know you left that photograph in my mailbox and I thank you for it," she said. She was looking me right in the eye.

"What photograph?" I said.

"All right," she answered. "Thank you anyway. I know you love my daughter."

Then they stood in the doorway, mother and daughter, and watched until Mother and I got in our car and drove away.

"I'm still glad we moved," Mother said. "I've been wanting a new house for fifteen years."

"May I use your phone?" I asked. "I need to call Jobe and tell him what's going on."

She pulled her phone out of her purse and handed it to me and I called Jobe and left a message to come over. "Sabra's with her mother," I said. "I don't think that will last long. If so we have a house full of food someone has to eat."

"That wasn't very nice," Mother said. "What if he thinks you think he eats too much."

"He does eat too much. He has a big brain. He has to feed it. He doesn't care. He doesn't think he's fat."

★   ★   ★

We had hardly gotten home when Sabra called and said she was coming over. "Are you going to spend the night?" I asked.

"I don't know. She might get her feelings hurt. I want to. You know I want to."

"Bring some stuff and stay if you can or don't. Our new house is right across the street from Dr. Ladner. It's 444 Rock."

"Okay. We'll be there in a minute."

She was looking more like herself by the time she got to our house. She had put on some khaki pedal pushers and a sweater and had traded the cashmere coat for a Windbreaker. Also, she had on some running shoes and socks. As soon as I saw her get out of her mother's car I ran down the front steps. I was totally back in Sabra's spell. There is no describing real beauty. It's just there and I love to look at it. Ever since she was a real little girl I would just go into these spells of looking at her and having this real art experience from it. I never was jealous of it and I'm not now. Sabra Larkin is my best friend and that is that. "Friendship is more than having fun," my mother always tells me. "It's being there for another person through thick and thin, no matter what happens to them or if they change for a while, you go on being by their side. And something else, you tell them the truth, about yourself and about them. That's the main basis for friendship, trust and truth saying."

My mother should know. She has more friends than anyone in town, plus the President of the United States and the First Lady. She stands by her friends and she never lets them down and she helps them out when they need help.

I decided Sabra needed help whether she knew it or not. Here she was in her hometown as a visitor. A visitor at her own mother's house and a visitor at her best friend's house and in a position where everyone she sees was going to ask her questions and she had to answer them and still keep up her pride.

My psychiatrist had told me that would happen when she got here and I saw it in her face. I pulled her out of the car. "Let her spend the night with me, Judy," I told her mother. "This is a terribly abnormal situation. Let's normalize it by doing what we'd do if Sabra had never gone to Canada."

"Good thinking," Judy said. "I have to go to an AA meeting at seven at St. John's. I'll call you when I get home and see what you're doing. Is that okay?"

"That's good," Sabra said and leaned over and kissed her mother on the cheek. "I love you, Momma. I'm so glad you're here and I'm with you."

Then she pulled a small bag out of the backseat and we stood on the sidewalk watching her mother drive away.

"Let's normalize," I said. "Jobe's coming over. We can walk down to Dickson Street and look at everything and tonight we can go watch them turn on the lights on the square." I hugged her to me. "Remember that night it snowed and we went down and walked all around in the lights in the snow. Listen, I have the whole collection of Audrey Hepburn movies now. Grandmother got them for my birthday. It's a five-movie set. Let's watch every one. You want to? Let's have an Audrey Hepburn film festival."

"I want to tell you about my school and all my new friends and this boy I like."

"Start talking," I said and took her bag. We started walking up the steps to our new house. I was so glad to have her by my side. I was bursting with a strange goodness or gladness or something. It was like I thought everything was going to turn out all right after all. Like I could make a difference in whether things turned out all right. Like I was right in the middle of it and I could affect it. No matter what people say who think the world is getting worse and it doesn't matter if you vote and you might as well give up and all of that, I don't believe that way.

"Listen," I said. "Jobe has discovered this place out behind the new Wal-Mart. It's back behind Shoe Carnival. It's this huge wall of rock where they dynamited down in the middle of a hill and left this sixty- or eighty-foot cut and on it you can see the whole geological history of this area. We will take you out there and see it. You weren't here when the woman came down out of the tree to stop them from cutting down the trees, were you?"

"Yes, I was. She came down right before I left. Did they put her in jail?"

"Not yet. They keep sentencing her. Anyway, that's how Jobe discovered the rock wall. He made his father take him out there to see the trees after they cut them down. We can go out tomorrow if you want to."

"I had forgotten what it was like to be with you." She stopped at the front door and turned those blue eyes on me and smiled an old Sabra smile from years ago. "I love you, Ginny. You're the best friend I'll ever have."

"Well, come on in. Let's get started."

So that is how I got her back if not for good at least forever. But now I have to go. I have cross-country practice and then I have cheerleading practice in the gym and then I have to do my homework. Later, Ginny.

Oh, yeah. One other thing. Sabra's mother is writing a book about how to stop drinking. "She met this guy at AA who's an editor for a book publishing company," Sabra told Mother and me. "He got her started on it. I read the first chapter. It's all about how she thought the only good thing about herself was that she was beautiful and when she started getting old she didn't know what to do so she started drinking. Now these AA people are teaching her that she has things to live for besides her beauty."

"It would be a happy ending to all of this if she'd finish the book and get it published," Mother said.

Jobe's comment is it's still about penises and vaginas no matter how old people get to be. But I don't buy that as much as he does because my vagina is not as much trouble to me as his penis is to him, only he doesn't really think it's too much trouble. It's worth it, he argues. Because you never run out of something to do in your spare time.

He will be glad when Sabra goes back to Canada. He thinks I act funny when she's around and talk like her instead of me. Maybe I do. I guess I do. And maybe she talks like me.

Light Shining
Through a
Honey Jar

IT WAS THE TWELFTH OF JANUARY and Miss Crystal and I were recovering from the cold we caught from Baby Eleanor when she was visiting us at Christmas. What a precious child she is. We could not resist picking her up even though mucus was running from her nose every minute we weren't cleaning it off with Puff tissues.

I wasn't over there much. I only work a few hours a week now that Mr. Manny has put me on retirement pay. There's nothing to do there anyway. King is in North Carolina with his family and Crystal Anne is in California working for a movie studio.

Things aren't much better in my family. My niece, Andria, has become so famous she spends most of her time in Washington, D.C., or Baton Rouge. Her little girls are watched over by their new nanny, who is from Iowa and doesn't think I'm a good influence on their grammar. Not that Andria goes along with her on that but I couldn't help noticing she smiled in a conspiratorial manner when "Nanny Jane" teased me about my accent. I like the way we talk down here. Mr. Manny was educated at Harvard University and has written papers about southern speech. He says our way of speaking English is a combination of African rhythms and Celtic speech patterns and that he thinks it is the most beautiful and seductive English spoken on the globe.

Also, he is having this big argument with a man who writes for the *New York Times* about who lacks irony. This man, Tommy, he's called, says no one below the Mason-Dixon line has any irony and Mr. Manny replies that he has been saying for years no one *above* the line has any and that Tommy stole that idea from the very people he's attacking.

They are carrying out this battle in the letters section of the *Atlantic Monthly Magazine,* and our phone, mailbox, and e-mail are full of messages defending both sides.

So that's where we are at the moment. Andria's little girls being kept from their blood kin by a girl with a degree in child care from the University of Iowa who is twenty-two years old. Mr. Manny locked in battle with Tommy Settle of the *New York Times* and Miss Crystal and myself taking Levaquin, Claritin, Deconsul II, and Robitussin. "If we were poor we couldn't get these drugs," she told me on the telephone yesterday. "If we were old and poor we couldn't pay nine dollars a day for prescription drugs to cure bronchitis."

"We might be better off if we couldn't," I replied. "This new antibiotic has torn my stomach up. My taste buds have disappeared."

Which is why, when I finally got out of bed this morning and realized I was feeling better, the first thing I did was get out the coffee grinder and make myself a cup of really strong P.J.'s French Vanilla coffee. Mark had already left for work so I had the house to myself. It was very quiet and I was just getting used to the idea of being well when I noticed a streak of gold on the flat black top of the stove. It was a piece of light shining through a jar of honey. This is the moment Buddhist monks wait for all their lives. To watch a piece of light penetrate the darkness of our selfish lives. Because we do not think deeply enough we sit around and worry about things and want things and think we are scared or bored and all the time light is shining through us and time is going on and our lives are being wasted in silliness.

In my case my life was being wasted by bothering to hate a young girl I didn't even know a month ago. What was an au pair from Ames, Iowa, doing being allowed to ruin my life and keep me from the dearest treasures of my life?

I watched the light for a long time, breathing in the beauty of the thought. Then I pulled my old prayer bench out of the closet and put it in the exact center of my living room. It is a beautiful little bench made of cherry wood by a carpenter Miss Crystal knew many years ago. He made one for her and one for me back when we were talking to some Buddhist poets about their beliefs.

I sat down on it and tried to think objectively about Nanny Jane. A young girl with a round face from a distant state arrives in New Orleans to nurse the twin daughters of a Creole anchorwoman for CBS. She encounters the Garden District, long hours, mosquitoes, a father who is gone all the time to medical school and a mother who is more interested in her career than in her children. She has to be scared to death as this is her first job.

The first time I came into Andria's house after the nanny got there the little girls ran to me and wouldn't let anyone else change their diapers. Of course she had to start finding fault with me.

I sighed. Once again lack of understanding had caused a problem. Could I find a way to set things right? It would have to begin in my own heart, as Jesus taught and I sometimes know.

I picked up the phone and called Andria's house on Philip Street. The nanny answered the phone. "This is Andria's Aunt Traceleen," I began. "We have met several times. How are you doing over there? How are things going with all of you?"

"Oh, pretty well, I guess. We're doing okay."

"That's good to hear. I have just recovered from a cold and wanted to spend a sunny morning in the park. I would like to take my great-nieces with me if that's all right with you. You could come along or stay there and have some time to yourself. Is Andria still there?"

"No, she has her morning show. She won't be back until one. Sure, that would be great. I have some work to do around here anyway. When would you like to come get them?"

"Now. As soon as I put on my walking shoes."

"I'll have them ready. Do you want the double stroller?"

"I would love the double stroller," I answered with perfect diction. "That would be helpful, Nanny Jane."

"Just Jane," she says. "Just call me Jane."

★   ★   ★

So that is how I cured myself of allowing a twenty-two-year-old girl with a nasal twang to high-hat me about my accent. My people are from Terrebonne Parish. Only people of great strength and courage could have gone to live in such a wild and barbarous land, and my people were there from the beginning. They fought off yellow fever and malaria and floods and hurricanes and lived to tell the story in one of the most beautiful accents in the English language.

As soon as I hung up from talking to Nanny Jane I called Miss Crystal to give her a report and see how she was feeling.

She said, "Traceleen, I'm proud of you."

"You think about that light," I said. "Keep thinking about it going into all of us all day every day. Don't lose the image. It is like the things Miss Horowitz used to tell us when we began our yoga."

"I'm coming to the park and meet you. I want to see those twins."

"I can use the help."

"I'll bring some snacks. Apples and carrots and crackers. The nanny won't object to that, will she?"

"We do not care what she objects to. She is only a young girl full of ideas she learned in college."

An hour later we were settled in the Little Children's Park with Kaleen and Hillary in the swings and us pushing.

"We must go back to yoga," Miss Crystal said. "We must never go too far from our deeper knowledge, Traceleen. Breathe in, breathe out, stay in the present moment." She gave Hillary a big push and Hillary giggled and beat her feet against the red plastic foot rest of the swing. We were pushing the girls from different sides so they could see each other as they passed.

"Breathe in, breathe out," I answered.

"Higher, higher," Kaleen yelled. "Go higher, Twaceleen."

So the morning passed and in a little while we put down blankets and had a picnic of fruit and carrot sticks and little biscuits, washed down with Evian in blue paper cups.

Then we packed up the girls in the stroller and Miss Crystal decided to leave her car at the park and walk back with me to see Andria's house now that the painters are finished with their work on the exterior.

Nanny Jane was talking to her mother in Iowa when we came in, arguing with her about something. She kept the phone to her ear the whole time she came to the door to let us in and while we brought the little girls into the foyer and took them into the kitchen to get some juice.

Finally she hung up the phone. "That's my goddamn mother," she says. "She's pissed off because she doesn't like my boyfriend. She hates him because he doesn't want to spend his life making money. What else is new with that generation? So how did things go at the park?" It is sometimes very hard to talk to Nanny Jane because she has a tongue ring and when she is wearing it you have to spend all your mental energy trying not to think it is the most disgusting thing you have ever seen.

"We fed them a nourishing lunch and I think they are ready for a nap," I answered.

"Well, thanks," she said. "Come take them anytime you want to. It's good for them to get out. I sure don't have time for it."

Miss Crystal was heading for the door. I could see she had had enough.

"Want to go with Traceween," Kaleen started screaming and Hillary came in with a chorus. "Twaceleen," they are calling, then they are crying, and of course I couldn't leave then so I got them to sleep before I left.

When I came back downstairs Nanny Jane was back on the phone. This time she was talking to her boyfriend who is in a halfway house in California. She kept saying things like, "It isn't the judge's fault," and "It won't be long now," and "She doesn't hate you. She's just worried about me."

I was embarrassed to be listening so I started for the door. She hung up and came after me. "Life's a bitch, isn't it?" she began. "Trying to keep my boyfriend from knowing my mother hates him. I mean, why should he care? You'd think my mother would be glad I'm happy, but no. She wants me to marry someone with money. All she cares about is money. It's her only motive, her only goal."

"What's your motive?" I asked.

"I don't know. To be happy, I guess. I mean that will do for a start, don't you agree?"

"No," I answered. "I do not think pursuing happiness is a worthy challenge. Besides, you cannot find it while looking for it. Searching for the ox while riding the ox is how the Zen masters put it. Think about that while you go about this day."

"Oh, God," she says and begins to cry. "I wanted to be in the theater. You know, show business, then I got into child care because I thought I could get to London or somewhere but all I'm doing is spinning my wheels and my boyfriend is so depressed they've put him on Prozac. I've been down that trail. It's okay when it's working but it takes the edge off life. I don't know. I don't know what to do."

She sat down at the kitchen table and put her head in her hands, only Andria doesn't have a kitchen table. She has this uncomfortable brick island in the middle of her kitchen. It is surrounded by uncomfortable stools made in the shape of bent coat hangers. Jane was doing the best she could to get comfortable on one of them while she cried.

I comforted her as best I could and made her a cup of herbal tea and some seven grain toast with jam. After she had eaten she got into a better mood and I took my leave, promising to come back the next day and take the girls to the park again. "You have too much work to do," I told her. "Twins are more than you bargained for. Andria will have to find you a helper. You are too young for so much responsibility."

I went outside and got into my car and drove slowly down to St. Charles Avenue and started to Andria's office. Do no harm, was my main motto of the afternoon. Don't go telling Andria to get rid of Jane until we find a replacement or I will find myself living over there like a slave.

Still, I do not want Hillary and Kaleen being cared for by a young girl so unhappy she has to take mood elevators, do I? A young girl with a boyfriend in a halfway house who doesn't like her own mother.

I am not a troublemaker. Quite the opposite, but I knew my

duty. I stepped on the gas and drove on down to Andria's office in the Shell Oil Building and told her what I had learned.

Then I got into my car and headed out to Metairie to the Wal-Mart to buy some car seats for my car. Until we find a replacement for Jane I will be on call twenty-four seven and I don't like to have to transfer car seats from car to car. It is too much trouble to move those big clumsy things into position and strap them down, which is a good metaphor for the way we live our lives in the year two thousand. How many hours a day are spent fixing it so we can transport our children all over the world when they would be better off just staying in one place and learning about the sun and moon and stars and how the trees take light and turn it into leaves and berries?

When I got home with the car seats I called Andria and apologized for overreacting. "We must not throw the nanny out with the bathwater," I advised. "Let me go over there every morning for a few days and continue to investigate. The girls seem happy and well cared for, she cooks healthy food for them, and is a stickler for them eating properly at the table, she is trained for medical emergencies and she's here. Just leave it to me for a week or so."

"I wasn't going to do anything anyway," Andria said. "Help is impossible to find and she was investigated thoroughly by the best agency in the United States. Just because her boyfriend gets in trouble doesn't mean she isn't okay."

"Well, it means something. Lie down with dogs, get up with fleas."

"Traceleen, that is the meanest thing I have ever heard you say. You ought to quit spending so much time with Crystal. She is so retrograde."

"It is because those little girls are the sun and moon to me. I do not want them spending all day every day with someone who cries at the drop of a hat. I'll go get them at nine tomorrow morning and take them to the park."

"Well, don't be mean to Jane. She's in a new situation. She's still nervous."

So I pulled my prayer bench out again and listened to my deepest thoughts and tried to remember everything that happens is multifaceted. We are in a web of being. Touch one strand and the whole thing trembles. I am not blameless in all this. I delight in Jane knowing those little girls like me more than they like her. And I am not above spoiling them if I forget not to do it.

Start at the place that's torn. The next morning when I got to Andria's I accepted Jane's offer of a cup of coffee and sat on the front steps talking to her and watching the morning heat overtake New Orleans.

"So what happened to your boyfriend?" I asked.

"He got in with the wrong crowd and started doing drugs and his folks sent him to a hospital and now he has to do six months in a halfway house. Then he's going back to school and start again. He's a really nice man. He loves me. Not many men have been in love with me." She hung her head. I was keeping an eye on Kaleen and Hillary, who were playing in the flower beds below the stairs. They were picking the little golden flowers we call Ham and Eggs. Hillary was picking them and giving them to Kaleen, who was holding them in her hand.

"It's seductive to be loved," I agreed. "It is the thing women like best. They like it more than good looks or money."

"Well, my mother doesn't like it. She hates his mother anyway. We go to the same church and she hates him. She wants me to promise not to see him anymore. Well, I won't do it."

"Did you ever do drugs with him?"

"No. I did not. I smoked some grass with him one time and it made me so paranoid I couldn't leave the house for days. He did all that while I was at the university getting my degree. He doesn't do it around me. He knows I hate it."

"Then how is he your boyfriend if he has this lifestyle you can't stand? It doesn't make sense to me, Jane. I'm starting to get on your mother's side."

"I'm all he has."

"Was or is your father an alcoholic?"

"How did you know that?"

"I am a counselor at my church. I counsel young people. I have seen this many times. The children of alcoholics find mates who drink or take drugs and then take care of them. There are two main things that happen to the children of alcoholics. Either they drink themselves, following the pattern, or they marry alcoholics and become codependents. It is the life they know, you see."

"Oh, my God. Then I am doomed." She got up and went down the stairs and picked up the twins and brought them up to where we were. She handed me Kaleen and kept Hillary on her lap.

"Don't eat those flowers," she said. "There are many

poisonous flowers in New Orleans. It is not a good idea to get in the habit of eating flowers until you are old enough to know which ones can be eaten and of course by then you won't want to eat them anyway."

"Give them a cracker," I suggested.

"All right." She got two crackers out of the sack we had packed for me to take to the park, breaking her vow of not feeding them between meals.

"It is not your doom or fate," I went on. "It is just a syndrome to be avoided. I have a list of Al-Anon meeting times and places. One is at the Presbyterian Church on Saint Charles Avenue. You can take the streetcar down there. I will bring you a copy. You should attend some of these meetings and learn all you can so you can protect yourself."

"So that will make me stop liking my boyfriend and then I will be alone?"

"No. Then you will be smarter and able to protect yourself. Also, there are very attractive young men at all these meetings. Plus, young women you might want to get to know."

"I'll go," she declared. "I always wanted to go to one of those meetings but I didn't want to do it in Iowa. I know too many people there."

I put the girls in the stroller and started on off to the park. I had done a good day's work already and it is a long walk from Philip Street to the Little Children's Park, so, at St. Charles Avenue, I boarded the streetcar, babies, double stroller, and all, and rode down to Octavia.

The park was full of young women and their children, even

some dark-skinned people, although this is mainly a white neighborhood. The world is changing about all that, but not as much as you would think from watching television. I have tried not to form too many opinions about civil rights and civil courtesy because I am still caught up in thinking about how many different kinds of "black" people there are in the South. I am a Creole, and we are very haughty by nature. My aunties and grannies were extremely prejudiced against people they called niggers and white trash. From that I learned that I am not responsible for the behavior of poorly behaved people of any color. From mine and Miss Crystal's study of yoga and Buddhism I have learned I am part of all creation and am responsible for the behavior of alligators and wasps and the most reprehensible humans on the globe, even Hitler himself or serial killers. I said I have learned it. I did not say I believed it.

Light shining through honey. Why would I think about who was black or who was white or who was the color of honey when I was in the park with my precious great-nieces, holding their hands while their minds dart here and there trying to decide where to begin to explore the park? The swings were full. That was a factor. An extremely overweight child was on one of the red plastic swings and a little girl was on the other one. The black swings, which are Hillary and Kaleen's second choice, were also occupied.

"That boy's on the wed swing," Hillary said.

"Get him off," Kaleen suggested.

"No," I said. "We have to wait until he stops. If we were swinging on them we wouldn't want someone to make us get off."

Hillary gives Kaleen this look that says, So what? and I just burst out laughing. They are the funniest little people I have ever known in my life and I cannot believe I get to have them in my own.

While we were standing there a young friend of Miss Crystal's comes up the sidewalk with her baby boy in a stroller that used to belong to Crystal Anne. It is this very beautiful dark blue pram Miss Crystal's mother-in-law had ordered from the Lylian Shop when Crystal Anne was born. It is lined with the most beautiful satin and looks like the inside of a coffin. We had kept it in the attic covered with plastic for many years and got it out in 1992 to give to the young girl next door. Since then it has been passed down to three babies. Now this big baby boy is bouncing along in it. He is sitting up and looking over the sides. His mother is named Alexandra and she comes over to us and we start talking. "Good God, Traceleen," she says. "They are beautiful. You should take them to a modeling agency."

"No, we would rather keep them to ourselves," I answered. "You take him to one. He looks exactly like one of those babies that are inside those Michelin tires. I bet they would snap him up for that."

About that time there is an accident. One of the swings has hit a tiny little girl who has run into its path and there is screaming and everyone gathers around the swings.

Alexandra takes over and starts ordering people to stand back. "I'm a physician," she says, and everyone obeys her. She examines the tiny little girl and says she is not injured seriously. The boy whose swing hit her is bawling louder than the girl who was hit. The good result is that everyone takes their children out of the swings to comfort them and after a few minutes I am able to put Kaleen in one swing and Hillary in another and they are happy.

"They are very territorial about these swings," I tell Alexandra. "I have examined my conscience about why I think that is funny."

"Being territorial is an evolutionary advantage," she answers. "Well, I hate to have blown my cover at this park. I take off every Wednesday to spend with William and now I guess I'll be giving out free diagnoses the whole time I'm here."

"How's the pram holding up?" I ask. "It was so grand I was half ashamed to push it when it was new."

"I think William's going to finish off the interior. It's highly impractical to line a child's pram with four-ply satin, don't you think?"

"Life was different a while ago," I answered. "We had time to mend and clean such things."

The morning passed and the sun rose in the sky and when I began to fan myself with my hat I decided to start home. Hillary fell asleep by the second block and Kaleen fussed awhile, then fell asleep beside her. It was twelve more blocks to their house, but I loosened my brassiere and decided to hike it no matter how hot it was. In my youth I walked to town from our farm many times in the middle of the day wearing my best clothes and never gave it a thought. I was the best student at every school I ever attended and thought I had to set an example of strength and courage at every point. Fortunately you can walk through the Garden

District in dense shade if you know what streets to choose. I walked along beneath a canopy of old liveoak trees and admired the gardens. Roses were peeping out through wrought-iron fences and many exotic flowers were everywhere. I will be fifty-nine years old on the twenty-second day of July, but you would never know it to look at me. I am extremely vain about my health and vitality and do not care if that is a sin. I do not think vanity is all that bad as it leads us to care what other people think and work for their good report.

I had made my way to Prytania and was waiting at a corner to cross the street when the police cars started coming from every direction with their sirens blaring. Hillary woke up and started screaming and Kaleen was right behind. I pushed on across the street and followed the police cars with both children screaming. I was just turning onto Philip Street when Miss Crystal passed me in the Saab. She threw on the brakes and got out and came toward me. "It's Andria's house," she screamed. "I was two doors away at a meeting of the Symphony Board and here they came. I thought the babies were in the house. I don't know what's happening. Where is Andria?"

"Not there," I said. "She has her program in the morning. She never gets back until one."

"Get in the car," Miss Crystal suggested. "Let's get the children off the street."

"We don't have car seats."

"Just get them inside the car. I won't drive fast. We can keep them from getting hurt for a block."

We folded the double stroller and stuck it in the trunk and

drove about five miles an hour toward Andria's house. Hillary and Kaleen had stopped crying now that they were in a car and were busy inspecting the ashtrays and windows.

We inched down Camp Street. Andria's house is just off Camp on Philip Street, a darling little brick house Martha Samuels found for her the first year she made her first six-figure salary check. One thing she liked about it was its fortress quality, since she was a Creole moving into a white neighborhood. That was working against the police now. It seems someone had Nanny Jane in the kitchen and was threatening to kill her if the police didn't deliver him some cocaine and an airplane to take him to Cuba.

We learned this from a bunch of neighbors on a corner. Andria was nowhere to be seen and I only prayed she knew the children were with me. I was certain I had told her I was going to get them every morning but now I began to wonder.

Miss Crystal was on her cell phone calling the television station and then Mr. Manny and then one of her cousins who lives on Camp and said for us to bring the babies there until it quieted down.

"Not until we find Andria," I insisted. About that time the television studio called back and said Andria was on her way home but still she wouldn't give us Andria's working cell phone number. "You have to be insane," Miss Crystal was shouting at her. "Her house is surrounded by police cars. Her children are on the street. Her aunt needs to tell her the babies are all right."

"I'll be glad to relay a message," is all the woman will say.

"Tell her we are on the corner of Camp and Prytania with a group. We'll wait until she comes. Call her this minute. What is your name, please? Could I know your name?"

But the operator had hung up on us.

Several large television vans had pulled up in the street. I was so upset I couldn't remember the name of the one Andria works for. Then there she was, running down the sidewalk in a pair of those three-inch wedgie shoes she has been wearing this year. She is such a gorgeous woman I get a lump in my throat to look at her. "What the hell?" she is saying. "What's going on?"

"You're the television personality," I answered. "We were hoping you would know."

"Mommie," Hillary is yelling.

"Momma, Momma," Kaleen is yelling too.

"My cousin, Sharon, said to come over there with the children," Crystal puts in. "She's only two houses away. Next to the Hall-Keith house."

"Take them there, would you please? I need to flash a press card. Do you think Jane's all right?"

"He has her in the kitchen and he's armed. All we can do is pray."

A deputy police chief comes up. He turns out to be Kane Thomas, a football player from Delgado Junior College who once was in love with Andria when she was a girl. He was shy talking to her so I guess he is in love still. "Your alarm system was going off. Your help managed to trigger the alarm before he over-powered her. All we have is the message she screamed out. 'Help me. He's here. Oh, God, please come and help me.' That and the message he has put on your answering machine. He wants co-caine and an airplane and he says he is ready to die so don't try anything. Is your place insured, Andria?"

"Against what?"

"We may have to make a mess."

"Just get Jane out of there. What are you waiting for? Send him in the coke and put something in it that will knock him out. That shouldn't take a genius. Give him what he wants and then go in with tear gas."

"I just wanted you to know we may mess up your house." He was standing with his hands clasped in front of him, a big, strong man like the ones I always liked. I like a man with heft and weight to him. Not the intellectual type Andria goes for. I like Andria's husband just fine and I am glad she is sending him to medical school but if it was my husband, Mark, or one of his brothers, they would already be there breaking in the place themselves.

Andria's husband had called from Tulane to see if she needed help, then went on to his anatomy class. He is just in his first year.

"Do anything you want to the house," Andria declared. "We can clean up a mess. A dead nanny is not an option."

So Crystal and I took the babies around the corner to her cousin's pretty little blue-and-white cottage and got them settled in a room watching *The Teletubbies*. Her cousin is a darling girl with two small children of her own so she watched them while we went back out on the street to see the fireworks.

The police had put up barricades and the closest we could get was half a block away in the Harters' yard. They had their maid serving iced tea and cookies to neighbors who were gathered there and Mr. Harter was making mixed drinks on the porch. This is New Orleans and anything is an excuse for a party.

Then there was a lot of yelling and a sound like an explosion and the New Orleans Police Department was through the new greenhouse and into the kitchen.

I was watching when they came out with Jane wrapped up in a blanket. A policewoman had her arm around her and they led her to an automobile. Of course the only newsperson she stopped to talk to was Andria. Later, Andria called us from the studio and told us what had happened. We had heard all sorts of things in the Harters' yard but none of it was true. What had really happened was Jane's boyfriend had a bad reaction to the Prozac. It had made him crazier and he had run off from the halfway house and come to New Orleans to kill her because he was having paranoid delusions that she was the one who told his parents he was taking cocaine. She is the one who told them but there is no way he could have found it out.

One week later we had things pretty well back to order. The greenhouse is being rebuilt. Jane has returned to Iowa and I have found a respectable black woman to take care of Hillary and Kaleen and a teenager to come in after school and help me take them to the park. The boyfriend is being represented by a group of powerful attorneys who are claiming he was the victim of police violence and Miss Crystal is delighted to report that because of the excitement she quit taking all her cold medicine and has recovered fully without it.

"It's people like that who are making viruses resistent to drugs," Andria said when I told her that. "If you fill the prescription, it is your public duty to take the full course. You all shouldn't have been given Levaquin for colds anyway. That is one of the new drugs we need to save for real illness."

"You need to spend more time with the children," I countered. "You can't just leave them with the help. You should come on home as soon as you finish your program in the morning and eat lunch with them."

"Traceleen, you do not have the slightest idea what it is costing me to keep this job. It's the razor's edge. I could be replaced any day. There are women lined up to take my job. I stay downtown to make sure they know I'm serious. I spend every minute I can with those babies."

She looked so hurt and downtrodden I was ashamed of myself for striking back and walked across the room and took her into my arms and apologized and said I hadn't meant it. "They wouldn't have hired you if they could replace you," I kept saying. "You are not some replacement part in the machinery of contemporary life, Andria. You are a once-in-a-lifetime miracle of passion and will and beauty and you have a voice that could have been in opera. Let me make you some herbal tea and let's go lie down on your bed while the girls are sleeping and talk some girl talk."

We went upstairs and cuddled up on her king-size bed. Although she is now five foot eleven and I am five foot six, we can still cuddle like we did when she was a child and I would go over to my sister Mandina's house and rescue her from the drinking they did over there.

"Jane's going to sue the halfway house for letting him get away. She says they weren't monitoring him."

"I don't think everyone should sue everyone all the time," I answered. "All that does is add to our store of fears. It stops people in their tracks when they are trying to help someone. And so forth."

"I'm glad she's gone. I'm glad to have my house to myself. She was such a constant presence. It was very annoying and she taught the children to fear things. She was afraid of thunder and they picked it up."

"What was the part about the airplane to Cuba?" I asked, to change the subject and keep myself from lecturing about spending time with the children. To keep myself from saying, Anyone can teach them bad things if you aren't there to watch them.

"That was Jane's finest moment. To keep him from killing her she told him to tell the police to send a helicopter, then a plane and they would take the babies for hostages. She let him think they were upstairs taking a nap. She said if they could get to Cuba, Fidel would take care of them. Of course, the thing that really worked was sending in the cocaine with an emetic in it. He started throwing up after he put it in his nose. I told the police to do that but they wouldn't let me put it on the news."

She sat up and started getting nervous and tight and anxious and all that but I kept pulling her back down onto the pillow and telling her about when she was little and we built a blue palace out of cardboard refrigerator boxes. "And we made little curtains out of paper and painted them blue with crayons and painted lace on them and I made you a real rug out of braided rags and got you some lace doilies to put on the doll chair and we painted roses by the front door and you said, Someday I'll have a real house as fine as this, and so you do."

Of course she fell asleep in my arms. I covered her with a knit coverlet my aunt Lily made years ago in Boutte and then I tiptoed into their room to see what the twins were doing. They were asleep like spoons, side by side as they were in the womb. Such is love. Such are the moments of our lives. Breathe in, breathe out, go and watch a sunset.